POPULAR PUBLICATIONS FACSIMILE EDITIONS

Terror Tales #6
(February 1935)

Starting in 1934, editor (and publisher) Harry Steeger unveiled *Terror Tales*: perhaps the flagship magazine in Popular Publications' so-called "Weird Menace" lineup of titles. Running for almost 50 issues, *Terror Tales* showcased some of the best suspense, mystery and terror stories to see print in the pulps. This facsimile of the February 1935 issue contains stories by Arthur Leo Zagat, Hugh B. Cave, Ray Cummings, and Nat Schachner, among others.

Authors:

Arthur Leo Zagat, Hugh B. Cave, Ray Cummings, Ben Judson, George Edson, Robert C. Blackmon, Nat Schachner

Illustrators:

Rudolph Zirm, Amos Sewell

Volume Two   February, 1935   Number Two

FEATURE-LENGTH MYSTERY NOVEL

THREE MYSTERY-TERROR NOVELETTES

SHORT TERROR TALES

Cover Painting by Rudolph W. Zirm
Story Illustrations by Amos Sewell

Published every month by Popular Publications, Inc., 2256 Grove Street, Chicago, Illinois. Editorial and executive offices, 205 East Forty-second Street, New York City. Harry Steeger, President and Secretary, Harold S. Goldsmith, Vice President and Treasurer. Entry as second-class matter pending at the post office at Chicago, Ill., under the Act of March 3, 1879. Title registration pending at U. S. Patent Office. Copyright, 1935, by Popular Publications, Inc. Single copy price 15c. Yearly subscriptions in U. S. A. $1.50. For advertising rates address Sam J. Perry, 205 E. 42nd St., New York, N. Y. When submitting manuscripts kindly enclose stamped self-addressed envelope for their return if found unavailable. The publishers cannot accept responsibility for return of unsolicited manuscripts, although care will be exercised in handling them.

Kidneys Cause Much Trouble Says Doctor

Successful Prescription Helps Remove Acids—Works in 15 Minutes.

Dr. T. J. Rastelli, famous English scientist, Doctor of Medicine and Surgeon, says: "You can't feel well if your Kidneys do not function right, because your Kidneys affect your entire body."

Your blood circulates 4 times a minute through 9 million tiny, delicate tubes in your Kidneys which are endangered by drastic, irritating drugs, modern foods and drinks, worry, and exposure. Beware of Kidney dysfunction if you suffer from Night Rising, Leg Pains, Nervousness, Dizziness, Circles Under Eyes, Acidity, or Loss of Pep.

Dr. Walter R. George, for many years Health Director of Indianapolis, says: "Insufficient Kidney excretions are the cause of much needless suffering with Aching Back, Frequent Night Rising, Itching, Smarting, Burning, Painful Joints, Rheumatic Pains, Headaches, and a generally run-down body. I am of the opinion that the prescription Cystex corrects such functional conditions. It aids in flushing poisons from the urinary tract, and in freeing the blood of retained toxins. Cystex deserves the indorsement of all doctors." If you suffer from Kidney and Bladder dysfunction, delay endangers your vitality, and you should not lose a single minute in starting to take the doctor's special prescription called Cystex (pronounced Sise-tex) which helps Kidney functions in a few hours. It starts work in 15 minutes.

Dr. W. R. George

Gently tones, soothes, and cleans raw, sore membranes. Brings new energy and vitality in 48 hours. It is helping millions of sufferers and is guaranteed to fix you up and make you feel like new in 8 days, or money back on return of empty package. Get guaranteed Cystex from your druggist today.

NEW!
Packed with Chills from Cover to Cover!
HORROR STORIES

In This First Great Issue
Spine-Tingling Mystery-Horror Novel
MUSIC OF THE DAMNED

Blood-Chilling Novelettes
MISTRESS OF THE BEAST
MEN WITHOUT BLOOD
HER LOVER—DEATH!

And

These Short Eerie Tales
THE NIGHT THE DEVIL WALKED
NIGHTMARE HOUSE
VILLAGE OF BONES
CLAIMED BY THE DEAD

Each one a masterpiece of horror—all written by men who know how to thrill you and chill you!

The January Issue Is On Sale Now!

A POPULAR PUBLICATION

Try these Knock-Out Punches of Champions

Can you knock any man cold with one blow? It's easy when you know how to land these famous punches on the *eight vital points* of the body! Learn them all for only 25c. Read this amazing offer!

Win Any Fight with these Sleep-Producers

Next time you find yourself in a scrap, just haul off and land one of these famous Knock-Outs. WHAM! The fight's over! Down goes your opponent. He's out! You walk off a hero.

Yes, it's as simple as that when you know how to hit—with the deadly knock-out blows of the great champions. A hundred wild swings don't do one-tenth the damage of any ONE of these paralyzing punches. Why take a licking when you can KNOW these amazing secrets of the knock-out? Now they are revealed so clearly and concisely that any man can quickly master them. For only 25c you gain the knowledge that may save you from insult, humiliation, ridicule—that may make you a CHAMPION.

12 GREAT PUNCHES 25c
Explained and illustrated—All for

No man living can stand up under the paralyzing effects of these expert punches landed on the vital points of the body. Here are the king punches of all the great masters—Corbett, Fitzsimmons, Kid McCoy, Jack Johnson, Benny Leonard, Gene Tunney, Carpera—every punch explained and illustrated—every move made clear. And here's an EXTRA SPECIAL GIFT:

FREE Chart showing the eight vital knock-out spots and vulnerable points of the body. Tells you where to hit a man to render him helpless and unconscious.

Rush Coupon—Offer Limited

Only a limited number of these sets of Knock-Out Punches and Free Charts on hand. Don't miss yours! Mail the coupon or write, enclosing a quarter, or 25c in stamps for your complete set. Money Back Guarantee.

The INSTITUTE of PHYSICAL CULTURE
55 East 11th St.   Dept. PP-2   **New York, N. Y.**

━━━━━MAIL COUPON━━━━━

The Institute of Physical Culture, Dept. PP-2
55 East 11th Street, New York, N. Y.

Please send me at once a complete set of the 12 Knock-Out Punches of Champions with Free Chart of Vital Points of Body. I enclose 25 cents in full payment.

Name ....

Address ....

Town........................., State.............

4

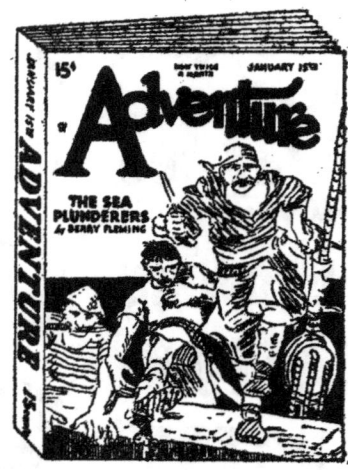

THE SEA PLUNDERERS
Part 1 of a Stirring Pirate Serial
by Berry Fleming

MURDER MILL
A Novelette of the West—and Just Another Jones
by Robert E. Pinkerton

BOARDERS AWAY!
A Story of the Q-boats
by William Chamberlain

WORLD HORSES
A Story of the Rodeo
by Palmer Hoyt

MAN CAN DO
A Story of the Aviation Service
by A. A. Caffrey

IT'S HOW IT FEELS
A Story of the Prize Ring
by Eddy Orcutt

STUNT MAN
A Story of a Wire Walker's Desperate Courage
by Alfred Batson

And Others—All in the January 15th Issue

on sale December 28th

15c

The only man who could talk to the Superintendent

For several years, he was just like a score of other men in the plant—a good, honest, fairly capable worker, but only that. There was nothing distinctive about him or his ability—nothing to make him stand out from the crowd—no reason, as a matter of fact, why he should ever receive a raise.

Then one fortunate day he decided that the reason he wasn't getting anywhere was because he lacked special training. He searched around a bit —asked a great many questions—and then enrolled for a home-study course with the International Correspondence Schools.

"Soon after I began studying," he wrote to us the other day, "we had a change in management at our plant. The new superintendent said that only men who had really studied their work were in line for positions as foremen.

"I certainly was glad then that I had decided to study in my spare time. For, thanks to my I. C. S. course, I was the only man in the organization who could talk to the superintendent in his own language. As a result, I was promoted over men who had been here from ten to twenty years."

What are *you* doing with the hours after supper? Can you afford to let them slip by unimproved when you can easily make them mean so much?

One hour a day, spent with the I. C. S. in the quiet of your own home, will prepare you for success in the work you like best. *Yes, it will!* Put it up to us to prove it. Mail this coupon today.

ENSLAVED TO SATAN

By Hugh B. Cave

(Author of "Death's Loving Arms," etc.)

THE Reverend Paul Norton reached the entrance to deserted Woodlawn Park at one-thirty a. m. Back in the road, the headlights of his small car stabbed fingers of light through the night mist, limned his tall young figure. His thin face was good-looking, though dark shadows of worry clouded his eyes.

Paul Norton thought himself a man of God. But a black-robed fiend came up from nowhere to tell him he had sold his soul to Satan, and blood-red letters flamed before his eyes to vouch the truth of his iniquity. Yet not till Satan's handmaidens had dragged him down to the foul depths of their pain-filled horror chamber did he believe that his eyes and ears had spoken truth . . .

He paced forward into the darkness of the deserted park. To his right loomed a huge sign. It was unlighted now, but the car lights reflected dimly against the glass tubing of the neon lettering. His mouth twisted a little as he read:

NOTICE

THIS PROPERTY HAS BEEN BE-
QUEATHED TO THE FIRST CHURCH
OF DENHAM AND WILL BE CON-
DUCTED HEREAFTER FOR THE BEN-
EFIT OF THE CHURCH. WE ASSURE
THE PUBLIC OF ENTERTAINING
PROGRAMS AND ASK YOUR PAT-
RONAGE.

The sign told a lie. Woodlawn Park had not been left to the church, but to Paul Norton and the board of deacons. To use for the benefit of the church, yes. But if Deacon Wyman didn't upset the apple-cart, the owners could assign themselves good salaries out of the operating expenses. Wyman, Paul Norton thought bitterly, could afford to be sanctimonious; he had money of his own. He didn't have to struggle along on a salary so pitifully small that he couldn't marry. He wasn't in love with beautiful Ruth Winward who had waited two years now and would have to wait indefinitely if Paul Norton didn't find some way to make more money. . . .

Norton shook his head to clear it of bitter thoughts, turned and strode on into the darkness. Gravel crunched throatily beneath his feet, husking a slow accompaniment to his advance.

Then he stopped, stood trembling. Ahead of him and a little to the left, on a dark expanse of lawn checkerboarded with man-high shrubs, was something alien. The wind moved sibilantly, carrying a strange and sinister odor.

Slowly he slipped forward, eyes unblinkingly wide. It was too dark here for human eyes to be sure of what the gloom might spawn, but it seemed to be. . . He took four more steps, each one an effort as cold dread mounted within him. Then he stopped, caught a hoarse breath, and stood as if impaled.

The thing before him was a cross—a huge wooden cross planted *upside down* in the lawn. Upon it, with bare feet reaching into the darkness, arms extended and head grotesquely dangling, hung a shape which was human.

"Oh, God!" Paul Norton whispered.

Men weren't crucified today. They hadn't been since civilization and men's souls were as dark as this dismal night. And even then, *not upside down!*

Paul Norton lurched closer, wide eyes staring. The man's feet, pointing grotesquely at the heavens, were pierced with an iron spike, and other spikes impaled his contorted hands. His naked body was a twisted question-mark of agony. And the face—that ascetic face contorted with suffering that had pulled each muscle out of line, was the face of Alfred Wyman.

Deacon Alfred Wyman—the man Paul Norton had been thinking of as a hypocrite, the one man who did not want the minister and the deacons of the church to make personal gain out of property which should be operated for the benefit of God's Church.

Norton gasped. The darkness around him was suddenly a black vale of horror. The blood in his veins went cold. Why had Wyman been put to death in such horrible fashion? Why was this cross *inverted?*

Hereditary fears festered in Norton's mind, gave horrible answer. This inverted cross, mockery of God and things holy, was symbolic of devil worship. In the long-dead past robed shapes had huddled over human sacrifices, knelt before uncouth shrines practicing the hell-born monstrosities of the Black Mass—*because they had sold their souls to the devil in the hope of worldly gain!*

And hadn't he and his deacons—all but Alfred Wyman—done just that? A week before prosperous old Jason Manley had sat up in his death-bed and signed a paper leaving Woodlawn Park to the minister of the Denham church and to the deacons, on the understanding that it would be used for God's work.

Paul Norton groaned in agony as he remembered how he had agreed that they feather their own pockets with the money made here. He had helped in working out some of the publicity schemes which would make the place more profitable. Well, they had their publicity now! The publicity of death and terror. And less than fifteen minutes ago, he had hated Wyman because the man had stood out against them, threatened to expose the whole scheme unless all profits from the park were turned over to the church and charity.

Then, with an effort, he wrenched his thoughts from their mad ramblings and fought for self-control. This was no work of the devil; it was murder, sinister and significant. Recent murder, for the body of Deacon Wyman was not yet cold.

Somewhere in Woodlawn Park, perhaps even now lurking nearby, would be the fiend or fiends who—

The crackling of a twig—or was it merely sudden premonition of peril?—whirled Norton in his tracks. The muscles in his legs went stiff; his body froze with a convulsive twitch. He was no longer alone.

LESS than ten paces distant, the darkness had spawned a majestic shape that did not belong there, had not been there before. Blacker than night itself, the shape stood motionless, arms folded on a broad black chest. It moved forward, lifted one massive arm, to point a dark forefinger at Norton's bloodless face. Words came out of the darkness, and Paul Norton was aware through the cold winding-sheet of dread that enveloped him that the words were emanating from that half-alive, half-spectral face which had no right to exist.

"You have done well, my servant." Crimson lips seemed to part in a mirthless smile. "You have done very well." The outstretched arm swayed sideways; the rigid finger pointed to Alfred Wyman's crucified corpse. "And here is publicity for you and your associates. Here is an obstacle removed from your path. The Prince of Darkness is ever eager to aid his servants!"

The leering smile vanished, and with a sudden rustle of dark garments the shape glided backward. It merged with another black hulk—one of the many shrubs that dotted the lawn. The monster was gone!

Seconds passed before Paul Norton found life. Breath wheezed from his lips and he lunged forward, hands outflung. The thing he had seen, the whispered words that had emanated from those spectral lips, were not real! Could not be real! And yet. . . .

His clawing hands made contact, but touched only the hard, brittle needles of the evergreen. He stopped, let his arms fall to his sides. The air that sobbed into his lungs was tangy with a taste of dew-wet balsam. Somewhere not far away a cricket was chirping. No other sound lived in the dark.

Norton's limp hands curled into fists and he pushed forward, walked a slow circle around the man-high shrub. Man-high. . . That was what had fooled him, of course! Staring in deceptive darkness, his nerves jangled by the discovery of Deacon Wyman's corpse, he had seen the wind-bent outline of this shrub and his imagination had done the rest!

Those whispered words? They had originated in his own mind, perhaps emanated from his own lips. Overwrought nerves could do as much as that, and more. Yet that red-glowing face—those shapeless lips curled in a soundless laugh of evil triumph. . . .

Well, he had imagined that, too! If a black-robed shape *had* existed, where had it vanished to? There was no possible hiding-place, except in the shadows of this particular shrub. And no one was here.

Staring around, he shuddered at shadows that seemed furtively to close in on him. The erratic chirping of crickets became an ominous muttering from hidden lips of horror. He wanted suddenly, consumingly, to get out of the park and race back to the twin headlights that gleamed so far away in the road.

The whole thing had been born of his own jangled nerves—yet that premonition of evil still persisted. That feeling of not being alone. . . .

He turned and stared at the corpse on the cross. That, at least, was real. Backing away from it, he sobbed with a realization of the agony that had preceded Wyman's death. But no dark-robed monster of hell had done that vile deed. Human beings, who could be brought to justice as soon as the police were notified. . . .

The police! Convulsively, Norton turned, strode across the lawn, along the gravel path that led to the park's administration building. Keys jangled in his hand. . . .

MOMENTS later, inside the small office, he lowered the telephone and knew he had done his duty. Then, with a calmness that surprised even himself, he rummaged in the office-desk, found a searchlight, and strode out again into the dark, toward the scene of the murder.

With the searchlight he studied again the torment engraved on Wyman's death-face. The frantic desire to get away from the park returned to him and he fought against it, steeled himself to investigate every angle of the horror.

Three times he paced between the inverted cross and the dark shrub where the monster with the glowing face—imaginary, perhaps—had seemingly vanished into thin air. Once, stooping to study the grass near the base of the evergreen, he thought he detected a faint sulphur-like odor that did not belong there. But that, too, might be a creation of his imagination.

But could a man's imagination conjure *words?* Had those whispered words been *real?*

He stood for a long while before the inverted body of the man who only last night had accused him and his associates of consorting with the devil. The beam of the searchlight swept the lawn beneath Wyman's dangling head. And suddenly Norton leaned forward, staring.

The thing he picked up was a button, small and oval-shaped and black. Not an ordinary button, and certainly not from the somber grey clothes of the man who hung dead. Moments passed while Norton examined it.

The squeal of a car's brakes, in the road beyond the park's entrance, aroused him. Mechanically he pocketed the button, turned and stared as shadowy figures came along the gravel path. A moment and uniformed policemen were crowding around him. And then, in slow, fretful tones he told his story. . . .

He said nothing, though, of having heard whispered words from the glowing lips of a red-faced monster. If he told them of that, they would think him mad. Even he himself was not sure. That evil voice had seemed real at the time, terribly real, but now it was only a vague echo in his brain. Perhaps it was his brain that had spawned it. . . .

He must wait, and be sure, before making any statements.

"You look pretty washed up, Reverend Norton. Better get on home and leave us to take care of this."

Slowly, Norton walked away. When he looked back from the road, before climbing into his own car, shadowed shapes were still gathered around the inverted cross and its ghastly victim. Searchlights winked like fireflies in the dark, and the murmur of men's voices rode the night stillness.

Half an hour later when Paul Norton

let himself into the little brown cottage next to the church, on Denham's main street, that scene was still indelibly printed in his mind. A dark, ominous picture, filled with vague threats of things abnormal and unholy. . . .

A white-enameled clock on the bedroom dresser showed the quarter-hour past three as Paul Norton undressed and clicked off the light. Ages had passed since he had tiptoed from this room, yet the clock then had said one A. M. So much had happened. . . .

Sprawled there on the bed, in darkness, he was strangely glad that he had refrained from blurting too many words to the policemen in the park. But why? What was the sensation that gripped him? Was it relief that Alfred Wyman was out of the way and could no longer balk the plans of the deacons?

He fought to drive such thoughts out of mind, and in the gloom of the room a picture took form—a picture of the inverted cross bearing its ghastly burden. Norton stared, gripped the bedclothes with stiff fingers and choked a scream that filled his throat. The picture vanished.

He dozed, but his tortured mind invented images that made him moan and toss in his sleep. Again he saw that strange robed shape with the leering face; again he caught that faint but unmistakable odor of burning sulphur. And this time the Prince of Darkness was bent above him, peering down at him with eyes loaded with threatening evil. . . .

Norton awoke with a start and pushed himself up on stiff arms. That image had been no dream! Instinctively he knew it, sensed the terrible reality of it. His wide eyes stared into the room's darkness, seeking. Somewhere in that darkness other eyes were watching him, gloating over his terror, and the gaze of those eyes was a tangible force pressing in upon him.

Suddenly he was rigid, unbreathing. Like a propped-up dummy he sat without motion, arms stiff as laths, shoulders bunched, head thrust forward. A sensation of unbearable cold began at his bare feet and crept through his body, stilling the beat of his heart.

Straight ahead of him on the room's rear wall, no more than twenty feet beyond the bed-end, a crimson message glared out at him!

BLURRED letters they were that made the message, swelling and contracting—yet slowly losing their bloated shape and assuming sharp outlines. Then the message glowed with hideous legibility, and he could not fail to read it. With spectral significance the words returned his stare, delivering their ominous message.

By not confiding too much in the police, you have proved yourself a good servant, Paul Norton!

Fear sapped Norton's strength, left his face white as the face of a corpse. The pupils of his eyes dilated. A sound, half moan and half shriek, accompanied his hoarse intake of breath.

Slowly the letters faded. Then others took their place on the wall's grim blackboard.

Take the button and go to Deacon Bingham's office tomorrow morning. Look in the third desk drawer. Remember, I am with thee always, my servant, so long as thou art faithful!

As the words faded, Norton's soulchilling numbness faded with them. His feet thumped the floor and he pushed himself erect, took a faltering step forward, hands outthrust.

But the wall before him now was bare and blank. No crimson letters marred its dark surface. No sound except the rapid wheeze of his own breathing disturbed the room's ominous stillness.

Some hidden well of fortitude gave him power to move forward, though the very walls of the room seemed closing in upon him with crushing force. His groping fingers, cold as if plunged into ice-water, found a light-switch, and as twin lamps glowed on the dresser he stood flat against the wall, staring into the chamber's every corner.

The room was empty.

Moisture formed on Norton's forehead, beaded the backs of his icy hands. His heart thumped violently. The room was empty—*empty*—yet the black wall before him, covered now with innocent brown paper, had twice spawned crimson words!

Had his imagination been playing mad tricks with him again?

He knew better, sobbed hoarsely with a sensation of utter helplessness. If only he could believe the thing a nightmare! But nightmares were seldom rational, seldom made sense. And those crimson letters had been so hideously significant. . . .

Slowly he made a circuit of the room, forced himself to peer into every niche, every corner. Opening the doors of two clothes-closets took courage, but he dragged them open, stared into the dark interiors. He found nothing. Then, as terror renewed its relentless grip, he examined every inch of the wall where some invisible hand had inscribed those scarlet letters.

The brown wall-paper with its lighter brown whorls leered back at him, mocking him. Trembling violently, he returned to the bed, sat down and put both hands to his sweat-drenched face.

"I am with thee always, my servant, so long as thou art faithful!"

My *servant!* Merciful God, what did it mean? At the meeting last night, Alfred Wyman had stood before the assembled deacons of the church and pointed an ac-

cusing forefinger into startled faces, thundered in a frenzy of sudden rage: "You have become money-changers in the temple! God is no longer in your hearts! You are servants of the devil, all of you!"

Servants—of—the—devil. Paul Norton's eyes widened, were suddenly rimmed with the whiteness of fear. He stared at the brown-papered wall and saw again the words that had glowed there. *"I am with thee always, my servant. . . ."*

Then he laughed, laughed hoarsely and with such violence that the sound startled him as it bellowed through the room. Lunging erect, he stood wide-legged, clenched his hands. "It's not true! I'm not a servant of the devil! I've done my best to preach the word of God. . . ."

His voice cracked, fell into a guttural mumbling. "I—I need the money. Ruth won't wait forever. If I don't get money enough to marry her soon, she'll turn to someone else. Oh God, what have I done?"

There was no answer, and those red letters, glowing now in his agonized mind, took form again and leered at him. What had they said? *"Take the button. . . ."*

What button? Dully he remembered, turned to stare at his clothes that lay piled on a chair. He had found a button in the grass near the foot of the death-cross. A black button. He had forgotten to hand it to the police.

Fumbling in his coat pockets, he found it, held it in his cupped palm. *"Take the button to Deacon Bingham's office tomorrow morning. Look in the third desk drawer. . . ."*

Hope smouldered in Norton's glazed eyes. When daylight came, he would do as those spectral letters had ordered, but not because they had ordered it. Geoffrey Bingham would know the answer. More than once, in the past, he had offered words of advice in times of trouble, and his sober middle-aged wisdom had been of infinite help.

In the morning. . . .

CHAPTER TWO

The Black Coat

THE mirror-clock over the windshield said nine-twenty when Paul Norton parked his car next morning in front of the Denham Trust Company Building. He made his way directly to the bank's private offices on the fourth floor, nodded to Bingham's secretary and waited impatiently while the girl announced his visit.

Evidence of last night's turmoil still clung to his face. His eyes were dark-rimmed, tinged with red from staring so long into shadows; his cheeks were gaunt, pale and twitching.

In the private office of Geoffrey Bingham, President of the Denham Trust Company, Bingham gazed at him and said anxiously: "You've had a sleepless night, Paul. Wyman's terrible death—"

"You've—heard?"

Bingham nodded. "The news spread quickly. In fact, Wyman's family has already offered a five-thousand-dollar reward for the capture of the killer. What I'm curious to know is how you happened to be out there last night."

Instead of answering, Norton fumbled in his vest pocket, drew forth the small black button he had stared at so long last night, and leaned forward. The torment in his face caused Bingham to gaze at him in bewilderment.

"Last night—" Norton mouthed the words thickly—"something happened. I'm in trouble. I want to talk to you."

He spilled forth his story. It was easy to talk to Bingham. The man knew how to listen. Compassion filled his round, sallow, moon-face and he sat with one heavy leg crossed over the other, his left arm

hooked on the desk-top to support the weight of his big shoulders. He was past middle age and the years had softened a face that perhaps had once been lean and hard. Soft grey hair made that face even more kindly.

Norton was interrupted only when the older man's hand reached out, at frequent intervals, to touch his hunched shoulder in a comforting gesture that seemed to say, "Take it easy, young fellow. When you're as old as I am, you'll learn to control your emotions."

In the end, Norton swayed erect, placed on the desk the black button that had come from the foot of the cross. "That's —all, Mr. Bingham. There's the button, and—"

Geoffrey Bingham smiled. "And you were advised to open the third drawer of my desk. Well, let's do it." Quietly he reached down, slid open the desk drawer. His smile changed abruptly to a puzzled scowl. Slowly, very slowly, he extended a trembling hand and drew forth a folded garment.

"You knew this was here?"

"No." Paul Norton's eyes were wide. "No. How should I?"

"Neither did I. It's not mine and it wasn't here yesterday. Someone must have put it here last night." Bingham shook the garment and held it at arm's length, frowned at it. It was a long black cloak, with broad sleeves and a row of oval-shaped black buttons!

The banker's eyes narrowed ominously; with stiff fingers he reached out, took the button from the desk and held it close to those on the cloak. Paul Norton stared at him, took a sudden step backward.

That cloak! A hideous vision stabbed Norton's mind and he suppressed a desire to shriek out the truth. That cloak was all too familiar! He had seen it before, had heard whispered words emanating from the glowing face above it.

The dark specter in Woodlawn Park had not been a figment of his mad imagination, after all! Here was proof!

But Geoffrey Bingham was seeing something else. Four buttons gleamed on the cloak's black breast. Four buttons—and a ragged tuft of black thread where a fifth had been torn loose. And the button in Bingham's fingers matched those that were sewn on the cloak's black satin!

The man's eyes smouldered. Violently he flung the garment from him, lurched erect and glared into Paul Norton's bloodless face. His chest rose and fell with the passion that fumed within him.

"It's a dirty lie! This coat isn't mine and never was mine! It was planted here!"

Never before had Norton seen a man change character so abruptly. But the answer came not from Norton's pale lips; it came from the far end of the room, in the sudden opening of a door that led apparently to a smaller office beyond. Bingham whirled. In the doorway stood a uniformed figure whose outthrust hand held a leveled revolver!

Geoffrey Bingham took a step backward, worked his lips soundlessly as the officer advanced. His gaze clung to the gun; color ebbed from his round face, left it limp and pasty. When he found his voice again it was a lurid shriek.

"It's not true, I tell you! It's a frame-up! The cloak doesn't belong to me!"

The officer's lips curled, formed a sarcastic sneer. With one hand he pushed the banker aside, snatched the cloak from the desk. His gun covered Bingham's every movement while he peered down at the black garment, narrowed his eyes over it.

"This isn't yours?"

"I tell you I never saw it before!"

"Maybe you can explain how your name comes to be on it, then."

Bingham swayed on spread legs, seemed glued to the floor. Slowly he came a step closer, and another, and peered down. A tiny white band inside the cloak's collar said, in the dull purple of indelible ink that had apparently been washed many times: *G. Bingham.*

A HOARSE sob croaked in the banker's throat. He gripped the desk with hands that were bloodless, wet with perspiration. Frantically he stared from the officer's face to that of Paul Norton. "Oh my God, it's not true! I swear it!"

Paul Norton shuddered, remembering the spectral shape in the park and the whispered words that had emanated from shapeless red lips.

"It's a funny thing," the officer said quietly. "Amateurs never get away with murder. Not for long." Methodically he rolled the black cloak into a crumpled wad and stuffed it into a pocket of his uniform. "In this case, we had a mysterious phone tip to come here and sort of hang around until something happened. Maybe your friend, Mr. Norton, sent it." He shrugged, made a sidewise motion with the gun. "Better not make any fuss, Bingham. Come along quietly."

Geoffrey Bingham's large body stood in the center of the small office, quivering as though made of jelly. No color remained in his face; his eyes were glassy grey buttons in danger of bursting in their sockets. He took a slow step backward, reached out both hands as if to ward off something horrible that menaced him.

"No, no! You can't take me to jail! I didn't kill Wyman! I swear I didn't!"

The officer sighed impatiently, again made movements with the gun. The gun was a loadstone for Bingham's horrified gaze. He stared at it, took another step backward, made incoherent noises in his throat.

"You'll hang for this, Bingham," the officer said indifferently. "The evidence is piled against you. After what you did to Alfred Wyman, and the way you did it, I wouldn't be surprised if the crowd took it on themselves to save the law a lot of trouble. Damn you, stop whimpering! You killed a man——"

A lurid shriek jangled from the depths of Geoffrey Bingham's soul. His trembling body spun abruptly like a monstrous top, hurtled toward the wall. Before either Paul Norton or the officer had divined his mad intent, he had reached a window.

With a wild lunge he gained the sill and hurled himself head foremost against the glass. Then, like a great black bat, he shot through the shattered pane and hurtled into space.

Broken glass cascaded to the floor as Paul Norton and the officer leaped forward with cries of horror. But Norton's outthrust hands were too late; that lunging body was already beyond reach, beyond sight. All that remained was a shattered window—and a wild shriek that ended, far below, in sudden horrible silence.

Norton was first to reach the aperture. Clawing the sill, he leaned forward and stared down. Muscles corded in his throat and a hollow sensation invaded the pit of his stomach, blurring his gaze to the sight that lay below.

A concrete sidewalk had stopped Bingham's fall. People in the street were running, shouting. The contorted shape on the sidewalk did not move, did not resemble anything human.

With a shudder Norton turned away, paced slowly to the desk and stood there, both hands gripping the desk for support. New horror had awakened the lethargic sickness in his soul; he swayed, would have fallen had not the policeman reached out a stabbing hand.

The officer's face had lost color, too. His mouth worked, made sluggish words.

"I guess he was guilty, all right. I guess he proved it."

Norton stared mutely at the black cloak on the desk, at the significant, damning black button that lay beside it. Then the officer spoke words that spiked Norton's soul with a blind, blood-chilling realization of the thing's full portent.

"You'll get a good wad of reward money for this, Mr. Norton. Maybe you don't know it, but Alfred Wyman's family offered five thousand for the capture of the murderer. And you're the man who produced the evidence. . . ."

Norton swayed blindly, leaned against the desk and closed his eyes. He was no longer in Geoffrey Bingham's office on the fourth floor of the Denham Trust Building. He was alone in a world of darkness, a black world peopled with leering shadow-shapes that mocked him, jeered at him derisively.

Somewhere in that dark void stood a majestic black-cloaked monster whose arms were folded on an enormous chest, and whose leering face glowed red. Shapeless lips were curled in triumph, uttering soundless laughter.

Paul Norton knew the truth. Knew that it *was* truth. An innocent man had plunged to hideous death, fearing black shame and reprisal for a crime he had not committed. And for the blood of that innocent man, Paul Norton was to receive five thousand dollars!

A hoarse cry gurgled in his throat and his hands gripped the desk-edge, holding his trembling body erect. And then his tortured brain conjured another vision in crimson letters, crimson words, that swam in a blood-mist before his eyes.

They were the words that had glowed on the wall of the bedroom, an eternity ago. *"You have proved yourself a good servant, Paul Norton! I am with thee always. . . ."*

THE face that stared back into Paul Norton's own, hours later, from the mirror above his bedroom dresser, was a gaunt and twisted, lined with torment. Hope had gone out of it; desperation and despair had sucked life from it, leaving only a thin, bloodless shell.

It startled him. And a moment later, when he descended the stairs to answer the insistent clamor of the front doorbell, it startled someone else.

Ruth Winward, standing there on the stoop, stared at him and took a quick step backward, as if seeing some strange cadaver risen from its grave. Her own face had been aglow with a happy smile; the smile faded as if wiped away with a wet rag. She said, "Oh!" in a sharp, quick voice. Then she reached out a trembling hand, gripped Norton's arm and cried anxiously: "Paul! You're ill!"

He shook his head. "I suppose you're wondering why I sent for you."

"What—what's happened, Paul?"

He made no answer. Mechanically she closed the door, followed him into the living-room. There she sat down in a straight-backed chair, stared at him intently and repeated her anxious question, "What's—happened?"

A feeling of utter hopelessness seized Norton's heart as he returned that anxious gaze. This was the end; dully he realized it, and the truth was a throbbing, relentless pain within him, more acute than physical agony.

This girl had loved him, promised to be his. She would know now that the dream was finished. She would realize that another allegiance had claimed him, had crept from some dark antechamber of hell to suck him into servitude. He was no longer free.

"Paul, what *is* it?" the girl whispered. "What's wrong?"

He wet his lips, forced words from his throat. "You've heard about Wyman?"

"Yes, Paul," she answered. "I've heard."

"And about Bingham?"

"Yes, but—"

"In a little while," he muttered, "the other deacons will be here. Mowry, Dwight, Miller, Shaw—all of them. I've called a meeting. I'm going to tell them the truth, a truth even you don't know. And I'm going to make them give up the whole deal. They've *got* to give it up!"

"I'm glad," Ruth Winward said simply.

His answer was a mirthless laugh. Glad? Yes, she would be. From the very beginning she had been against the evil scheme to which he had pledged allegiance. But even she did not know how far that pledge had carried him, into what black hell it had led him.

"I want you to stay here when they come," he begged. "God knows I'll need your help!"

She sat on the arm of his chair and tried to comfort him. "I'm sure they'll see how wrong the whole thing is, dear." Her voice was soft, soothing, as if she were talking to a child afraid of the dark. "They're not wicked. Remember, they are all rather poor; they need money. Under the circumstances, almost any group of men would have been tempted."

Norton looked up into her face and found courage. He murmured half-audible words that sounded like "God bless you!"

How long he sat there with his head cradled in her warm arms, his face against the soft satin of her throat, he did not know. The drone of the doorbell aroused him, prepared him for the ordeal that was to come.

He stood up, dragged a deep breath as he paced into the hall. When he returned to the living-room, accompanied by the men who had come in answer to his summons, his fists were clenched and his courage bolstered for the impending battle.

They were an assorted group, these men who seated themselves in the living-room and gazed at him expectantly, waiting for him to speak. Clinton Miller and Mark Shaw, the two youngest, were bachelors, leaders of the Young Peoples' Club at the church. Edwin Dwight, blimp-bodied and shabbily dressed, owned a small shoe-store on Main Street. Erwin Mowry, wearing horn-rimmed glasses too large for his wedge-shaped face, had a shrew-ish wife and three small children at home. Alexander Pierson, short, fat and dumpy, was a florist.

Deacons of the church, all of them. Brought together by the similarity of their spiritual beliefs, but otherwise hav-ing little in common.

Yet they had one common desire which would make them fight bitterly the sug-gestion on Norton's lips. They were men of average means, perhaps even less than average, and had already, in their minds, spent the fortune that Woodlawn Park would bring them. They would not give up that added income without a fight!

PASSIONATELY, Norton began to talk, and the touch of Ruth Winward's hand on his arm gave him courage. But he dared not tell them of all the things he had seen, and he knew the answer be-fore he had spoken a dozen sentences. The expression on every face was against him.

It was Alexander Pierson, the florist, who put that answer into words. Hunched forward in a chair too big for his dumpy body, he scowled blackly, fingered an out-thrust chin and snorted: "Are you mad, Norton? Good Lord, man, we can't give up now! That er—crucifixion at the park has drawn thousands of people there. The place is mobbed; the restaurant's doing a thriving business; all the conces-sions are booming—"

"We've laid our plans carefully, Nor-ton." It was Clinton Miller who interrupt-ed. "It's too late to back out. We've gone to a good deal of expense. Tonight the first two of our Biblical dramas go on—*Daniel in the Lion's Den* and the one about the Flaming Furnace. We've rehearsed our parts, bought stage set-tings and equipment that cost money. We can't quit now."

"Then—you're determined to go on with this unholy business?"

"Who said it was unholy? We're work-ing in the interests of the church, aren't we? These dramas are Biblical plays, even if they are a bit sensational. You've got to give the public what they want, or they won't come to see it. And if they don't come, how can you tell them about God's work?"

Norton shut his eyes and groaned. The word "God," linked with such mad schem-ing, was blasphemy.

"As for this stuff you've been telling us about—" Miller shrugged— "this busi-ness of being disciples of the devil—it's sheer nonsense, Norton. You've been having nightmares!"

Norton knew that further argument would be futile. These men were poor; the sudden vision of wealth had burned itself into their souls to the exclusion of all else. He turned away, walked stiffly from the room, shuddered as he slowly climbed the staircase to his bedroom.

Later, when the deacons had gone, Ruth Winward found him there, sitting disconsolately on the bed. She sat be-side him, put an arm about his shoulders.

"You mustn't take it so hard, Paul."

He laughed. The laugh was a hoarse, throaty cackle that made her stare at him with sudden apprehension. And if she heard the muttered words that came half-audibly from his curled lips, she surely did not understand their meaning.

For Paul Norton, staring dully at the

floor, growled out incoherently: *"You have proved yourself a good servant. The Master takes care of his own. . . ."*

THAT night, alone, he sat in an over-stuffed chair in the living-room and watched in torment the crawling hands of the clock that leered at him from the mantel. Eighty-twenty. Shadows filled the room's corners and a lamp on the table glowed yellow. In half an hour or so, the program at Woodlawn Park would begin.

For hours he had paced the floor, trying to think. But thinking had not driven the black doubts from his mind or made him indifferent to his failure. Thinking, brooding, had merely brought mental visions of horrible things better forgotten.

In the shadows of the room a ghastly, featureless face had taken form, glowing with crimson significance—a majestic, dark-robed shape, standing with arms folded. And a cross, planted upside down and bearing its crucified victim. A shattered window, three stories above a concrete sidewalk where lay a broken human body. And carmine letters glowing through a blood-mist. . . .

Terror stalked the room. Beads of cold sweat glistened on Norton's forehead. He had wanted to be alone, had sent Ruth Winward away; now he dreaded loneliness and was afraid of what the room's crawling shadows might spawn.

The clock struck once. Eight-thirty. . . . Norton rose from his chair, walked slowly up the stairs, closed the bedroom door behind him. Mind and body were exhausted from waging a futile battle against intangible foes; yet he dreaded sleep. Sleep would bring a parade of new horrors.

Without undressing he sprawled on the bed and lay there, staring mutely at the ceiling. Through an unshaded window beside him a thin shaft of ocher, from a gas-burning street-light outside, angled down to yellow the floor. The rest of the room was in darkness.

Somewhere in the hall beyond the closed door, a clock was ticking—and the sound clucked hollowly, maddeningly, in a silence otherwise unbroken.

And then, with a sudden sucking intake of breath, Paul Norton jerked erect and gaped with bulging eyes at the room's rear wall!

Red letters were forming there in a carmine blur that extended the length of the wall's brown surface. Slowly the letters moved into focus, became legible. And the crimson message glared back at him as if inscribed with a brush dipped in blood.

You have served well and been rewarded, Paul Norton. But think not that you will be allowed to cancel your bargain! Your soul belongs to the Master, and the Master retains his servants through all eternity!

A shriek jangled in Norton's throat and he flung himself from the bed, staggered forward with both arms extended. Terror had snapped the color from his face and numbed him. Yet the same terror had brought him courage—mad courage.

He lunged toward the wall, then jerked to a stop and stood stiff, his mouth open and drooling saliva. The wall was blank! The crimson message had been wiped away as if swept by a blackboard eraser!

Then, sobbing, Paul Norton did what he had done before—blundered blindly about the room, peering fearfully into every shadowed corner, every dark niche and closet. He found nothing.

Failure angered him. He stood wide-legged, shook a clenched fist and snarled with the fury of a trapped animal. Rage brought a dull red flush to his gaunt face and hooked his drooling mouth. Lurid words husked from his throat.

"I've not made any bargain, damn you! I'm not a servant of the devil!"

The words bounded back from the blank wall, mocking him. A shudder shook his body; moments passed while fear and madness fought for supremacy in his tortured mind. Then he thrust a clammy hand to his face, mopped the sweat that gleamed there.

"By God, I'll show you whose servant I am! I'll put a stop to the whole rotten affair! Right now!"

He stormed to the door, flung it open with such violence that it thunderclapped against the corridor wall. Breathing in great gulps, he strode down the stairs, snatched hat and coat from a rack in the lower hall and slammed the front door behind him.

Not until he was pushing open the sliding doors of the garage, a moment later, did the fury go out of his heart and leave him prey to renewed terror. But desperation urged him on. Hunched behind the wheel, he drove the small coupé at reckless speed out of the yard, and turned its blunt nose toward the maze of lonely roads that led to Woodlawn.

Rain spattered the windshield. The clock on the instrument board showed five minutes past nine. Occasional lighted homes swept past, and then Norton strained his eyes to see into a misty darkness broken only by the car's headlights.

By now, the crowd at the park would be watching the curtain rise on the first of the sensational Biblical dramas which would stuff the pockets of the deacons with unholy profits. But the dramas would not go on! He, Paul Norton, would demand a showdown!

He wondered dully if he would have courage enough to go through with it. The ordeal of the past two days had done things to his mind; his head throbbed viciously and he found it hard to think, hard even to concentrate on the immediate task of driving. The darkness around him was a wet winding-sheet, closing in relentlessly. . . .

He groaned, took one hand from the wheel and brought the flat of his palm against his cheek. The shock stiffened him, cleared his blurred vision. But the shadows came back; his head spawned a dull droning sound that weighted his brain. The road was an ill-defined aisle of misty gloom that refused to be still.

It was a treacherous road, too, that wound like a wet black serpent between walls of massed trees. Rain made it slippery; rain dripped from the car's windshield and the heat of Paul Norton's laboring breath fogged the glass on the inside.

Again and again he wiped it clean with the palm of his hand, but new mist formed and the effort of fighting it only added to his exhaustion, fed on his remaining strength and brought moaning sounds from his lips. And the fog in his mind could not be wiped out; it grew thicker, more impenetrable. Driving was an effort. Thinking was an effort even greater.

He knew then that his mind was no longer his own. Out of the darkness around him, some malignant power had extended sucking tentacles to claim him. Bloody words formed in his brain, swam in a red mist before his staring eyes.

"Your soul belongs to me, Paul Norton. . . ."

Black fear clawed at him, blinding him to the tangible perils ahead. His hands were white, clutching the wheel. His foot trembled on the accelerator. Every fiber of his being screamed at him to apply the brakes, pull the car to the side of the road and wait for that numbing, nerve-tearing sensation to depart. But his muscles refused to obey. The car roared through darkness, careening madly from side to side.

Ahead, the mammoth neon sign of Woodlawn Park blazed in darkness, and a sob of relief welled in Norton's throat. In another moment. . . .

Sudden rain swept the windshield, blinding him. Frantically he wrenched his foot from the gas-pedal, jammed it on the brake; but sluggish muscles responded too slowly. The car swerved; the wheel spun from his numbed hands. With a sickening lunge the machine careened sideways, roared off the road-shoulder into sodden sand.

Gaunt trees loomed in the glare of the headlights and Norton's hands clawed madly at the wheel. A scream spewed from his lips. Abruptly, the bole of a huge pine rushed toward the leaping lights of the machine.

Creation upended. Sudden agony stabbed Paul Norton's rigid body. A roar of deafening thunder burst in his brain.

His last conscious sensation was of flying through space—hurtling in a contorted, battered heap, at express-train speed, into a black void of horror whence mocking laughter accompanied him into oblivion.

CHAPTER THREE

Sworn to Satan

ALL about Paul Norton the world was in motion—a jet-black world that flowed over and through him, filled him with a strange buoyancy as of gliding through deep dark water with the light of day far above and death terribly close.

Death—terribly—close. The thought grew in the laboring agony of his mind until now he was running in nightmare terror—running with every ounce of strength, spurred on by stark fear and desperation—yet unable to escape the cruel chains that bound him.

His eyes opened and he knew now

that actually he was being carried, but darkness hung all about him and his blurred gaze failed to make out the forms of his bearers. A taste of blood was in his mouth and a crushing pain pressed his skull. He heard the tread of slow-moving feet, many of them, and knew that he had been borne from the scene of the accident and lugged deep into the woods.

The sandy ruts beneath him were part of an old tote-road. Somewhere in here, about half a mile from the main highway, lay a crooked body of water called Fletcher's pond, with an abandoned icehouse looming at the road's end. . . .

He fought the hands that held him. Oblivion returned. Yet through agony-racked darkness he was aware of the passing of time, felt new torment as his bearers occasionally stumbled, jarring his limp body.

He knew at last that his captors had stopped and were talking in low whispers. A door creaked; he was carried over a wooden floor that groaned protestingly. Ungently he was dumped to the floor. Warm hands tore his bloody shirt, stripped him to the waist. He was pushed backward until his naked shoulders made contact with a wall.

Then a light glowed, and with an effort Norton forced his eyes open, stared until his dazed brain recorded his surroundings.

This was a room somewhere in the old ice-house. He had been here before, while hunting small game in the thickets around Fletcher's Pond. But why had he been brought here? What earthly reason. . . ?

And *who had brought him?*

Torment surged through him when he turned his head. Blood had run from a throbbing gash above his eyes, a gash probably inflicted by broken windshield glass. The cords of his neck were stiff, leathery, and seemed to creak their protest at being stretched.

The room was empty. A worm-eaten floor ran crookedly into bare walls that bulged upward in gloom. Some kind of ice-chute angled downward in the far corner, extending apparently from a chamber above this one to a chamber below. A soot-blackened lantern was the room's sole source of light.

In a daze he looked down at his feet, saw that his ankles were roped together. For the first time he realized that he could not move his hands; they were fastened behind him. Dully, without much ambition, he tried to pull his wrists free; and the creaking of a door interrupted him, caused the muscles of his aching body to go suddenly rigid.

Then, staring at the sight before him, he doubted for a moment his own sanity.

THE door in the wall opposite him had groaned open, and across that time-worn threshold came a company so strange, so utterly out of place in such surroundings, that he shook his head violently, hoping to clear his brain of what must surely be a vision born of suffering and pain. But the strange creatures came slowly toward him, and they were real!

Women! Young women, half naked, their sensuous bodies gleaming in the pulsing light of the lantern! With an effort Norton closed his eyes, blinked them open again, yet though his mind was still dazed and his vision blurred, the creatures before him did not fade!

Yet something about those near-naked bodies and gloating faces was unreal, unholy! Every pair of eyes was filled with hunger. Every one of those too-beautiful faces was pale with a paleness as of death!

A scream welled in Norton's throat, died there unuttered. He stared with enormous eyes at the leader of the strange procession. Stared, and leaned forward as that sensuous body came nearer.

The bloodless face was terribly familiar. It—no, no, it could not be! His overwrought nerves were playing tricks upon him. He stared, held his breath as the girl came closer with a slow gliding motion that seemed inhuman. Then at last his lips writhed open to utter a hoarse babble of sound.

"Ruth! Oh, God, no! No! . . ."

For the leader of that mad company was indeed the girl who but a few hours hence had tried to comfort him. The girl who had promised to be his wife!

As she advanced, she drew her naked right arm from behind her back, and the slender too-white fingers of her hand gripped a thing that glowed dark red. That glowing thing was a heated iron rod, its tapered point pulsing as if alive!

As the members of the unholy clan closed about their terrified victim, Ruth Winward stood rigid, stared down into Paul Norton's face and said in a low monotone: "The Master punishes those who plot to disobey him. Prepare yourself, Paul Norton—for the punishment will not be light!"

Norton felt his eyes leaving their sockets, felt the blood in his stiff body run hot, then cold with terror. He knew that his face was a mask, gaunt and horrible.

As from a great distance he heard more words issuing from the lips in the blurred face before him. "The mark of the Master, Paul Norton. . . ." The misted face swayed closer. Norton's gaze focused on the glowing tip of the iron rod, as the red needle-point made contact.

A nerve-numbing horror was his soul, and the touch of the hot iron seemed ice-cold. Somehow it did not hurt. He stared down at it, saw the flesh of his bare chest turn black as the iron burned a deep design that was vaguely familiar.

Where had he seen that mark before? It was a cross—an inverted cross. Years ago, in darkness, he had wandered into a place called Woodlawn Park and seen the same kind of cross, with a man crucified on it. Yes . . . a crucified man . . . and the unpleasant odor that was choking his nostrils now was a stench of burning flesh. His own flesh. . . .

Wearily he raised his head. He knew now that he was in pain, yet the pain was not acute; it was like a dull headache, days old. One got used to such pain. It was like being drugged, doped. The agony was there, but the brain was too dead to heed it. Too tired. . . .

"You are a servant of the Master, Paul Norton, just as we are." That was Ruth speaking. His head lolled on his neck as he tried to look up at her. The iron bar still glowed in her hand, and its dull rediation made a carmine statue of her half-naked body. But that body was like something in a diffused photograph, with no definite outline. It had soft white breasts and a sloping bare abdomen, but he could not see it clearly. . . .

"You are a servant of the Master." The girl's words come slowly, ominously. "At first you served well and were rewarded. Then, foolishly, you planned to disobey the Master's commands."

STRANGE words to be issuing from the lips of Ruth Winward! In mild amazement Norton gazed into her blurred face, frowned at her. She seemed to be waiting for an answer. When he made none she stepped back, muttered something to one of her companions. Then, taking a small vial from the companion's hand, she leaned forward, forced Norton's mouth open and upended the vial's liquid contents in his gaping mouth. He was too weak to resist.

The stuff trickled down, forced him to swallow. It had a bitter burning taste.

Slowly then, he became more aware of the agony that stabbed his branded chest.

"Listen to me, Paul Norton!" his torturer said. "You are a minister, a man of your word. The Master demands your solemn promise that never again will you try to interfere with his plans!"

Paul Norton's reply was a moan of pain. Impatience filled the corpse-face of the woman before him. She took a short step forward, and the glowing iron bar hung within inches of his face.

"Would you care to lose your eyes, Paul Norton?"

He stared, and the red end of the rod became a mammoth blur, menacing his bulging eyeballs. Abruptly, then, he knew the truth. The liquid which had been poured down his throat was an antidote for some unholy drug that had long gripped his mind. A drug-deadened mind would not suit the purpose of these fiends. They wanted him to feel the agony they were about to inflict!

Agony was already in him. His burned chest throbbed viciously. Terror was a living, crawling thing upon him.

"I give you ten seconds," the girl rasped. "Either you give your word of honor to obey the Master's every wish, or. . . ." The glowing rod moved nearer, searing Norton's eyes with its heat. *What is your answer?*

Somewhere, Paul Norton found courage and defiance. "I won't do it! I won't!"

An evil smile curled the lips of the girl he loved. As if moved by some hypnotic power that claimed her soul, she swayed closer. A scream jangled in Norton's throat as he cringed from the menacing iron bar. The wall stopped him.

The glowing rod inched forward to make black wells of agony of his eyes. Stark terror seized him, left him limp. Incoherent words babbled from his lips.

"I promise! Oh, God, leave me alone! I can't stand any more. . . ."

The bar receded. Once again Ruth Winward stood over him. Vaguely he was aware that the ropes on his ankles were loosened, and he was being set free.

Warm arms gripped his armpits, helped him to his feet. The same hands pushed him toward the doorway through which those half-naked mistresses of hell had entered. And a low, triumphant voice was saying: "Go, Paul Norton. And remember that the Master is all-powerful. If you break your promise, your torment will be greater than that of a lost soul in Purgatory!"

Norton's feet stumbled on the threshold; the door rasped shut behind him. Alone, half-naked and branded with a mark that would live with him through eternity, he stumbled into the night, sobbing with a realization that he had pledged his soul to some dark monster who would watch over him, checking his every word, his every movement, even the thoughts that festered in his tortured brain.

WHAT time it was when he emerged from the woods, Paul Norton could not tell. Ages of agony and bewilderment had passed since the car had crashed. His brain had wandered in darkness. He had been drugged, then given a restorative.

He stood in the road and peered around him, saw a black contorted shape which was the wreck of his own car. Helplessly he stared at it, then trudged toward the mammoth neon sign of Woodlawn Park, a few hundred yards distant.

The sign was a blazing red emblem in the dark. The hour, then, could not be so very late. The park was still open.

Only half aware of his near-nakedness, of the sinister hell-sign branded on his bare chest, he passed beneath the crimson letters and trudged along the park's main path, toward lighted buildings. This end of the park was deserted; a wave of sound rolled toward him from the huge dance-hall where Mowry and the others had planned to put on a double bill of sensational entertainment.

People were massed about the hall's entrance, apparently clamoring for admission. The deacons had been right. This place would coin money. If tonight's crowd were any indication of what would follow, it was obvious that the park would be a gold-mine. But the church would see little of that money. And old Jason Manley from his beath-bed had demanded solemn promises that the church would benefit.

Mechanically, Norton plodded on, staring at the milling mob of people under the floodlights that blazed from the dance-hall's roof. It was a young crowd, the type of crowd that ordinarily would have come to dance to the jangling jazz of some popular orchestra. Good-looking girls, attractive young men, happy, noisy, eager for the thrills that had been promised them. They paid no attention to the solitary figure of Paul Norton.

And Norton, peering ahead, did not see the dark shape that stood in the doorway of the office as he went past.

That shape suddenly stiffened, gaped, then strode forward. An outthrust hand seized Norton's arm.

"Norton! Good Lord, man, what's happened to you?"

He turned slowly and peered into the fat, dumpy face of Alexander Pierson. Fear had leaped into Norton's eyes, but now went sluggishly out of them. He mumbled thickly, "Oh. It's you. I thought—"

Pierson's searching gaze darkened with suspicion. His grip on Norton's arm tightened and he said softly: "Better come into the office and I'll fix you up. Dwight and Miller and the others are in costume for the Fiery Furnace number. They left their clothes here." With significant patience he ushered Norton over the sill, led him to a chair.

A moment later, when he returned to the chair after taking a shirt and coat from a peg in the wall, he peered darkly at the mark on Paul Norton's chest, caught a slow, noisy breath and said: "What have you been doing to yourself?"

"It's nothing. Just—a burn."

"A *what?*"

"I don't feel like talking, Pierson. I —I'm tired." Sluggishly, Norton thrust his aching arms into the shirt, stood up and put on the coat that Pierson held for him. "You said Dwight and Miller and the others are taking part in—what?"

"The big sensation of the evening." Pierson's wet mouth curled in a grin. "The casting of black-souled sinners into a fiery furnace. The furnace is the real thing, and so are the victims. A great little act. Miller's the man who doped it out."

"But—"

"Oh, it's perfectly safe. No one'll get hurt. Miller himself is one of the lost souls. On the floor of the dance-hall, right next to the orchestra platform, we've got a big iron tank about six feet deep. The victims will be herded across the platform and forced to leap down into the flames, to the accompaniment of much screaming and wailing for mercy. And if you don't think Miller and the others can do a good job of wailing, you should have heard them in here half an hour ago, rehearsing!"

NO ANSWERING smile touched Norton's gaunt face. He said slowly: "How can they be thrown into the flames without being hurt?"

"Easy. Miller got all the dope from Houdini's book on magic and we tried it out beforehand. All it takes is a little careful anointing."

"And this is the second act of the evening?"

"Second and last. The first was *Daniel in the Lions' Den* and yours truly himself played the part of Daniel." Pierson's thick neck pulsed with a triumphant chuckle. "We had a big cage rigged up with sandbags and painted canvas to look like a den, and the French Brothers Circus gave us the loan of four ferocious-looking lions. It looked like the real thing, I'm telling you!"

Norton paced to the door, stared out across the park. An unreasonable sensation of terror crawled through him; his hands were white on the door-frame, his face pale. Hesitantly he said: "I—I want to see this." Then he strode forward, with Pierson behind him.

The thing happened as Paul Norton reached the edge of the crowd and began pushing his way toward the entrance. Happened as though timed to his arrival. On the stage the Fiery Furnace scene was in progress. From the interior of the dance-hall, an interior choked to the very walls with a sea of sensation-seeking humanity, came a vibrant scream of horror —from the throat of a young woman who realized the truth before those about her were aware that anything had gone wrong.

Then as others realized what was happening up there on the stage, countless hundreds of human voices took up the terror-cry. The milling mob went mad. A shrill storm-wind of sound poured against walls and roof, shook the wooden frame-building to its foundations and went wailing across the park in soul-searing crescendo.

Paul Norton's blood ran cold as he battered his way forward. How he got through that terror-crazed mob and reached the scene of horror, he was never sure. The borrowed coat and shirt were torn from his body; reeling, staggering, sobbing for breath, he fought through to the huge tank that stood near the platform.

Heat blasted his face and a roaring wall of scarlet flame blinded him, but he saw what was happening. Saw a group of flame-reddened shapes struggling frantically to pull a shrieking, burning thing over the tank's iron rim.

Blasted by the fury of the flames, they dragged that writhing shape clear, lowered it to the floor and beat desperately at the crimson hell that enshrouded it. Other men were staring with horror-wide eyes into the tank's inferno, and one of them—Clinton Miller—was screaming lurid words that tocsined above the din of the mob.

"Mowry and Shaw! They're still in there! Oh, God—!"

After that, Paul Norton was not sure of what happened. A blackness filled his brain and the torturing heat sent streaks of fiery agony through his already weakened body. Dully he was aware that he tried to help, tried to stumble forward and take a pitifully small fire-extinguisher from a gibbering idiot who had no notion of how to use it. But someone else pulled the thing from Norton's grasp and pushed him away. He stumbled, went down.

People were screaming the names of Mowry and Shaw. Frantic men were stumbling in one another's way in their blind efforts to help; yet none knew what to do or how to be of assistance. The writhing shape on the floor, the blazing human torch that had been dragged from the tank, was moaning in agony as fevered hands tore the smouldering clothes from his body. His face was a blackened, distorted gargoyle of pain, and it was the face of Edmund Dwight.

Half-dazed, Paul Norton pushed himself up on hands and knees, tried to gain his feet. But lunging shapes crashed against him and tumbled him off balance again. A tidal wave of darkness blotted out his last conscious vision—that of a seething, surging mass of flame-reddened humanity gone mad.

CHAPTER FOUR

Blood Message

ANXIOUS-FACED men were standing around him when he came to. They had carried him across the park to the administration office and lowered him into a chair. Peering into their faces, Paul Norton read the horror that was engraved there. His hand went out to clutch the arm of Alexander Pierson.

"Mowry—Shaw—" he said. "Are they—?"

Pierson nodded and his lips formed the word "dead," but no sound came. Clinton Miller stood like a propped-up corpse, his large, shabbily dressed body trembling from head to foot, his face drained of color. It was Miller who had invented the fatal fiery furnace and prepared the victims. . . .

"You've been unconscious nearly an hour," Pierson said dully. "We're the last ones here. Dwight's been taken to the hospital, and they've carried Shaw and Mowry away. If you're strong enough to go home. . . ."

He did break, on the long ride home. Sobs shook his big body and incoherent words blubbered on his lips. "Oh, my God, it was all my fault! But I didn't know! I thought I'd taken every precaution against accidents. Something must have been wrong with the solutions I used. . . ."

His companions were grimly silent. Pierson's dark eyes watched Miller's every move and were clouded with suspicion. Suspicion burned in other eyes, too, but Paul Norton was too tired to notice. When at last the car stopped before the rectory, he climbed wearily out, let himself into the house and went straight upstairs to the bedroom.

The events of the past few hours were strangely jumbled in his mind. They seemed diffused, blurred, as if spawned in the distorted ramblings of a nightmare.

The wreck of his car, the torments inflicted on him by those death-faced women in the old ice-house near Fletcher's Pond—those things could not have happened! They were unreal. So, too, was the hideous accident that had claimed the lives of two of the deacons, Mowry and Shaw, and injured Edmund Dwight.

Yet those things were real and he knew it. Horror had stalked the night; devil's laughter had triumphantly ridden the darkness. And he, Paul Norton, minister of the word of God, was branded with a hell-mark that would disfigure him until death.

Standing naked before a mirror, he gazed at the inverted cross and·saw again the living-dead face of the girl who had tortured him. Her name whispered in torment from his lips. "Ruth! Ruth—"

How he got downstairs to the telephone, he was not sure. When he gripped the instrument and called Ruth's number his face and neck were drenched with cold sweat and his body shook as with the ague. Breath wheezed in his throat as he waited. Merciful God, would they never answer? Would they never come? . . .

A voice droned through the receiver, the voice of Ruth's mother. The woman was vexed at being roused out of bed at such an hour.

"I—I want to speak to Ruth," Norton mumbled. "It's important. Please—"

"Is this Paul Norton?"

"Yes. Yes, it's Paul."

"But Ruth's in bed. She went to her room hours ago and I don't like to wake her. She wasn't feeling well, Paul."

"In—bed—hours ago?" Norton said weakly.

"Why, yes. Is something wrong?"

"No. It's all right, Mrs. Winward. I'm sorry. . . ." The receiver slipped from Norton's fingers. Slowly he climbed the stairs again, closed the bedroom door behind him. Ruth, in bed hours ago? Then how—?

His brain refused to think any more. Groaning, he threw himself on the bed, buried his face in a pillow. Everything now was blurred by a dark mist of torment that would not dissolve.

He dozed. A sensation of impending peril aroused him, dragged him out of a half-sleep that was loaded with evil forebodings. Instinctively he sat up, stared at the wall.

Crimson letters glowed there, as they had glowed twice before!

Tonight's torment was merely a warning, my servant! If you again dare to disobey me, I shall drag your soul to the torment-pits of hell! I shall come as the woman you love, and destroy you!

Snarling, Norton surged erect. But the sinister message faded before his eyes; he sagged back again. He had come to realize now the futility of fighting intangible evils. Moaning dully, he closed his eyes, lay in a cold sweat until sleep came mercifully to relieve him.

SUNLIGHT was in the room when he awoke. A clock on the dresser said eight a. m. and he remembered dully that the day was Sunday. . The first Sunday in the month, and he must give Holy Communion.

Downstairs, he called Ruth. This time it was Ruth, not her mother, who answered the phone.

"You—you were home last night?" Norton demanded.

She seemed to hesitate. Then: "Yes,

Paul. I went to bed early because I didn't feel well. I must have slept soundly, because I woke up only half an hour ago. But—but it was a queer sleep, full of the strangest dreams—"

"You'll be at church?"

"Yes, of course."

"I'll see you there, then. I must talk to you."

Scowling, he hung up, tried to think.

So she had not slept well. She had dreamed strange dreams. . . .

Black doubt festered in Norton's mind and stayed with him, filled him with uneasiness as he shaved and showered. Standing in the shower he again fingered the hell-mark on his chest, and shuddered. With the brand of the devil upon him, he must go now to administer the Holy Sacrament. . . .

It was late when he reached the church, and he knew by the lifeless tone of people's voices as they greeted him, and by the fixed, dead expressions of their faces, that the news of last night's horrible disaster had traveled through town. Alone, he went to the vestry, closed the door on himself and approached the linen-covered table near the wall. He would barely have time to prepare the wine. . . .

He froze in his tracks, stood staring. A dark brown bottle lay on its side on the linen-covered table—the same dark brown bottle that should be standing upright, filled with wine. But the red liquid that had run from the bottle's mouth, forming a scarlet pool on the tablecloth, did not look like wine. It was too red, too thick.

On leaden feet Norton moved forward, stared down. Like thick red paint the liquid from the overturned bottle flooded the cloth. And it was not wine. Even before extending a trembling hand to touch that viscous pool he knew the truth. It was *blood!*

And on the only portion of the cloth not stained by the pool itself, some fiendish forefinger had traced a *bloody inverted cross, symbol of sin!*

Blood! The red liquid—the wine he was supposed to serve to those who took Communion—was blood! They would be damned, all of them, just as he was damned!

But no one had seen him come in here! He stared frantically around, reeled backward. There was a side door by which he could escape without encountering any of the congregation. He *had* to go!

Frenzy seized him and darkness beat in his brain as he wrenched the door open. Then he ran. Ran with terror sapping the strength from his legs and his half-crouched body a shuddering, stumbling thing that refused to obey his will. Thank God, the distance home was short, through the back yard of the church and across his own back yard to the rear door! If it were any longer. . . .

The back steps of the rectory tripped him; he sprawled against the door, reeled inside and slammed the barrier behind him. The thud of his footsteps along the hall beat a jangling sing-song. *Blood—blood—blood—blood!* A red mist of madness swam before his eyes as he lurched into the living-room and slumped, sobbing, into a chair. . . .

How long he sat there, frantically gripping the chair-arms and staring straight ahead of him with eyes that saw only blackness, he was not sure. Someone was insistently ringing the front doorbell.

He went to the door and opened it mechanically, stared into the bewildered face of Alexander Pierson. Pierson gaped at him, pushed over the sill and began talking in a quick, harsh voice.

"Norton! For Heaven's sake, man, don't you know this is Communion Sunday? We've been holding up the service, waiting for you. You—"

"I don't feel well," Norton mumbled.

"Then why didn't you let us know? We've been frantic! Dwight and Miller and I have looked all over for you!"

"Dwight? I—I thought he—"

"He's up and around, in bandages. Wasn't hurt as badly as we thought. But look here, Norton, if you're sick, let me get a doctor. You can't just stand there and say you're ill without doing something about it!"

"I—I'll lie down for a while," Norton said slowly. "Yes, that's the best thing. Come back later."

He closed the door, turned wearily and climbed the stairs to the bedroom. It took a long while and the stairs seemed endless, reaching upward into infinity. Something was wrong with his brain; it was an effort to think, even to concentrate on such a simple task as climbing a flight of stairs. Things were blurred and unreal, just as they had been before he had driven the car off the road.

He was conscious of closing the bedroom door behind him, and of walking slowly toward the bed. The shades were down and the room was filled with a pale half-light that confused him.

Then he saw something and his feet stopped their sluggish advance; his hand went out, cold as ice, to grip the bedpost. A shriek climbed from the depths of his rigid body and came in a weak chatter from his lips.

Words were on the wall. Crimson words glaring out at him. Like a drunken man he stood gaping at them, struggling to make his brain decipher them. In a daze he moved forward, reached out to see if they were real.

And this time the words did not vanish when his stiff fingers made contact. The tips of his fingers smeared through a line of crimson letters and came away wet and sticky. The words were written in blood!

You are to murder three men—Miller, Pierson, and Dwight—within the next twenty-four hours! It is the Master's command! Do not fail, or terrible punishment will be meted out to you by the hand of the woman you love!

NORTON stared until the crimson words blurred before him, became a red mist of horror. He stumbled back, sank shuddering to the bed. Moments passed; the clock on the dresser ticked on. Still he sat staring, while black terror mounted within him.

"By the hand of the woman you love!" What did that mean? Was it a hideous confirmation of the dark belief that had shadowed his mind ever since the brand of sin had been burned on his body?

What else could it mean? The half-naked girl who had burned that brand on him had acted abnormally, as if under some strange influence. And Ruth Winward had admitted not feeling well, had confessed to strange nightmares. . . .

In a daze he made his way downstairs, closed the door of the living-room behind him and sat down stiffly at the Governor Winthrop desk. For the best part of an hour he used pen and paper, filling many sheets with a complete, truthful account of everything that had happened to him. When his task was at last completed, he folded the sheets, pushed them into an envelope and stuffed the envelope into his coat pocket. Then, bareheaded, he left the house.

The Winward home was less than half a mile distant, but he used thirty minutes getting there. Time meant nothing now. Walking slowly, he looked around with wide eyes that were anxious to miss none of the day's beauty.

It would be the last time. In a little while sunlight and green trees and the sound of birds twittering would no longer be of his world. His world would be a deep chasm of darkness peopled with sinister shapes and prowling specters: a place of everlasting torment and agony.

When he climbed the steps of the Winward home and hesitantly rang the bell, Mrs. Winward opened the door to him. She, at least, had not changed. White-haired and motherly, she gazed at him with worried eyes. "Paul, you're not well," she said anxiously. "What has happened?"

He followed her inside and saw that Ruth was not at home. "She is at church," Mrs. Winward said in answer to his question. "She should be here soon."

An aroma of burning food came from the kitchen and Mrs. Winward hurried away. Alone, Norton sat in the parlor, amid dark shapes of Colonial furniture that seemed solid and comforting.

Then—she came.

She stood motionless in the doorway, staring at him. A single anxious word left her lips— "Paul!" —and then her hands gripped his shoulders and she gazed down into his face, trying to read what lay there. "Paul, what's wrong?"

"I want to talk to you, alone."

She seemed to understand. Quietly she closed the door leading to the kitchen, then came back, sat facing him. "Yes?" Her voice was low, pleading. "Yes, Paul?"

With trembling fingers he pulled from his pocket the envelope he had stuffed there. "Read this. Read every word of it. Then you'll understand."

It took her a long while. He had written a full account of everything, beginning with the discovery of Deacon Wyman's body on the inverted cross in the park, and the appearance of the nameless dark shape that had so inexplicably vanished; and ending with an account of the final command that he commit murder.

Color seeped from her face as she read the written lines. Long before she had finished, her breast was rising and falling as if in danger of bursting, and her hands shook as they tried to hold the pages steady. In the end she looked up, said in a hesitant whisper: "Oh, God, Paul, what does it *mean?*"

"It means I can't stand any more of it. It's the end." He stood over her, reached down and took her hands. "There's only one way out, dearest. A week ago, if anyone had told me that the devil had power to enslave human beings, I would have laughed and accused him of living in the Dark Ages. Now I know better. There's only one way out and I'm taking it."

"Oh, God, no! *No*, Paul!"

"It won't be hard, dear." Strange, that he should be trying to console her, at a time when his own soul was black with torment.

She stared at him as if hearing her own death-sentence. Loveliness had vanished from her face, leaving it bloodless. Abruptly her hand gripped Norton's wrist.

"Paul, promise me you'll wait! I know something—something that you don't. I'll go with you to the park tonight and show you!"

"It's no use, dear."

"I tell you I know something!" Desperation blazed in her eyes and the grip of her hand was so savage that it purpled his wrist. "I've lived in Denham longer than you have! I was here when the park site was cleared and the buildings were put up. You've written here—" She stabbed a trembling finger at the letter—"that a dark shape seemed to vanish into thin air. I'll show you how it was done!"

"You—know?"

"I think so, Paul. Oh, God, I hope I'm right!"

"Then we'll go out there now, and—"

"No." Her voice was suddenly low, almost a whisper. "Wait for darkness, Paul. Then no one will see us. Promise me you'll wait."

His answer was slow in coming, came at last as if forcefully dragged from his lips. "I'll wait. We'll go tonight. . . ."

CHAPTER FIVE

Into the Pit

THERE was no moon and the road through the woods was an ink-black aisle of crawling shadows, evilly dark on both sides. The big neon sign at the park's entrance was unlighted. This was Sunday, and the park was closed.

Norton had spoken but a few words to the girl beside him since the start of the journey. He stared at her now, and a feeling of uneasiness wriggled inside him, filling him with apprehension. The blood-words of that last message were in his mind and seemed to blaze luridly across the road ahead, warning him. " . . . By the hand of the woman you love!" He shuddered. Something about Ruth *was* strange.

Her face was abnormally pale, just as the face of the merciless creature who had branded him had been pale. He didn't remember much about that particular interlude. It had been a dark blur of agony even at the time, and he had been drugged, dazed.

The neon sign loomed overhead and Norton braked the car to a stop, climbed out. The sudden sharp glance that Ruth Winward threw at him startled him; he took an involuntary step backward as she climbed from the car. Something was wrong, dead wrong! But he had to trust her. Had to believe in her!

Her hand found his arm and clung there. Whispered words left her lips as she stared fearfully into the dark. "I— I'm afraid, Paul. I feel so—so numb— the way I felt last night."

He scowled. So she felt "strange" again. Sudden terror clutched him. He,

too, had felt "strange" the last time he had driven out here. Had been unable to think. Some hellish power had owned his mind, bending his will to another will possessed of fiendish strength. Now it was Ruth. . . .

"Let's get out of here!" he said sharply.

"No, Paul. I've got to show you." She broke from his restraining grip and almost ran toward the gate. When he caught up with her she was striding resolutely along the gravel path toward the administration office and the dark expanse of lawn beyond it, where that inverted cross had loomed blackly in the dark.

The cross was not there now. Miller, Pierson, Dwight and the others—the others who were now dead!—had removed it. Only the dark man-high hulks of evergreen shrubs rose above the lawn's level. And Ruth was striding toward them.

Passing the ragged hole where the death-cross had been planted, she shuddered but did not stop. Straight to the nearest shrub she went, and it was the same shrub that Norton had examined so carefully, eternities ago.

She stood motionless and her face in the dark was ghastly pale, stiff as a plaster-mask. "When this park was originally laid out," she said harshly — so harshly that the metallic rasp of her voice made him gape at her in amazement—"the administration building was to be right here. They laid the foundations, then changed their plans. They filled the hole up again but left a tunnel, planning to use it later for some kind of amusement device—an underground boat-ride or railway or something. Anyway, the idea was abandoned and the entrance blocked up. I never would have remembered it if you hadn't said in your letter that a—a dark shape disappeared without leaving a trace."

She forced a mirthless laugh, reached out and pushed against the shrub. Norton's eyes widened, filled with sudden comprehension. He stepped forward. When he stooped, put both arms around the evergreen and hauled, the shrub came up, dragging with it the big wooden tub in which it was planted.

At Norton's feet a rectangular pit of blackness extended downward. He leaned forward, cupped a glowing match in his hands. Matchlight disclosed a flight of concrete steps.

He sucked a deep breath, straightened again. "So that's where the killer went to!" Triumph blinded him to the strange glint in the eyes of the girl who stood watching him. "I'm going down there! Going to see what's at the end of that tunnel!"

Even before his declaration had died to silence he had one foot on the top step. Here at last was something tangible, that might lead somewhere! These steps were real, not spawned in a hideous nightmare. Eagerly he descended, then remembered that he was not alone. Abruptly he stopped, looked up.

At the rim of the pit Ruth Winward seemed to hesitate, and her slender body, silhouetted against the dark of the sky, seemed for a fleeting instant to sway on stiff legs. "Wait, Paul!" Even her voice was abnormal, queerly inflexible. "Wait for me. Don't leave me alone!"

Then the tunnel narrowed; Norton dropped the girl's hand, went more slowly. The scrape of his boot-soles on hard concrete was like thunder. In his eagerness he widened the distance between Ruth and himself.

Her low cry pulled him up short. He turned, could see nothing in the solid blackness. A sudden premonition of danger stabbed through him. The girl's scuffing footsteps came nearer.

In that lampblack gloom he neither saw nor heard the thing that crashed down on him. It came from nowhere, grinding against his head. Blazing lights of agony roared in his brain and a giant cannon-cracker exploded in his skull.

THE blazing lights that had accompanied his plunge were again in his brain when consciousness began slowly to filter back, lifting him up through a swirling world of blood-rimmed shadows.

No, the lights were not in his brain. They were out in front of his eyes—deep, vivid blotches of scarlet mist that lunged, twisted, leapt like frantic flames. And he was still in the tunnel, but not alone.

The agony in his head did things to his eyes, so that the tunnel walls, glowing dark red now through the blood-mist, seemed to move and sway as he stared at them. He knew he must be delirious. The strange half-naked shapes that stood around him could not be real!

Yet they were real. Vaguely he remembered having encountered them before, after the smash-up of his car. These were the same chalk-faced women, the mistresses of hell who had tortured him!

He groaned, flattened his hands on the stone floor and tried to push himself up, but other hands clamped on his shoulders and forced him down again. A face swam toward him through the red mist and hung above him, peering down. He stared into it, opened his mouth to scream, but no scream came. The face was twisted in a mirthless smile. It was her face. Ruth's. . . .

His black fears had come true, then. He had made no mistake about that other occasion. *Ruth, too, was one of the devil's disciples.* Oh, God!

But why did that crimson glare still fill the tunnel? He had regained full consciousness now; the agony-mist in his brain should be clearing and the tunnel should be dark. Yet that red glow persisted, and the passage was unbearably hot, bringing sweat to his face and to the near-naked bodies that crowded around him. . . .

Strong hands seized his ankles and yanked his legs clear of the floor. The jolt rocked his shoulders back and his head cracked against solid stone. New agony coursed through him.

Now he was being dragged along the tunnel. Every irregularity in the floor inflicted torment, but his captors did not stop. Relentlessly they pulled him along, and the crimson glow brightened around him as they hauled him deeper into the earth's bowels. The heat grew more intense, more unbearable.

Suddenly the walls fell away on either side; the passage widened, became a subterranean chamber—a hell-chamber filled with roaring redness and savage heat that was like a breath from some mighty blast-furnace. Half-naked shapes bent above him. His clothes were being ripped from his body.

Always, above him, hung the living-dead face of Ruth Winward, gloating over his helplessness. . . .

Then, as savage hands jerked his naked body to a sitting position and propped him against the wall, he saw something else, and terror crawled like a monstrous maggot through his veins. A scream burst from his lips.

The floor before him sloped gently downward; the far end of the room was a roaring hell-pit of flame. And now clutching hands had taken hold of him, gripping his armpits, thighs, ankles, and were hauling him forward toward the pit!

This was a torment-chamber of hell's inferno. These near-naked women were slaves of the Black Master. *And he, Paul Norton, was to be the victim!*

Stark terror gave him strength to struggle; he fought with mad fury, raking with both hands at the hot, bare flesh of his captors. But they outnumbered him, swarmed over him and pinned his arms, held him helpless. Step by step they dragged him forward, down that sloping floor of stone. And with each forward step the heat grew more devouring, the crimson glare burned more viciously against his seared eyeballs.

Then there was something else, something he had not seen since that first black night in the park. As if spawned by the flames themselves, the monster himself stood like some huge statue, arms folded, shapeless face staring triumphantly through the red hell. Norton shuddered.

Paul Norton, stark naked and racked with a thousand agonies of flesh and spirit, had no strength left for fighting. The mouth of hell was waiting, the roaring furnace hungry for its victim. This was the end. . . .

And above his terror-frozen face, as he was dragged relentlessly forward, hung the leering face of the girl who had loved him. *She* was the ring-leader, the chief handmaiden of the Black One! When his naked body was flung to the flames, *she* would revel in his dying shrieks of agony!

"Ruth!" The name croaked from his throat. "Ruth! Oh, my God—!"

His cry brought strange results. Behind him, sounds of conflict came from the tunnel's entrance, and an answering scream in a girl's terror-laden voice shrilled through the rock-walled chamber. "Paul! *Paul!* Oh, my dear, my dear—"

He stiffened, managed somehow to jerk his head around. Dark horror welled over him in a viscous wave. In the doorway that led from the tunnel, a second group of hell's mistresses were parading forward, dragging a second victim. And like himself, the other victim was stark naked.

The glare of the fire made a glowing thing of her struggling body, crimsoned her heaving breasts. Flame-glow reddened her writhing thighs, made a carmine gargoyle of her twisted face. But he knew that face, knew the voice that shrilled from the girl's fear-torn mouth!

He had been wrong! Horribly wrong! The face he had seen above him was not Ruth's. This second victim, being dragged behind him into the same fiery mouth of hell that would devour his own body, *was the girl he loved!*

MADNESS tore at Norton's soul and the shriek that ripped his throat was an inhuman sound filling the room with wild echoes. His own life had not mattered; he had not dreaded death itself but the manner of it. But Ruth! . . .

His soul shrieked a prayer and the prayer jangled from his drooling mouth, to tocsin above the roar of the flames. "Oh, God, give me strength! Help me!"

But he had more than a prayer. He had arms and legs, fists and feet, teeth that could tear flesh! Madness showed him how to use them.

With mad-dog fury he fought free of the clutching hands that frantically sought to subdue him. Near-naked bodies reeled away from him, battered and bloody from the raking blows of his fists. He staggered forward, flung himself upon the hell-born demons who held the girl he loved.

And he knew now that they were not hell-born. They were human. Human enough to shriek out in terror and scatter as any group of women would have scattered before the murderous charge of a madman. Some of them went down, battered to unconsciousness by his blind blows. The others staggered clear, choked the tunnel mouth in their frantic anxiety to escape.

Like a great white ape gone amuck, he stood straddling the sobbing form of their abandoned victim. Sweat poured from his body; his chest rose and fell with great gulps of breath. He stared down; madness died in his eyes, and words mumbled from his mouth. "Ruth! Thank God—"

Her arm shot out and her answering cry was a scream of terror. "Behind you! Look out!"

Norton whirled, jerked rigidly to his toes. Facing him across a distance of less than ten paces, not behind the flames now but in front of them, stood the Black Master himself!

That shapeless, red-glowing face was an unholy mask of hate. The fiend's robed body, huge and bloated and smouldering with flame, stood darkly silhouetted against the red mouth of hell. And in one of those blackened hands, rising slowly to a level with Paul Norton's branded chest, was balanced a revolver!

Norton lunged sideways, crashed against the wall as the gun roared. The sound of the bullet past his cheek was a dull sob, so close that he heard it above the echoing thunder of the gun. The gun roared again as he hurtled forward, head down, shoulders hunched.

Hot pain seared his arm, spun him off balance. Then he made contact with the fiend's legs.

Madness was in his soul again and he pistoned erect, with crushing force, inside the monster's outflung arms. The gun rose, fell, but Norton's teeth sank savagely in the demon's wrist and the clubbed weapon spilled from paralyzed fingers. Above the roar of the flame-pit the Master's howl of pain rose in lurid crescendo, and he stumbled back.

But strength was going out of Paul Norton's body, going fast. He felt sickness writhing in the pit of his stomach, crawling up into his chest. And the black-clad arms of the Master were locked around him, crushing with savage power.

Norton's knees went limp, gave way under him. Behind him, miles away, Ruth Winward screamed wildly, "Oh, God, help him! Give him strength!" But her voice was only a mocking echo. Hooked fingers had found Norton's throat; his face purpled, he gasped for breath.

Above him, the Master's unholy countenance was twisted with hate. Creation was slowly turning black, and through the blackness came livid streaks of scarlet lightning that were shafts of agony, piercing Norton's soul. The world was a roaring abyss. . . .

Suddenly then, close beside him in that black chaos, someone else was fighting! A naked girl, sobbing with terror, was using her small hard fists to batter at the hideous face of the Master!

But not for long. Throttling fingers whipped clear of Norton's throat, balled themselves into fists and leaped toward the girl. Savagely they hurled her aside. She crashed against the wall, fell, lay moaning.

Then Paul Norton went mad. Animal growls jarred his throat as he hurled himself on the girl's assailant. His hands shot out, ripped and clawed at the glowing hell-face. His hooked fingers smeared through greasy make-up, tore loose a layer of putty-like plaster.

With strength that amazed even himself, he buried a clenched fist in the fiend's uncovered face, and the sound of the blow was a sickening, thudding crash.

The face reeled backward. No longer did that unholy red glow emanate from it. The red stuff was on Norton's fingers instead. The face was a shrieking, sobbing lump of terror, and as it shot backward it was human and ghastly white against the red hell of the flame-pit.

Norton stood swaying, staring, breathing fire and heat. Horror choked him as the black-robed body staggered back, failed to regain balance. The room was full of a soul-retching shriek of terror.

For a moment only, the black-clad Master rocked on the brink of his own lurid hell, his face a flaming horror. That face belonged to Edmund Dwight.

Then the hell-pit claimed its victim.

PAUL NORTON was not sure what happened after that. For an eternity he stood staring, mumbling over and over: "It was Dwight! It was Dwight who did all those terrible things. . . ."

Madness had given him strength, but now the madness was gone, taking the strength with it. In a daze, he stumbled to the naked form that lay against the wall. Stooping, he tried to gather it in his arms, only to realize that the task was beyond his ability. The girl was unconscious. In another moment he, too, would give way to exhaustion, and—

He heard voices, low voices that came muttering through the tunnel, but they meant little to him. And when, moments later, the tunnel vomited forth a group of uniformed men, Paul Norton was unconscious on the floor, his arms around the unclad form of his sweetheart.

He did not know that the policemen covered her body and his with their coats and carried both limp bodies through the tunnel, into cool clean air. . . .

Hours passed before Norton's fear-blackened brain reacted to restoratives and he wandered back through a world of darkness into conciousness. He was lying on his own bed, at home, and Ruth Winward sat beside him gently massaging his face and throat. Staring past her, Norton saw Alexander Pierson, Clinton Miller, and a third man who was a stranger. The other man must be a doctor. . . .

Miller came forward, stared down. "Miss Winward owes her life to you, Norton. For that matter, Pierson and I do, too, for we surely would have been next on Dwight's death-list."

Norton tried to think, but was too tired. Later he would be able to reason the whole thing out. And right now, Miller wanted to talk.

"Ruth has shown us the detailed report you made out," he blurted. "I think I can clear up a lot of things, Norton. In the first place, Dwight's big motive was to kill us all off so the park would belong exclusively to him. He murdered Wyman because Wyman opposed the park business in the first place and might have prevented the deal from going through.

"He committed that murder sensationally for the sake of publicity. Then he saw a way to get rid of Bingham, by framing Bingham for the murder. It worked; Bingham committed suicide—maybe because he was in with Dwight on the earlier deed and feared exposure. After that, Dwight murdered Mark Shaw and Erwin Mowry by doctoring the preparation that I made to protect them from the flames in our Fiery Furnace act. He threw suspicion off himself by letting himself get slightly burned at the same time."

Miller's fists were clenched, his eyes blazing. "Dwight picked on you from the very beginning," he rasped, "because he thought he could terrorize you into murdering the rest of us, and so save himself the dirty work. That's why you received those messages on the wall of the room here, and why the sacramental wine was turned to blood. Maybe you'll be interested in knowing how the messages were put on your wall. Here!"

He snatched a small, box-shaped object from the table and thrust it forward. "This is what's know as a mirrorscope, a magic lantern. Small, yes, but big enough for Dwight's purpose. We found it in the attic upstairs, and there's a neat round hole drilled in the ceiling, with a wooden plug to be used in masking the hole when not in use. The crimson messages were printed on lantern-slides and projected through the hole onto the wall here. A damned clever arrangement and

hard to detect, because this machine is too small to throw a noticeable light-beam.

"All I can say is," Miller finished hoarsely, "that Pierson and I owe our lives to you. We'd have been the next to be lured into that hell-hole and flung into the flame-pit."

"As it is—" The interruption came quietly from Pierson— "Dwight is now very dead, thanks to Norton. And you—" He peered at Norton— "are due to stay in bed for at least a day or two. Both you and Miss Winward were somehow doped, drugged, many times. And we have a problem on our hands as to what must be done with the group of unwholesome women who were working with Dwight. One of those girls looked remarkably like you, Miss Winward—which is probably why Dwight gave her the leading role in his fanatical program.

"The girls were part of his wild publicity scheme and undoubtedly he promised them a great deal of money. Now they are in jail, terrified of the consequences. They might have escaped, if Miller and I had not phoned the police and followed you two to the park, thinking you were—" He forced an apologetic smile— "acting suspiciously."

Ruth Winward did not answer. And when Miller began again to speak, he stopped abruptly, let his voice sputter to silence. For the girl and Paul Norton were oblivious to what was going on around them.

Norton's head was cradled in Ruth's arms and he was asleep with his lips pressed against the warm satin of her throat. And she was murmuring soft, intimate words, so personal that Miller, Pierson and the doctor glanced meaningly at one another and tiptoed silently from the room, closing the door behind them.

THE END

In the Next Issue—

Blood-Chilling Yarns by
GEORGE EDSON—ARTHUR J. BURKS—MINDRET LORD
And a Host of Other Masters of Terror Fiction!

—Out January 25th!

The House of Doomed Brides

By Ray Cummings

In the dim past, a wizard-husband laid a potent spell upon the Frane women: Daughters they might have, but the mother's death must pay for every birth. . . . Yet Earle Kennison married Gretna Frane, and learned too late of the monstrous fate reserved for those who scoff!

The statement given here is filed among the official records of the London Branch, Scientific Club of Anglo-America. There are several brief affidavits attached to it: One from the attending physician; another, the opinion of a noted British Scientist; a seismograph record of the night in question from Clarkson Observatory, with a learned, technical and lengthy paper on the geologi-

cal formation of the British Isles in relation to the possibility of earthquakes; an attempted psychical explanation of the strange affair, from a member of a Psychical Research Society; and a very earnest dissertation by a British clergyman who evidently felt called upon to review the case from a religious aspect.

All these papers are accessible to the public; anyone may find them as A-49371, "The Case of Sir Robert A——". I transcribe the main statement substantially in its official form. For obvious reasons attending publication, however, I have altered it both in names and dates—disguised it in other small details for the protection of a well-known English family.

—The Author.

MY name is Earle Kennison. Details of my early life, my family, are unimportant to this narrative; little is of interest before that August 4th, 19— which was my twentieth birthday. With Gretna Frane I was wholly in love, though I had not seen her or heard from her since the previous June. I did not, indeed, ever expect to see or to hear from her again. But on August 4th, unexpectedly, her note came. It gave me her home address—even that had heretofore been denied me. I stared at her few written words.

> I think, if you still love me, it will be all right for you to come. Oh, how I do hope so.
> Gretna.

I had known her at the University for two years. No family of hers had ever come to her school to take pride in her education. I knew little, almost nothing about her, for early in our friendship she bade me not inquire. Nor had she ever been willing to meet my family; nor would she have me speak of her to them.

A strange, queerly matured girl of sixteen, boarding at a school adjacent to mine. Small, slim, dark, with coal-black braids dangling like a child's. A singularly odd personality, half child, half woman, queerly intermingled. From the first, I had sensed an invisible black shroud of mystery enveloping her. It seemed endowing her with a wistfulness — a settled, wan melancholy which all the laughter of healthy girlhood could no more than drive into the depths of her dark eyes. I

had often noticed it lurking there. Perhaps, to my own romantic youthfulness it was at first an attraction. But soon I grew to fear it.

She did not seek my friendship. I realize now that with all her little strength she was fighting always against every normal instinct with which an abundant nature had provided her—fighting, and losing.

That last night of June, I stood bidding her goodbye for the summer vacation. Her hair was up around her head in a thick, black coil. I saw her suddenly not as a strange, wistful little child, but as a vibrant woman. And I felt myself a man. There was no need for love-making. It blazed from our eyes; it flowed like a stream between our fingers as they touched . . . But she tore herself away; to separate us sprang the monster of that lurking tragedy in whose grip she was enveloped. Her plea was a sob of terror: "No! No, Earle—don't love me! No one must ever love me!"

I stared now, this August 4th, at her note. My promise, given at her tragic pleading that June night, was released. I could come to her—if I still loved her! I was on the Scotland train that night, bound for the small town near the border which she had named as her home.

THE village of Grath is an out-of-the-way place; it was mid-afternoon of August 5th before I reached its neighborhood. I dismissed my conveyance, walked the last half-mile through the somber forest alone, in a tumult of emotion . . .

And I stood at last before a small, crumbling stone gateway with an unhinged rusty gate, set off the main road at the end of a path which the summer vegetation had crept over and almost obliterated. A lost and forgotten spot in this new Twentieth Century. Here in the dark, hushed recesses of the enveloping forest I could have imagined the Black Prince standing with his huntsmen, imperiously winding his horn at these humble portals.

I pushed the tangle of ivy aside, entered, and saw the house. A castle such as might have graced a North Sea headland of Saxon England lay hidden here. But a castle all in miniature, for this was a small stone structure, looped and turreted but no larger than an unpretentious country home. Solemn and brooding, it stood enveloped in trees which by contrast seemed fantastic giants.

There was no garden about the little castle; no flowers, no paths save one leading from the gate to the small main doorway—a path with ferns and leaves and underbrush encroaching upon it unmolested . . . The afternoon was overcast, windless, oppressive. I stood breathless in the heat, an intruder upon the past. It was as though all this had for centuries remained untouched by the hand of man. The gate through which I had passed, the little castle walls, stood with mute evidence of the fingers of Time plucking at them. Decrepit walls, crumbling stone, rusted ironwork, wormy wood, chipped and broken masonry . . . . Age everywhere; an aspect ancient, venerable, but all with a strange pathetic dignity, for in outward form, the building was unbroken save where perhaps the ivy mercifully hid its scars. A sturdy little castle in its bygone day, and still bravely standing.

How long I remained motionless with the ghosts of the past crowding me I do not know. But presently I was advancing, kicking away the forest creepers on the forgotten path. This was the home of Gretna Frane . . . her family . . . What ancient tragic mystery was here? I could feel the specter of it standing at my elbow as I thumped the rusty knocker.

Then Gretna was in my arms; soft, clinging, with her lips on mine; her greeting ringing in my ears.

"Earle! You came! Earle, I think I dare say it now—I love you! I love you!"

No specter here! I held her, and the specter fled. I held her with a surge of love; and in her kisses felt a love divine and a very human passion unrestrained.

"Earle! Let me go! I can't breathe!"

SHE lived alone with her grandfather. No servants—seldom, if ever, any visitors. I was to stay with them for a few days, they said. Amid the friendliness of their welcome, no questions were permitted me. A spirit of gayety was upon Gretna. I had never seen her like this. It brought to the interior of the castle a cheer and laughter which suddenly I knew was false. These ancient rooms, beamed oaken ceilings dull with the smoke of centuries; oak planks worn black and smooth beneath my feet—I was conscious always of their brooding age.

"After dinner this evening," the old man said, "we'll talk then, young Earle."

The night came; the long main hall, with its raised end whereon Gretna had set the black oak table for our evening meal, was shadowed in the candle-light. We sat over our coffee. Figures of a modern world—Gretna in a filmy dress of white; the old man erect and smiling in black dinner clothes for all the heat. Figures of a modern world; yet to me, the shadows of King Alfred and his fellows might have been dining there with us.

"You have been very patient, young Earle. You are all that Gretna said you were." His lean old hand went impulsively over mine on the table-top. "I like you. I only hope that perhaps this love you and Gretna have found may be allowed its fulfillment." His smile had faded; a shadow had swept to Gretna's face; I felt the specter nudging my side.

"Why, I thank you—" I began awkwardly, but he checked me.

"There was a reason why Gretna could not let herself love you—or anyone. I may, perhaps, have removed it now. I don't know. That, I think, we may find out—tonight." He added, "You've been patient; be patient a while longer. This family into which you would like to marry has a history—a tragic one. The present, young Earle, is but the past in the making. The future too, will advance to be the present, and fade away into the past. And we are—or at least we have been—a tragic family. It is that Gretna wanted to spare you—our fear of the future."

He would not let me speak. "No! It's your right to know the past—and if tonight we can just glimpse the future—"

I sat in the candle-light, and his slow, quiet old voice took me back among the shadows which all evening had been enveloping me . . .

"I was a handsome young devil when I was your age, young Earle, as handsome as you are, and as typical of that other half century as you are of this one. I came here to this house, wooing its young mistress. A motherless, fatherless girl—dark-eyed, black-haired, slight and beautiful—like Gretna. Her mother had died when she was born, her father had committed suicide with his grief. It seemed too bad, but not significant. I loved her, well, perhaps as you love Gretna.

"Our little girl, Gretna's mother, was born—and the birth killed my wife. I did not commit suicide—" His voice was quivering. "Perhaps I was too brave, or not brave enough. My wife died, and I put all my love into the little girl. She grew to maturity—at seventeen, like a small, dark rosebud. Like Gretna . . . I told the young man when he came asking for her what I have told you. There were to be no children. Yet that was my own idea—against God's law—perhaps,

too. That now is part of the punishment, for I made them promise.

"A coincidence? Or a physical defect of the women of our breed? There was no physician who honestly could say it was that . . . My girl was married. She confessed afterward she yearned to have a child. She knew it would be a daughter." His voice raised sharply. "Gretna! You—as you know things are now—do you want to be a mother?"

I thrilled to Gretna's voice. "Yes! I do! Grandfather, you know I do!"

"That too, young Earle, is perhaps the heritage of our women. Gretna says it frankly. You could not shake her in it . . . Her mother died in giving her birth. Her father blamed himself. We found him dead, that earnest young man who had come asking me for her only a brief year before. Found him dead in the bottom of a ravine near here. I like to think he fell from the path above by accident. But I do not think so. And all these years I have watched Gretna maturing, her womanhood budding, swelling from springtime into summer, preparing to blossom—" His voice broke. "To blossom with our next tragedy."

SHE was huddling now against him. His fingers stroked her hair, but his somber eyes held mine. "I had to tell her, warn her, years ago. I could not spare her. There is a tragedy in that, too. The mysteries life holds, the sorrow and conflict eternal—not to spare even childhood is in itself a tragedy. At fourteen, Gretna knew, that for her at least, love and marriage could only mean a child. A daughter, like an obsession, always that longing for a daughter. That was more than pathetic, tragic. Why, at fourteen I found—when I had always been so careful to keep dolls away from her—at fourteen, I found her once crooning to a little thing of rags she had made. . . ."

I sat staring, unblinking, with eyes that

smarted in the smoke of my neglected cigarette. This blight upon a breed of women, each to bear another like herself, and die! What destiny was this? What power greater than all our little mortal strivings, was exacting this penalty? And why? . . . And now I had come like a wind-blown puppet to play my part! Mysterious workings of nature! Awesome, unfathomable business! A physical defect of these women, an understandable, medical fact unquestionably. Yet back of it, must there not be the guiding hand of Omnipotence? The innocent shall suffer for the guilty. Back, somewhere in this line, had been woman's sin, no doubt. And the innocent shall suffer—

Woman's sin? It was almost as though I had spoken the thought aloud, so that the old man was moved to answer it. His quiet gaze was on my face. He said:

"I have not told you quite all, young Earle. There was a tale my wife told me. She was motherless, fatherless. A tale told to her by the old family nurse. Perhaps it was only from a generation previous—or perhaps from several generations, so that it had come down like a legend.

"An old woman's fancy? Call it that, young Earle. I would not have you believe it. My wife believed it. And to me it has become very real."

Gretna had come close beside me. I felt her trembling. It was real to her also, this thing the old man was about to disclose. His eyes held me.

"There was a time when one of the women of this family, cast off her husband. Her child was to be born, but its father was a man of evil, a necromancer, by profession a juggler of the secrets of nature. A juggler of things evil, who put his skill to such evil purpose indeed, that he ended by being hanged upon the gallows. His wife had previously left him, when first she learned what manner of man he really was.

"And for that, he cursed her. A tangible human curse, young Earle, a curse laid upon her and her issue with all the man's human hatred and his power of necromancy. A curse, so that she in childbirth, must die—and her daughter live on, in turn to die . . . Gretna child, stop shuddering. . . ."

I held Gretna closer. The old man said, "That is nothing but the tale of a servant woman, told to my wife. You need not believe it. But imagination is a very strange thing. To me—"

He was obviously trying to speak lightly now. His lips showed the trace of a grim smile. "To me—so many years have I brooded on it—that man of evil who laid so diabolical a curse upon a line of women—he is very real to me now. In fancy I conjure him, a fellow in doublet and hose, with lean face and burning eyes. So real that sometimes, Gretna and I fancy that the evil spectre of him still hovers within these walls.

The spectre of him here within these walls? How could I doubt it? I, who ever since I had been here had felt a spectre nudging at my side! Imagination! Call it that, you who read this, and toss away the menace. But I, who was there, could not, with every word of the old man, that apparition hovering near me became more real. A man . . . I stared across the shadowy room. The thing was here with us now! Doublet and hose. Long and lean and evil face. Eyes that burned and leered at me with a gloating, fury. Eyes seeing its new victim . . .

But I tried to fling away the vision. I heard my voice crying aloud in the welter of my thoughts. "If the decision is mine, I want Gretna! She—I'll protect her—she shall remain the last of her line. We'll stamp it out, whatever it is—Gretna and I the last of our line—"

"No!" burst from Gretna. "I want—I must have my little daughter—"

I was on my feet. What I would have said I do not know. Old Frane raised his hand sharply. "Wait, young Earle! You and Gretna, so young, thinking you must decide the future! That's decided for us, lad! Sit down, Earle—"

He pushed Gretna gently away; he smiled at her and at me. "We sent for you, young Earle, because I think that tonight I shall be able to let us glimpse what the future holds. Perhaps if we knew what lay ahead of us three we could advance to meet it more courageously—"

He was speaking quite calmly now. "This is not wholly mysticism, lad. I am no seer, but—what you did not know—I have been in my day, well, to some extent, a scientist. Yet even in science, a measure of mysticism creeps. For years, as I watched Gretna's womanhood unfolding, I have wanted to know the future. To transport myself ahead of my time—with a drug, a mechanism, a crystal ball—anything with which even for an instant, I could lift the veil.

"The past is less difficult to envisage. It hovers always quite close to us. The future is equally as real an entity. Advancing into reality, as the past recedes ... Why, Gretna! You were happy over this when we sent for Earle!"

But she was shuddering now. White and silent and shuddering. Was it a premonition, a sense beyond the normal, which already was giving her a glimpse of what our future held? I think it was that. And upon me too, the future was resting an impalpable, icy hand ... or was it the spectre of that nameless thing which I sensed always was in the room with us. Was that what was touching me now? I started into sudden physical alertness as though I had felt a ponderable touch. Or was it a wraith conjured only by my thoughts, perhaps? A gloat-ing, menacing thing, with burning eyes watchful of our movement ... ?

"Come," said old Frane. "Come, Gretna—let us see—"

AT the inquest they pounded me with scientific questions which I could not answer because I am no scientist. And if I were, the confusion of those moments, my own stress of emotion, would befog me out of all credibility as a witness. Did old Frane explain to me any scientific principle for the conquering of Time? Did he talk of Time and Space as one blended Entity? Yes, that I remember. Time was to be crossed like Space. As though there could be a geography of Time; as though the Future were a Location in Time, to which we could move at least our Minds ...

I know definitely, and I testified, that he led us to Gretna's bedroom. A place sanctified by her girlhood. Her little bed, a dressing table, a chair ... A faint perfume in the air which to me had come to mean her. A dim, sanctified place, shadowed now with shadows that moved as he set down the candelabra he had carried in to light our entrance.

"This, young Earle, is the room in which Gretna was born. To me, it is redolent of the past—"

The crowding past! I could feel it pressing around us. This emptiness here—an emptiness crowded with the past. And the future! I became aware that the future was here, as well as the past. Crowded empty Space, with only Time to hold separate its myriad events ...

Three of us here, the old man, Gretna, and I. No! We were four! Those watchful eyes still were upon us. I could feel, rather than see, them. Yet how easy, here in these flickering shadows of the candlelight, to conjure that lean and evil face—that evil man of doublet and hose! Hovering shape from the Past, stalking us here in the Present—ready to go with us now into the Future . . .

The mechanism stood on a small table. A crystal ball? It seemed no more than that. It stood a foot high in the center of the table, poised on a small wooden base. I recall that to my mind, for all those uneasy spectres of which I was so utterly conscious, there sprang a vague contempt. This old fellow—half mad, or wholly mad perhaps—was no more than a charlatan, a necromancer. And a sudden hope came to me. Was all this tragedy a figment of his own warped brain? Was Gretna his dupe? And now, for his own unreasoning, irrational purpose, was he trying to make me a victim too?

But the thing was more than a crystal ball. At each corner of the table stood a small apparatus, a tiny brazier, like an ash-tray. A light-shield stood in front of it, and above, a small lens, held horizontal in a bracket. Over that, a mirror; and a tiny prism, and a small metal cylinder like the barrel of a microscope, pointed at the crystal ball. At each corner of the table, the small cylinders pointed at the crystal ball.

We sat by the table. Frane said, "This apparatus would not operate without your being here, young Earle, because quite evidently your future is interwoven with ours. Without your consciousness to advance with ours beyond the veil, it resisted us. So we sent for you. Gretna, sit by him, child—"

We sat together. Her trembling body huddled against me. Her fingers as she clung to mine were dank with the premonitory chill of death . . . The old man stood behind us. He moved about the table; into each of the little braziers, from a glass vial, he poured a small quantity of powder . . . The touch of Gretna's fingers seemed to communicate their chill to me . . . Was this science, or something diabolical or both? To lift the veil which the Almighty in His infinite wisdom has placed between us and our future—was this thing permissible? Or was it something that man may not do?

With a puff, old Frane blew out the candle. The darkness sprang like a monster with a great black cloak flung over us . . . The old man was fumbling with matches. Gretna sobbed, "Earle, I'm afraid!"

A match lighted with its yellow flare; showed me the old man's grim face; bloodless lips; gleaming, eager eyes, probing a mystery no man may probe! Eyes that sought to see the unseeable! His old fingers were trembling with eagerness as he held the match to one of the braziers. The powder ignited. It burned with a dull purple light—a slow, steady glow. In a moment, all four of the braziers were lighted. The lens caught the glow, projected it upward in a tiny, concentrated beam; bent by the mirror to the horizontal; through the prism, into the projecting cylinder—a beam spread flat like a tiny rainbow of weirdly confused color, yet all dimly purple.

The old man's voice was saying, "In that burning powder is the secret of Time. A purple beam of vibrations to overtake the seconds, the minutes, days and years—"

I SCARCELY heard him. Gretna was stiff beside me. The crystal was dim in the flat shadow from the brazier shields. Then from each of the pointing cylinders at the table corners, the purple beam sprang forth. I was aware that the old man had opened tiny shutters to release it. The crystal was bathed in their strangely lurid glow. One of them, from behind me, passed close by my shoulder. I sensed a vibration from it. A soundless whirr; a breath of impalpable heat. . . .

I bent to Gretna. "Don't be afraid. It's nothing—"

A burning powder. I could smell it now like some heavy, exotic incense. It seemed to make my head reel as I breathed it. Was this a trick? A madman's trick to drug my senses—make me think I saw what I did not?

"Ah—" His sigh was exultant. The clear depths of the crystal were filled with purple shadows. Taking form; tiny images—myself, in them—my intent face, with Gretna beside me. Vague outlines of the room in miniature.

"Ah! You see? See us three? That is the present, but in a moment it will move forward. Slowly, at first—then faster, rushing us into the future!"

Wholly mad or at best a trickster! Of course the present was mirrored in the crystal. A reflection of us as we sat at the table was all I was seeing.

There was just an instant when an utter terror swept me. I felt that I was about to see what I had no right to see. And I was afraid. But whatever the crystal was about to disclose, its secret remained forever hidden. Yet what a vaster thing unfolded! Frane was no trickster, for he was now as frightened, as surprised as Gretna and myself. The four purple-glowing braziers reflected a dim glow everywhere about the room. The perfume of the burning powder was escaping, and so was the light. Not confined to the tiny beams, but glowing everywhere; and everywhere seeming to gain intensity. Something was going wrong! And suddenly to my consciousness, the crystal ball, the four mechanisms, the table—everything, all of us—were lost in a wild glare of purple light. Like a living monster, it had escaped its confining prisms and projectors. The air around me was tingling, snapping. A hum filled my ears; then a roaring. A numbness had come to me. A lightness of body; physical chains dropping away. A wild sense of freedom; my senses were fading. I heard the sound of old Frane as his body fell to the floor with a choking cry; felt Gretna sag against me, and vaguely felt myself slump inert in my chair. This thing—this science—was a Frankenstein monster risen to destroy us!

But my consciousness went on. Will you who read this think me mad? Or lying? It does not matter—I can only tell what I remember . . .

A dim, glowing chaos was around me. Melting shadows; formless movement; a soundless humming; and within me a faint tingling to mark a spark of the physical still remaining.

Formless shadows for what seemed an endless time. But they were shadows of old Frane, and Gretna, and me. The sound of music; slim little Gretna standing beside me, white-robed. Our marriage—it swept by as though upon the whirring wings of fancy. Yet it was very real. An instant impression, dissolving, crowding into other shadows of its kind.

A bedroom—this bedroom, in which, like a dead shell I could feel my body slumped in purple light . . . This bedroom—Gretna, my wife . . . Ah! That fleeting vision of love melting into other visions, nearly always here in this room. This crowded space, yielding now its future secrets! Within these walls . . .

Then I knew these were not visions. I was living these fragments . . . Whirling forward through them, leaving them behind me as memories . . . Riding upon a winged steed . . .

A CORNER of the beamed ceiling showed a wide, opening crack. Water had come through in the heavy rain. Gretna said, "Earle darling, we really ought to repair this old house. Grandfather never would. He never will, if you leave it to him."

And I said, "Yes." And kissed her . . . Another year . . .

"I noticed that last year, Earle. It's

getting really too old, this house—"

Last year. This year. And other years. They sped away. Happy years, with only a shadow of fear upon them. But it was a shadow made more vivid by the sunlight of our happiness. Gretna, my wife, old Frane, myself, living here. The house and all of us were getting older. No children had come to bless us . . . Ah! one now was coming. I was very happy, but the shadow stalked me closer . . .

Shadow? It had always been with me, a vague nameless weight upon my heart, a shadow of fear upon my happiness. But when I was told that a child was coming, the shadow suddenly leaped again into form—the face, horribly familiar now, leering at me. Jibing! Did I hear the voice? It seemed that there was a voice, a taunt, a gloating mocking taunt, hideously terrible . . .

The months went by. . . . The nurse said: "A perfect, wonderful little girl, like her mother." But I burst into the room, shuddering. She was still alive, my Gretna, there in the bed, her face with closed eyes a white waxen mask. . . . The baby was crying with its puny new-born wail. The doctor said gravely, "We had —she had rather a bad time, but it's all right now. Rather a bad time, eh, nurse?"

But it wasn't all right. The doctor said, "You go now. I'll call you, if we need you." It wasn't all right, and I stumbled out to sit with old Frane. . . . And presently the nurse called, hastily, with alarm in her tone. . . . And I went back—

"Earle, my husband—" Her dear voice, dim with distance as it rode away on her bravely riding spirit. "Earle, take care of our little daughter—don't be too sorry, about me . . ."

Desolation. Loneliness. . . . And then, in the black darkness of my stricken life, the jibing monster out of the past revealed itself with a sudden, complete clearness. Monstrous, triumphant ap-

parition, dangling here over me with outstretched arms; fingers quivering as though raining upon me the full measure of its curse. And my head rang now unmistakably with its eerie jibing voice. Horrible mocking laughter. Diabolic triumph—noisome with evil—noisome with the stench of the grave . . .

I sat numbed, beaten and pounded at last to where no longer had I the strength of mind even to be terrified. . . . Emptiness, filled only with jostling memories. Here in this bedroom the still, white shape of Gretna lying now in bed. Old Frane had fallen with his grief. . . . The infant lay in its bassinet with a white aura around it. . . .

I was trembling. Or was it the floor beneath me which was trembling? The room was filled with a purple glow. A light run rampant. It seemed to be eating at the floor, the walls, the ceiling, eating like soundless purple flame. The room, the house was shuddering. Old Frane staggered to his feet.

I gasped: "An earthquake! It's shaking us—"

I heard his wild laugh. A rumble sounded outside. Something fell. Crashed. The house was crumbling—falling. Ten years! It had not seemed ten years since Gretna and I were married. But it was. And the old house had come to its end. A rift somewhere, a last crumbling keystone, a foundation twisting, sliding. The old house was falling. . . .

Something heavy hit my shoulder. I was on my feet. I must get Gretna out. I ran to the bed. Lifted her up, held her so white and soft against me. A cloud of falling débris enveloped old Frane; but I was past it, staggering with Gretna so white and soft in my arms. The infant was buried in a choking cloud. The purple glow was gone; the house rocked, clattered behind me as I escaped out into the starlight. Into the cool air of dawn, where to the east, over the forest, a pink flush was mounting.

My head cleared. Normality came to me. Under the trees beside the line of willows, the castle lay a tumbled mass of ruins. I sank down insensible beside Gretna, and there they found us. . . .

THEY tell me they found the castle in ruins; found Frane's body, but no infant. And there was no earthquake. It was only August 6th. I had been in the castle, so they say, only over night.

My physician examined me. I was twenty years old when I entered that castle. But I was thirty, that next morning when I emerged. I looked thirty. The police said it was only mental shock. But I know I lived those ten years, crowded into that one night of the world's slow-moving Time. And my physician says I aged ten years. Not only my looks. My organs had aged. My arteries, my blood-pressure had changed as only the living of ten years could change them.

Gretna, too, physicians say, was a woman of twenty-six that next morning. Evidently that much, at least, is an established fact. Gretna's memory of those ten years we lived together in the old castle agrees with mine.

There is little more to tell. Gretna and I were married in London a few days later. Our child, our little daughter, was born the following year. Who could ask me to picture what agony of mind was mine those hours while I waited for what the doctors would tell me? The child lived. Ah! I had known it would! But Gretna? For days she hovered upon the brink. Then she was restored to me. Several years have passed now. Gretna lives, healthy, happy with me in the treasure of our daughter.

For this that I have recounted we ask no one's credulity. Have we an explanation? Yes; it is this:

Before each of us, in life, the future stretches like an open road. At every instant of our life there are branch roads turning from it. A word, a deed, and we plunge down one of them. The course we take—that is the route of our life to the destiny we each of us makes for himself.

And we think, Gretna and I, that upon the old castle and its inmates lay that curse. A spell of evil, call it what you will; something not to be defined. But within those walls the family of Gretna Frane was doomed to disaster.

We lived there, man and wife, for ten years. And the ravages of time, those ten years, were too much for the crumbling old structure. It fell, and with it fell the curse. As though the jibing monster himself were engulfed, his evil spirit falling with those walls. And Gretna and I were released. By a merciful Providence, we have been given those ten years to to live again.

You who read this may well say, "Ah, now you are actually living those ten years. You lived them that night in the castle only in fancy—a fancy born of your own imagination, or perhaps under the spell of a drug from old Frane's strange device."

Perhaps so. Perhaps we lived them in fancy! Lived them, to put them in the past, with vivid memories remaining! Perhaps that is all life is! Metaphysicians have said so. I do not know.

But I think, of all the learned reviews of our strange experience, the Reverend Abercrombie comes nearest to the truth. Gretna thinks so too; and to woman is given a spiritual insight which few men possess. The Reverend Abercrombie says, "Science is sometimes too presumptuous. There are some things about which we seek to know too much."

I am coming now to believe that is so.

EARLE KENNISON.

Riverfront Horror

By Arthur Leo Zagat

(Author of "When Love Went Mad!" etc.)

THE night it all happened, we were feeling pretty high in the hut that Jim Hawks and I had made out of wood scrap and old tomato cans. Marge Beals had started to sing a song. *Mother Machree* it was, and I forgot everything else listening to the kind of husk in her voice that makes it hard for me to swallow. I didn't hear the yowling of Red Connors and Rat-Face Floyd from under the railroad embankment over their smoke—that stuff they stew out of

The Thing that came up from the fog, to strike fear to the hearts of the wretched inhabitants of New Deal Town, was only a ghostly black horror glimpsed in the greyness. Yet it struck with rending claws of steel, leaving behind it mangled, headless tokens. It was spawned of hell, no human thing —but one by one it was driving them, screaming, from their last refuge!..

rubbing alky and throw into their lead-lined guts. I didn't hear the slither of the river sliding by under the fog. I didn't even hear the bawling of the ferry-boats — till that one hoot, so close and loud it drowned out the quivery sadness of Marge's singing—and ended in a high, thin scream!

Wow! It was like somebody stabbed a knife right through the dark, and the shack wall, and into my chest. I saw the girl's mouth stay open without any sound coming out of it, and her eyes were all of a sudden big and round and black with the scare of that shriek. I saw Jim's face go the color of a dead fish's belly.

Then the scream came again, wire-edged with pain and something more terrible than pain, and it cut off right in the middle. Then there wasn't any more noise except the hoot of boats feeling along in the fog like blind men and the rasp of our breathing that made the silence more silent and scary.

In the bunch of lopsided shacks made out of broken boxes, rusting sheet-iron and what have you that we called New Deal Town, we were used to screams. But this one was different. It wasn't any souse that had made it, nor any cokey. You knew the guy that had screamed that way had seen something a man wasn't supposed to see, and it had killed him, and he'd gone crazy before he died.

Marge moved first, twisting to the door and reaching her little hand to open it. That got Jim and me started. We jumped up together. I shoved the kid aside, barking, "Stay here. We'll go!" And my buddy and I jammed in the doorway.

In the seconds it took for us to get through, the yellow fog outside came alive with guys yelling and the squeals of rusty opening hinges and the pound of running feet.

I pushed hard, tumbled as I came out, scraped my face with mud and cinders. As I twisted to get up Jim pounded by me towards the hollering of the gang, that was going away towards the other end of the muck plot. There was someone else alongside of me. Marge said, "Hen, is that you?" and I felt her little hand on mine. She helped me get up and I started to follow Jim.

"Wait," Marge whispered. "Wait, Hen." I could hear her teeth clicking through her words.

I started to whisper something. Only started—I didn't finish. Because just then the light from the shack-door was gone, and something big and black and shaped like nothing God ever made was there instead, and it was lunging at us like a big bird come out of the fog. I saw a tremendous black wing and hooked claws flashing silvery like, and I yelled and threw myself at Marge. The two of us went down in the mud and the big thing missed us and pounded past.

My yell was answered by yells from the gang and I heard the bunch coming. But I heard something else that made gooseflesh all up and down my back-bone. It was a laugh, a laugh thin and loud and screechy and terrible. . . .

Marge pulled at me, pulled me up. "Come on," she gasped. "Come on. It went this way." Nuts. The girl was nuts, but she started away and I couldn't let her go alone.

I didn't catch her till she was stopped by the river. I grabbed her. "What's the big idea, Marge?" I said. "Running—"

"Hush," she whispered. "Hush. Listen."

I SHUT up. I couldn't hear a thing, nearby, except the oily *lap-lap* of the river along the rock. The gang hadn't seen us go, and we were alone there.

We were alone, and we weren't. There was someone else there, someone or some *thing* else. I couldn't see it. I couldn't really hear it. It just *was* there, if you know what I mean. A feel like eyes on the back of my neck. But no sound, not anything to let me know I was right. Nothing except the little shiver of Marge's slim, cold hand in mine and a whimper from her throat that told me she felt it too.

And then, like the snap of a finger, whatever it was was gone. But a footfall thudded over to one side of us. I jerked around, started to go after it, stubbed my toe in something soft, and tumbled again. Tumbled and came down hard on something limp laying there. My arms flailed out. One hand splashed into the cold wet of river water. The other touched something wet too—a warm, sticky wetness on skin—on *human skin*.

I gagged, fought to get away from what I had fallen on. I pushed myself up. Right under me I saw a red face, a face that was red because it was drenched with blood like as if someone had poured a bucket of the stuff over it!

It was lopsided and all twisted around, but I knew it. "Baldy Thomas!" I said, and looked at the top of his head to make sure. My stomach came up into my throat. Because there wasn't any top to his head. His skull had been peeled open like you peel the shell off a soft-boiled egg. And the mess inside was awful.

I was sick. So sick that I didn't think to wonder where the light was coming from that I saw by. But something clicked, and it was dark again. I managed to get to my knees, and to my feet, without touching it again. Then I knew that the light had been from a flashlight and none of us had one, and I grabbed at where I judged the light had come from.

I caught hold of a coat lapel and held on tight. The sounds I squeezed out of my throat didn't make words, and then they did. "Who're you? What—what are you . . . ?"

The man kind of gasped and jerked away. My hand slipped along the coat edge, caught against a button. A fist exploded against my jaw, rocked me back. And in that minute the fellow tore away. I heard foot-thuds running off.

I shook my head to clear it. Marge yelled, "Hen! Are you all right? Hen!" and I felt her grab hold of me. Then there was a lot more shouting all around, and I knew the bunch had found us.

Someone scratched a match, cursed, and I knew he had seen what was left of Baldy. I pushed against Marge, pushing her out of the mob. That wasn't anything for a dame to look at.

"What was it, Hen?" Her voice was like silk tearing. "What awful thing was that behind us just before—before you jumped away from me?"

IT TAKES a woman to crack to the kernel of a nut. As soon as she talked about it I somehow knew that what had happened to Baldy was only the beginning. No, I haven't got second sight, or anything like that, but I knew just like I had seen them that there had been hate in the eyes watching us from the fog, and a yen to kill that wouldn't be satisfied with just the one stiff. What had been done to Thomas was a giveaway on that too. Back home—don't ask me where that is—there was a sheep-dog went killer once, and something about Baldy's corpse reminded me of the ewes we found in the field the next morning. But this time it was us the killer was after, and not sheep.

"Listen," I said. "Listen kid. Where's Mom Stone?"

"I don't know. In our shack, I guess. She was lying down when I came over to yours."

Mom was the little old dame Marge lived with. A sweet-faced old lady with hair white and soft as the little clouds you see in the morning sky. Kind of gentle too. She and Marge made a pair, though the kid was nineteen and Mom three times that. There wasn't a guy in New Deal Town wouldn't lay down and let either of them walk all over him if it did them any good, and that goes for Red Connors and his mob of hoboes as well as the rest of us what have hopes of going back to our trades sometime.

I say to Marge, "Well, I'm taking you to her, and you're barring the door, and then I'm going for the cops." While I'm saying this I start walking, shouldering her gentle-like toward the little rise about the middle of the lot where their hut is.

"The cops! Hen, some of the boys—"

"Yeah. I know some of the boys won't like it. But they've got to take their chances. This thin—"

I stop as wood crashes somewheres ahead and there's another shrick. It's a regular banshee howl, but Marge plops out, "That's Mom," and starts running. I take out after her, catch up and pass her just as Mom yells again.

I feel the ground lift under me. Sudden-like there's a lighted doorway in front of me and there's something coming out of it. A man? Well, maybe. But all I see as I jump for it is fluttery blackness, big as King Kong, it seems like, and two green spots of light like cat's eyes.

I spring, throw an overhand left jab at those eyes. It lands square. . . .

But it seems like my knuckles just smash! An awful pain shoots up my arm. I screech. Then a locomotive hits the side of my head and I slam up against the side of the shack, slam into blackness. A screaming, crazy laugh follows me out, a laugh that turns my blood cold. . . .

CHAPTER TWO

I Put Her on the Spot

THERE'S hammers pounding in my head. Light and shadow do a crazy jig in front of my eyes that are open but don't see anything. My left fist feels like pulp and my left arm is paralyzed. A nutty thought slides through my head that I must have hit rock or metal. My other hand is clenched tight too, and there's something hard in it, something small and hard. I wonder dumb-like what it is.

I'm laying on my side in the doorway of Marge's shack. I'm facing in and the floor gets clear to me, the floor a couple of us have made for Mom and Marge out of boards we lugged from a wrecking job on the Boulevard. It's the only wood floor in the settlement and I remember the feel of the old dame's thin lips when she kissed me for finishing it. She scrubbed it every morning to keep it clean.

It isn't clean now. It's all over mud from the broken shoes that's trampling it. I look in between sockless ankles and frayed pants bottoms, and see the white sheet hanging down over Mom Stone's cot.

But that isn't white either. It's red. It's dripping red and the smell of the blood that's making it red comes to me through all the other smells, warm and sickish.

Then someone moves, and I see the old dame is still on the cot, and I see where her head ought to be. Gees! I get sick all over. Hell! I've been through a lot, and I've seen a lot, and I can take it. But I couldn't take that.

There was others couldn't take it too. There's a squeal like a stepped-on dog and Rat-Face Floyd comes busting out, howling. His face is like jello without any color in it and two little coals for eyes. "I'm getting out of here!" he squeals. "Fast as my dogs will take me."

And that, for some reason, gives me a laugh. Only this afternoon we were all sort of celebrating because the papers tell us we're gonna be allowed to stay in this God-awful place!

I can still see that clipping, which all of us had read so many times. It had sure enough given us a kick!

NEW DEAL TOWN TO CONTINUE
G. Watts Condon's Plea for
Squatters Wins

An application for condemnation of waterfront property occupied by homeless men and women was today denied in the Supreme Court. In his decision Judge Barton said that the prospect for private profit so overshadowed any public interest in the proposed development by the applicant, the Riverbank Corporation, that he saw no reason to disturb the squatters who have found refuge on the land in question.

"I wish particularly to commend," he continued, "the self-sacrifice of Mr. Condon, owner of the property, who appeared before me in opposition to this motion. I happen to know that Mr. Condon refused a munificent offer for the property solely because of his reluctance to deprive unfortunates of the asylum they have found on his land. The gentleman has this once again added to the philanthropies for which he is publicly revered."

Richard Barkley, the young attorney representing the Corporation, again refused to reveal the identity of its backers.

We'd been feeling pretty high—then. For though New Deal Town ain't no luxurious place, it's sure enough a devil of a lot better than city flop-houses and the like of that. And we ain't got any other place to go . . . . Now, though, it don't seem so healthy.

Someone else shoots past me so fast I can't see who it is, and this bozo steps on my busted hand. That pulls a yell out of me my old man must have heard in Wyoming. Everything goes dark for a second, and when I can see again Marge is on her knees beside me, shutting out sight of what's in the shack, and she's blubbering, "Hen! You're hurt. You're terribly hurt."

THERE'S a girl for you! Not pretty. No, not pretty at all. But I'd a damn sight rather look at her pushed-up little nose and her eyes that's always been crinkly-cornered with smiles, and her mouth that's kind of—kind of clean and sweet—than at the best looker in Minsky's chorus. When she looked at you, straight and level, you got uneasy and a little ashamed thinking of all the rotten things you'd done in your life. She's sort of boylike, with her short-cut hair that's like a cap of curly fur. Boylike in the grinning way she takes the tough breaks that's brought her to New Deal Town from—no, I can't tell that, even now. If I told her real name you'd know it, and you'd remember a piece in the paper along about November 1929 about a certain banker and his wife taking a dive from a top-floor hotel window. Or maybe you wouldn't because there was lots of pieces in the paper like that just then, and you might of forgotten all about it, like Marge's ritzy friends forgot all about her. No. I can't tell you no more. I promised her not ever to spill it.

But boylike as she was, Marge was all woman, make no mistake about that. If things had been different with me . . .

There's no smile in her eyes now, but she ain't thinking of herself. "You're hurt, Hen," she says again, and pulls at me, trying to get me straight.

"No," I push through teeth that I can't get apart. "No. I'm all right. Just —knocked cuckoo for a minute. I'll be all right." I'm trying to stop the squirrels that's running around inside my braincage, trying to think what's best to do for her. "Where's—Jim?"

"In there." Her lips twitch when she says it. "Looking at—Mom."

"Call him."

Jim's mug is frozen, when he gets to us, but his shirt's torn just above the rope holding up his pants and I can see his belly-skin quivering. "Waddye want, pal?" he grunts.

"I want—out of here and I can't make it," I groan. I didn't really know if I could and I wasn't trying. "You'll have to—help me get to—our dump."

There's a flicker in Jim's eyes that makes me guess he's tumbled, and what he says tells me he has. "Sure. You oughta get inside. But you're no light weight and—"

"I'll help," Marge sticks in, just like we'd put the words in her mouth. "Take his shoulders Jim, and I'll lift his legs." You see, I was figuring on getting her inside our hut. With the three of us together, and something jammed against the door she ought to be fairly safe till someone gets sense and calls the cops.

But they've just got me to the shack when the third yell cuts the fog, this time from the top of the railroad embankment.

A S LUCK would have it, I'm facing that way and just then the fog all lights up with the searchlight of a coming loco. I see the big, black, shapeless *thing* up top there, see its arm like a huge wing come down again on a smaller black shadow, and hear—hear, I tell you—the crunch of crushed bone.

What it's hit flings down off the wall. Another black head shows. The killer twists toward it and it ducks back. The train roars out of the fog. The car windows make a streak of light sweeping by, but there isn't anything up there. Not anything at all! The tracks are right along the edge of the stone. God, I think, has the loco cut the killer down?

The cars screech around a curve, scream away into the night. Silence pounds on my eardrums—and give way to a laugh, the crazy laugh of a loon coming out of the yellow dark. Wow! No, the killer isn't cut down. He's alive.

Or is he alive? Is he alive like what we call being alive? Could any *real* thing have stayed on top that wall and escaped the wheels of that streaking train?

Scared? Say! I'm that scared I can't hardly breathe. This killer that's loose in the night ain't something you can fight. It's a devil that's sneaked out of hell, it's a doom that's been sent to wipe us out. All of us. We can't get away from it. We can't get away!

Jim almost drops me, but the kid hollers, "Hold it. Hold on!" We're inside the shack, and the light kind of calms me, kind of lets me think again. Cops! I snicker. There ain't going to be no cops called tonight. There ain't anyone going across those tracks to call the cops.

Jim shoves the door shut with his shoulder. They drop me on the bunk, and he dives back to grab up a broken-handled axe and wedge it under the jamb. The kid's making little whining noises I know she doesn't hear herself. Her hands are like ice when she pulls me around to make me comfortable, but they're rock-steady as she lifts me to pull my coat down off my shoulders and down over my fist that's swollen ham-size by now.

"Jim," she says, low and calm. "Put a pot on the stove with water to heat. We've got to get this hand in water as hot as it can stand."

I couldn't have said anything just then, and I'll bet Hawks couldn't have squeezed out a word, but she did, and there wasn't a sign of a shake in her voice. Not even when the pound of running feet came through to us, and Red Connor yelling, "It's got a face of iron. It's got claws of steel. Oh Jesus, it's made of iron and it almost got me! It got Rat-Face! Oh Mother of Mercy, it's a fiend from hell itself!"

He goes past, and I hear other steps pounding after him, and I know all hell is loose out there. Their fear strikes through into me, and I see it flare in Jim's eyes as he stands back to the door, his arms spread out either side of him and his palms against the wood.

But Marge says again, "Put a pot on the stove with water." She doesn't yell, she doesn't even turn around, but there's something in her voice that gets him going. That girl . . .

Her fingers are on my right hand. "What have you got in there, Hen? What are you holding so tight?"

Funny, all through everything I'd kept that fist tight closed on something little and hard and round. "I don't know," I says, kind of slow. "I don't know."

"Well, open it up and let's see."

I open it. And what is in it is a button, a brown button off a man's coat, still sewed to a scrap of brown wool.

"For the love of Pete," Jim rumbles, coming over to see. "Where did you get that?"

I DON'T answer right away. I'm choked up, kind of, with something heavy that had been in my chest lifting off. Devils don't wear coats of brown wool buttoned with brown buttons. And they don't use flashlights. The killer wasn't a devil, he was a man. He was the man whose fist had bounced off my jaw and who had run away from the corpse of Baldy Thomas. Run away to kill again, to kill Mom Stone. And being a man he could be stopped.

"It's from the coat of the murderer," I say finally. "I had hold of it when he sloughed me and it tore out when he pulled away. This piece of bone and rag is going to put someone in the chair to burn. All we've got to do is match it up."

Jim whistles. Marge takes the thing from me, and looks at it with a funny look on her face, a look I can't understand. I start to say something, don't. And my scalp all at once goes tight.

The bunk I'm on is right up against the wall that was just thin boards patched together and covered with flat-pounded cans on the outside to stop the chinks. It did keep wind out, but it didn't keep out sound. It don't keep out the soft sound I hear now, the scrape of cloth against tin—cloth, or my name's not Henry Trent, like the scrap that button was sewed to.

The wall don't keep sound out and it don't keep sound in. The killer's up against it and he's heard every word I said! He knows what I've got and he knows it'll burn him if he don't get it. *And he knows there is only one way he can get it.*

I'm shaking like jelly inside. I'd brought Marge inside here because it was the safest place I could think of, and now it's the most dangerous.

I'm thinking fast now. I've got to get Marge out of here. I've got to get her out right away. But the very thing I'd used to get her here would keep her here. She wouldn't leave me, thinking me as sick as I'd made out I was.

"Listen," I croak, "this thing's got to stop, and the only ones that can stop it is the cops. Someone's got to get them."

"Yeah," Hawks grumbles. "That's right. But you seen what chance anyone's got to get over the tracks and out. You seen what happened to Rat-Face and you heard Red Connors yammering."

"There's another way." I roll over, far away from the wall as I can. "Look." I'm talking so low they've got to bend down to hear me. "He's watching the embankment, ain't he? He's got to stay thereabouts to do that, don't he?"

Jim just grunts, but I see in the kid's face she catches on. I don't stop, and I don't look at her. I'm talking to Jim, see. "That means the river bank is clear. You can swim like a fish." He could, but Marge could leave him tied to a post, and I knew it. "He won't expect anyone to go that way. You slip down, swim with the tide, a half-mile or more, and get to shore. The rest is easy."

JIM licks his lips. He's afraid. He's afraid to go, and he hasn't got the guts to say no. But Marge butts in, just like I counted on. "I'll go," she whispers. "I can swim better than Jim and I can move quicker. I'll go."

"No," I say. "It's no job for a girl."

"And is there anything a man can do I can't do better?" she flares. I'm laughing inside of me, she falls for it so neat.

"Goodbye, Hen," she says. "I'll be back with a gang."

She tosses her hair back, straightens up, kicks the axe out of the door and is through it like a flash. Jim makes a pass to stop her but she's so quick he misses. Then he's out too. God! I hadn't figured on that. I hadn't figured he'd hang back and then be ashamed to let her go alone. I hadn't figured on being left alone in the shack to wait for the killer.

With all I could do for Marge done, I got time to think of myself and now I'm afraid for myself. Afraid! So afraid I'm like a lump of ice laying there and waiting for the killer to come. I don't want to die. *I don't want to die!* It's a scream that makes no sound, a million separate voices yelling, "I DON'T WANT TO DIE!"

I'm going nuts. Sure as shooting I'm going nuts. I got to think of something else. Of the button. I got to hide it. I—Cripes! I ain't got it! *I ain't got the button!* MARGE HAS IT!

Marge has it, and she's outside there in the fog where he can get at her without taking any chances! I've sent her out to get killed! I've sent her out to have the same awful thing happen to her as happened to Baldy and Mom and Rat-Face! I've killed her just as if I'd stuck a knife in her throat myself.

I push up to go after her. That is, I *try* to push up. I bang my bum fin against the wood and the whole damn shack whirls around me like all possessed, and I drop down again with a thud. My head seems to split open. I wasn't kidding about not being able to move myself. I wasn't kidding. The slough I'd gotten must have been tougher than I thought.

I lie there waiting for her to scream. Waiting to hear the scream that will mean the killer's got her. The scream that will mean the top of her head . . .

CHAPTER THREE

Alone With the Killer

AFTER a few minutes I try to get up again, but it's no go. The light, from the busted stove and a couple candles stuck in bottles, goes bleary, and my arm pumps like a plugged fire-hose. My head, too. *Pump. Pump. Pump.* And I can't make out if things I hear is real: shivery hoots of fog-horns from the river; a kind of rumble that might be the voices of the fellows nearer by; the growl of the big city that's spread all along the river.

All the noises blur like the light, and I'm crying a little with weakness, and still listening for Marge's scream. And I'm beginning to hope a little that maybe God has had mercy on her and let her get by, when a sound gets through the blur to me. It's the soft thud of a footfall right outside the shack door—and the fumble of a hand on its wood.

Maybe it's one of the fellows. Maybe it's Marge come back, or Jim. But I know it isn't. I know it isn't anyone that's been in the shack before. There's a little trick to opening that door. Nothing much —but whoever's there don't know it.

I go cold all over, and try to yell for help. The squeak I get past my tonsils can't be heard two feet away. And I can't move. All I can do is lay there and watch that door. Watch it start to open. I see the opening grow between the door-edge and the sash, and see the fog show in that space. Not yellow now, but a kind of dull red, like blood—drying blood.

Afterwards I find out the fellows have built a big bonfire on the flat and it's the light of their fire makes the fog red. But I don't know that, and the color of mist to me then is just the color of bloody death, reaching in a hazy arm to take me. Not making any sound, but getting solid and black in the space opening slow between the door and the jamb.

It gets to be the black shadow of a man and comes in. It closes the door behind itself, and stands there, all blurred because my eyes is blurred, and shuts the door on any help that might come.

Funny how your brain works sometimes. I'm afraid. Sure I'm afraid, like nobody's ever been afraid before. But under my fear there's a couple of thoughts. One is that if the killer is here he can't be after Marge. Maybe she's got away, maybe he didn't catch her.

The other thought is different. I'm thinking it at the same time. How could that be? There is the feeling of being scared, and at the same time there's these two thoughts. One the hope for Marge. The other that the killer is so sure of getting me he's letting me see that he's a man and not the big black thing with wings, kind of, and no face except for two green lights where its eyes ought to be.

He's a man all right, in a brown suit and without a hat. I don't see his face yet, because he's turned around, like as if he's listening through the door. He isn't bothering about anything I can do, and he's right. I *can't* do anything. Not if my life depended on it.

That's funny. My life does depend on it. Because Marge has kicked the axe over against the bunk and if I can pick it up I can fling it at him and knock him down. I try to get my hand moving to it —God knows I try.

Maybe I do move it a little. Maybe I make some sound moving it. Because he turns around, quick, and he's looking at me. And I'm looking at him, and I know who he is. It's Barkley. It's Richard Barkley, the young lawyer that's been doing the dirty work for the Riverbank Corporation!

HIS face is white and his eyes is like— like fire would be if fire could be black. But he don't look like a murderer. His mouth kind of twists, and all of a sudden I'm sore at myself for being paralyzed with fear of him. This guy's scared to death himself.

"Where's the girl?" he croaks. "They told me she was here."

"What—what the hell's that to you?" I say. And I'm listening again, with one ear, for the sound I'm afraid will come to tell me the answer. Because if he isn't the killer . . . Part of me's doing that, and part of me's remembering how he's looked at her the couple of times he's been around with G. Watts Condon, arguing with him to put us off the plot. How he's looked at her, and how she's looked at him when she thought he wouldn't see. "What do you want her for?"

His hands go up to his throat as if he's choking. "I—I want her. I want her to . . ." I don't hear the rest of what he says, because his hand comes down just then, and I see the front of his brown coat. And fear blows up inside me like a shot in hard rock. Because I see the front of his coat now, and the top button's missing, and his other buttons are of brown bone. . . .

There's no doubt about it now. Richard Barkley's the killer and he's come to get me because I know about the button even if I ain't got it any more. And there's no doubt about something else, too. He wouldn't be here if Marge was still alive. Marge and Jim. He's gotten them first, outside somewhere. And now he's come to clean up.

My mind goes black and then it's red—hot red with hate. But it turns cold after that—cold as sly. He's stalling. For some reason he's stalling for time, making believe he's looking for the kid where he knows damn well she isn't. Maybe I can use that stalling. Maybe I can pay him off for Marge. ". . . and the rest of you had better get out, too. If you stay you'll all get it." All that must have gone through my head in no time, flat, for he's still talking. "You can't stop it. Tell that to the rest. Tell it to them. They won't believe me."

So that's the game! He isn't going to bump me—yet. He's giving me a message for the crowd. Buying the plot hasn't worked, nor getting it condemned. We've got to be chased off and that's the way he's doing it. Killing. Killing like a maniac. Sending me with the message.

He takes a step toward me. And another. But it's funny. I'm so scared I'm not afraid any more. Now that I know the kid's gone and he's just plain human, just a filthy murderer, I'm not afraid. I'll either go out like a candle or go somewhere Marge might be. There's a chance I'll get to see her again, and there's no chance if I stay alive.

But if I'm kicking off he's going with me. That's the only thing I'm afraid of now, that I'll go and leave him behind, and I'm more sore than afraid. So sore that I get a little strength back, and feel that I can move my good arm. That'll have to be enough.

"All right," I say, weak. "All right. I'll tell them. Call them in here and I'll tell them."

Barkley stops, and his eyes slide to the door. For a minute I'm stumped. Is he going to do it? Is he going to call the gang in here? I can't make that out.

But I see his hand come up and fumble at the torn place the button come out of. And he turns back to me. "No," he says. "I've got to go and find her. You call them."

"Hell," I say. "Can't you see I'm bunged up? I can't move. I can't yell that loud."

Whatever else, he's a good actor. He fidgets, starts for the door, starts back. "I can't," he husks. "I don't dare chance getting held up here. You'll have to manage it."

"All right." I talk mush-mouthed. "I'll try. But give me a drink. For the love of God, give me a drink from that water can on the table. Maybe then I can holler loud enough to bring someone."

HE TWISTS to the can. That takes his look off me just long enough for me to drop my hand over the side of the bunk. Then he's turned back and is coming towards me with the can. He's bending over—the can's to my mouth. . . .

I grit my teeth and jerk up my bum arm. I jerk it around his neck in spite of the red-hot irons shooting through it. I pull him down on my chest and jerk up my other arm with the axe in its hand. . . .

But it don't come down! Someone screams. Wet fingers grab my wrist, pull the axe out of my hand! Barkley slams a fist into my belly, slams himself up and away from me, twisting.

Wow! It's not the pound of his knuckles in my solar plexus that's got me winging. It's who I see standing there. It's Marge! Dripping wet, her hair plastered around her pale face and her dress pasted to her so that there might as well be no clothes on her at all, Marge is standing there, the axe in her hand. Her lips are blue, she's shaking like a leaf in the wind. But she's there, alive!

Everything's frozen like a movie with the film stuck and the light still on. There's the kid, not boylike now. Not with the round of her breasts heaving, kind of, as she gasps for breath. And her eyes sort of swallowing Barkley. And there's him, half-twisted to her and meeting her look while a little muscle twitches at the point of his cheekbone.

Just for a second it's like that, then things start moving again. But slow at first. His arms coming up, slow. And she swaying toward him. And me fighting for voice, but not getting it because a half-dozen things I want to say get jammed up together. And inside me a jumble of gladness that she's not dead, and fright at what he's going to do to her, and something else. Something that hurts more than my arm or my busted fist. Something I see in his face and hers.

The axe drops out of her fingers, pounds to the ground, and brings me up sitting. "Marge!" I yell. "Marge! Look at his coat!" Foolish, I guess. But it's the best I can manage. "Look at his coat."

Does she hear me? I don't know. Because he's yelling something, too, something I don't get. And he's swept her up, lifted her right from the ground and is plunging out. Oh, Mother of Mercy! He's carrying her out of the shack, out into the fog that's dripping with blood!

I roll out of the bunk. My feet tangle in the blankets, and I pound down—down on my swollen arm and my busted hand. Ten thousand devils rake me with white-hot pitchforks, but I roll, get clear, get to my feet and reel for the door that's slammed behind them.

I can't see it. I feel something, though. Wet clothes. Rough, wet clothes and someone inside them.

"Hen!" someone yells, and I can see again. I can see Jim, wet as hell, water running off his hair and down his face. "Hen! Where's Marge? For God's sake, where's the kid?"

"He's got her, Jim!" I yammer while he holds me and my legs are rubber under me. "The killer's got her! Just now! Lemme—" I try to push past him. "Lemme go after him. Leggo!"

But he hangs on to me, and I see that his eyes ain't sane. They're like red glass marbles with lights inside them, lights that don't show anything but fear. I paw at him, and twist to get away from the death-grip he's got on me, but I'm weak as a babe and I can't do anything.

"Jim!" I shriek. "Let go!"

THAT gets to him, starts him moving. But not the way I want. No. He barges in, carrying me with him, and then he drops me to twist to the door and slam it again.

Jim turns around and is backed up against the door like he was when the kid told him to put a pot on the stove. He looks down at me crawling toward him, and his eyes clear a little.

"Hen," he mouths, "I seen the killer. It's—"

Zowie! The wood slashes in, right at his head! Something slashes through, slashes into his skull. It's metal! Pronged metal!

It pulls back, pulling through bone and wood, jamming Jim back against the door. His face is gone, it's just a mess of spurting blood and pulped brains, and he pounds down. Through the gash in the door I see fluttery black, and I hear the screaming laugh of the killer. Then the splintered wood frames nothing but red fog, and what was once my buddy is just an awful mess on the ground.

My throat tears with a shriek I don't know I'm letting out till it's out. I'm scrabbling the ground, dragging myself toward it, toward Jim. I don't get to him, because my shriek brings the pound of feet, and shouts. The door busts in, pushing Jim along the ground, and there's the bunch.

They've got scantlings in their fists, and iron bars, and such things, and their faces are all grey and their eyes bulging like Jim's was when he had a face. Their yells are all mixed up in my head, but there's one voice that's bawling the others down. That's Red Connors yelling: "We've got to get out! We've got to get out of here or the devil will get us all. Come on! All together we can make it. Come on!"

From where I'm layin', I see their faces work, like inside them they're fighting between being afraid to stay and being afraid to go. He howls again, "Come on! All together. Up the embankment and out!" And someone else yells, "I'm with you, Red!" and then they're all yelling that, and they're streaming out of the shack. They're streaming out and pounding away through the fog and the mud, and I hear them yell as they go.

And I know the yellow curs have left me here for the killer. Left me helpless on the ground that's all blood, and mucked brains.

Left *me* helpless, and left Marge somewhere out on the flat where the killer has carried her. . . .

How long I lay there I don't know. I'm like someone dead and in hell, but the hell is all inside my head. It's a picture of the kid, laying out in the mud and fog with—Oh, Mother of Mercy!—with the top of her head. . . .

How long I lay there and think of that I don't ever know, but somehow I feel strength coming back into me, strength to get up on my feet and stumble towards the axe so that I can beat the killer to it. I whirl to the door and through it as a scream rips to me from out there!

"Hen! Help! *Help!* It's Marge!"

Marge's scream cutting off, and the killer laughing his mad laugh that's like a crazed loon crying in the marshes. . . .

CHAPTER FOUR

Good-bye to Marge

I GET out the door, twist to where that scream has come from, towards the river. Towards where the killer must be.

Devil or human, I'll get him. Devil or human, I'll tear him to bits with my bare hands. He's killed her. He's killed Marge and he's killed Jim, and he's not getting away with it.

Maybe I'm crazy right then. I guess I am crazy. I've got the strength of a crazy man, anyhow, and like a crazy man I don't care what happens to me so long as I can do what I want. And what I want is to kill Barkley. That's all that's left for me to want.

I plough like that through the fog, and I veer towards where a kind of red glare shows the fire the crowd has built. Why, I don't know. I just run.

Then all at once I trip on something in the mud, and flop. I skid in the slime, bring up against something soft. I roll to get up again and see by the firelight what it is that's stopped my slide. Marge. Marge's body, limp in the mud and red. Oh, God—red with. . . .

But it's *not* blood. It's the firelight that makes her red, and the water on her face taking the red of the fire. At least the killer hasn't ripped her skull. At least her lips are still there for me to kiss goodbye. Lips I'd never dared even think of kissing when she was alive.

Oh, God! They are still warm to my lips. Warm! And they move. Great Almighty, *they move!* She isn't dead! Marge isn't dead!

She moans. . . .

Right then a shadow falls across me—

a black shadow that cuts off the firelight. I twist around. A black form towers above me, high in the fog. The black is all fluttery, and the firelight plays on where its face ought to be—and there's no face there, but only a blankness shining like silver, out of which two eyes look that are green lights from hell itself.

I see that, and I scream like Baldy Thomas screamed out of the night, and like Mom Stone screamed. The Thing lifts an arm like a huge black wing, blanking out the fire. At its end there's metal prongs shining, the same metal prongs I've seen pound through wood and through Jim Hawks' skull.

I roll. I roll over on top of Marge so that I'll cover her. So that maybe the killer won't see that she's alive and'll kill only me and leave her alive.

That brings me face down so I can't see the killer's arm come down. I can see only Marge's face under mine, and feel the warmth of her body against mine, and I kiss her again. And I wait for the slash of those prongs into my skull.

But it don't come. A clang comes instead, like a rock on a bell! I roll over again. The killer is leaping away into the night and a rock does splash down into the mud, just missing my hand.

I heave up. I grab up the rock, and pound into the dark where I hear the thud of running footfalls. Two sets of footfalls, the killer and someone he's chasing. Whoever it is that's saved me by throwing that rock. I've got to save him now.

The chase pounds along shore, through the fog. The killer pulls away from me, and the one he's chasing pulls ahead of him, but that isn't going to do him any good. The railroad embankment curves in to the river a ways ahead, twenty feet high and straight up. It can be climbed, but not in a hurry. Not quick enough.

I try to run faster. But they pull away. . . .

IT'S hours we run like that. Minutes, of course, seconds, maybe, but it seems like hours. Then the grey loom of the embankment shows ahead, and against it a shadow that's a running man, and behind him a bigger shadow that's a man maybe, or a devil.

A street lamp above makes the light that shows me that, and there's another shadow up there, a man peering over. It's funny that I think, even then, that the man up there ought to come down and help instead of looking down like a ninny.

Then there's the thunder of a train coming, and the first man in our chase comes up against the embankment and starts climbing. I'm going faster and yelling, and the killer is just ahead of me, reaching up with his black wing and just reaching the first man's coat with the prongs, and sinking them in.

Everything seems to happen all at once. A locomotive roaring around the curve, and the killer tangled with the other man in front of me, and my jumping about ten foot and landing right behind them, and my swinging my arm with the rock and bringing in down *kerplunk* on blackness that I know covers the killer. I feel bone crush under that swipe that's got the weight of the rock, and the swing of my arm, and the pound of my jump behind it. And right then I hear another sound above me, a shriek like hell let loose, and something pounds down alongside of me.

There's yelling up above, and the scream of brakes locking, and sparks spurting as car wheels slide along steel. There's a yell down here where I am, and I fall forward on top of the killer and get all tangled up in a lot of black cloth. I feel him quivering underneath me, and somehow there's a lot more light all around than there's been before.

My head comes clear of the cloth and I'm looking up into the light. I see a face over me, a face with lips snarled back from white teeth, and eyes burning black in whiteness, and my insides turn over. For I'd felt the spine of the killer crunch under the rock I'd brought down on it, and he must be dead. But he wasn't dead. It was Barkley's face looking down at me. Barkley's face! The face of the killer!

It's white, that face, a queer kind of dead white, except on its forehead and one cheek, where it's smeared with blood. . . .

I'm gone then. I know I'm gone. But I'm still going to make a fight of it. So I jerk my good arm free and throw its fist at Barkley's jaw.

Anyhow, I think I'm throwing it, but the killer's head floats away into mist. There isn't anything there but mist full of white light, and that blurs and gets dark. Hoarse voices rumble in my ears but don't make sense, and I go down, down the side of a black wave into blackness.

Then the wave lifts me up into light again, but my head's spinning and I'm seeing things. I'm looking along the ground, and there's a mound of black cloth and out of it is sticking a carrot-topped head that it seems to me is the head of Red Connors. And right beside it there's another body all twisted so that I know every bone in it is smashed. The face that belongs to it is thin, and grizzled, and from the corner of its mouth blood dribbles down into a pointed grey goatee. Then I know I've gone nuts altogether, for that's the face of G. Watts Condon and what would he be doing laying all crumpled up in the mud?

The white lights move around and shadows move on the ground, and I look up to see what's throwing the shadows. And I'll be a crop-eared donkey if it isn't a man and a woman clinching, his arms around her and their faces so tight together you can't push a piece of paper between them. The light gets stronger, or

my eyes clearer, and I see who they are, and the ground seems to rock under me and I groan out loud.

They jump apart and Marge swoops down on me. "Hen! Hen, dear! Are you—are you all right?" And Barkley bends to look over her shoulder, and he says, "How comes it, old man?" in a hearty voice.

THIS all has got me winging. It don't make sense at all. I push up and look around. I see a couple of guys in overalls holding lanterns and whispering together, and I hear a loco puffing overhead. Then I see a kind of mask laying near Red Connor's head, a mask of polished steel, and inside it a couple of little green bulbs and wires, and I begin to get a glimmer of the truth.

I look back at Marge and try to say something. But all I can manage is, "What—what the . . .?"

But the kid catches on. She smiles, kind of sadlike, and says, "Yes. The killler was Red Connors. He had a mask, and a cloak of black cloth that he could get in and out of very quickly, and a heavy fork with five curved steel prongs with which he did the killing."

"But—but why?"

"For money. For money paid to him by—" her voice kind of broke— "by G. Watts Condon."

That *certainly* don't make sense. My lips move; maybe I ask the question. Maybe she just reads it in my eyes. Anyways, she turns to Barkley and says, "Tell him, Dick."

He uses a lot of big words, but I kind of untangle what he means. And it's plenty. Seems like this: Condon's been caught in the market and if he don't get what the Riverbank Corp's ready to pay him for the flat where New Deal Town is, he's going to have to move down with us, but if he does he can save near all his cash. But he's always been nuts about being an all right guy and giving till it hurts and the way people kowtow to him for that means more than a flock of autos and yachts and dames to other guys in the money. If he puts us out he figures everybody will be thumbs down on him and having the money ain't going to be no good to him, so he's s. o. l. either way. But he's a nut, see, crazy as a bedbug, and. . .

But this is the way Dick Barkley puts it: "But if you were driven off, the dilemma would be solved. And so this great philanthropist evolved the scheme that's made horror here tonight. I came down tonight to see Marge." I winced at that. "I'd seen her here several times and I couldn't get her out of my head. I had just gotten across the tracks when I heard a scream down by the river. I ran down there, flashed my light, and as you jumped up realized that I, a stranger, would surely be accused of the crime. So I pulled away from you, ran away.

"Then I heard a woman scream, and, remembering some things Condon had let drop, guessed what was up. I was frightened for Marge, started to hunt for her. . . ."

"Dick may not have been able to get me out of his head," the kid put in, blushing. "But I wasn't much better. I saw him when he flashed the light on poor Baldy, recognized him. And something inside of me told me he couldn't be the killer. So when you showed me the button I got it from you and grabbed the chance you gave me to get out and warn him. But Jim went with me and I had to start swimming. I managed to lose him. I came back, and as I landed I saw Red Connors just putting on his black cloak. I ran to the shack to tell you and got there just in time to save you from killing Dick. Then, when he carried me off—"

"I had to get you away, dear. I didn't know when the killer might break in and go for you. . . .'"

"I told Dick what I'd seen. Connors must have overheard us, because he loomed up suddenly in the fog. I screamed, and his first wild swing stunned me—"

"And I pounded a fist into his mid-riff. It staggered him. I ran off, keeping just near enough to him to make him think he could catch me. That was to lure him away from Marge. But suddenly he tumbled and turned back. I followed, saw him bending over you and threw a stone I'd picked up. . . The rest I guess you know."

"Yeah," I say slowly. "Except—" I pointed to Condon. "How'd he get what was coming to him?"

Barkley looks grave. "That, Henry, was just one of those things we can explain only as the inscrutable justice of an omniscient God. Condon must have been hanging around to see how his scheme was working, gotten so interested in the chase down here that he didn't hear the train coming, and—there he lies."

Marge shudders. "Oh, it's been horrible. A horrible thing. I'll—I'll dream about it forever."

Barkley pulls her to him. "It's been horrible, all right," he says. "But it gave us one thing that's worth it all. It's given us the knowledge of our love."

That hurts. It hurts like hell. Then I think what it means for Marge, and it don't hurt so much. . . .

THE END

IN THE MARCH ISSUE—

Another Spine-Tingling Tale by Arthur Leo Zagat

—Out January 25th!

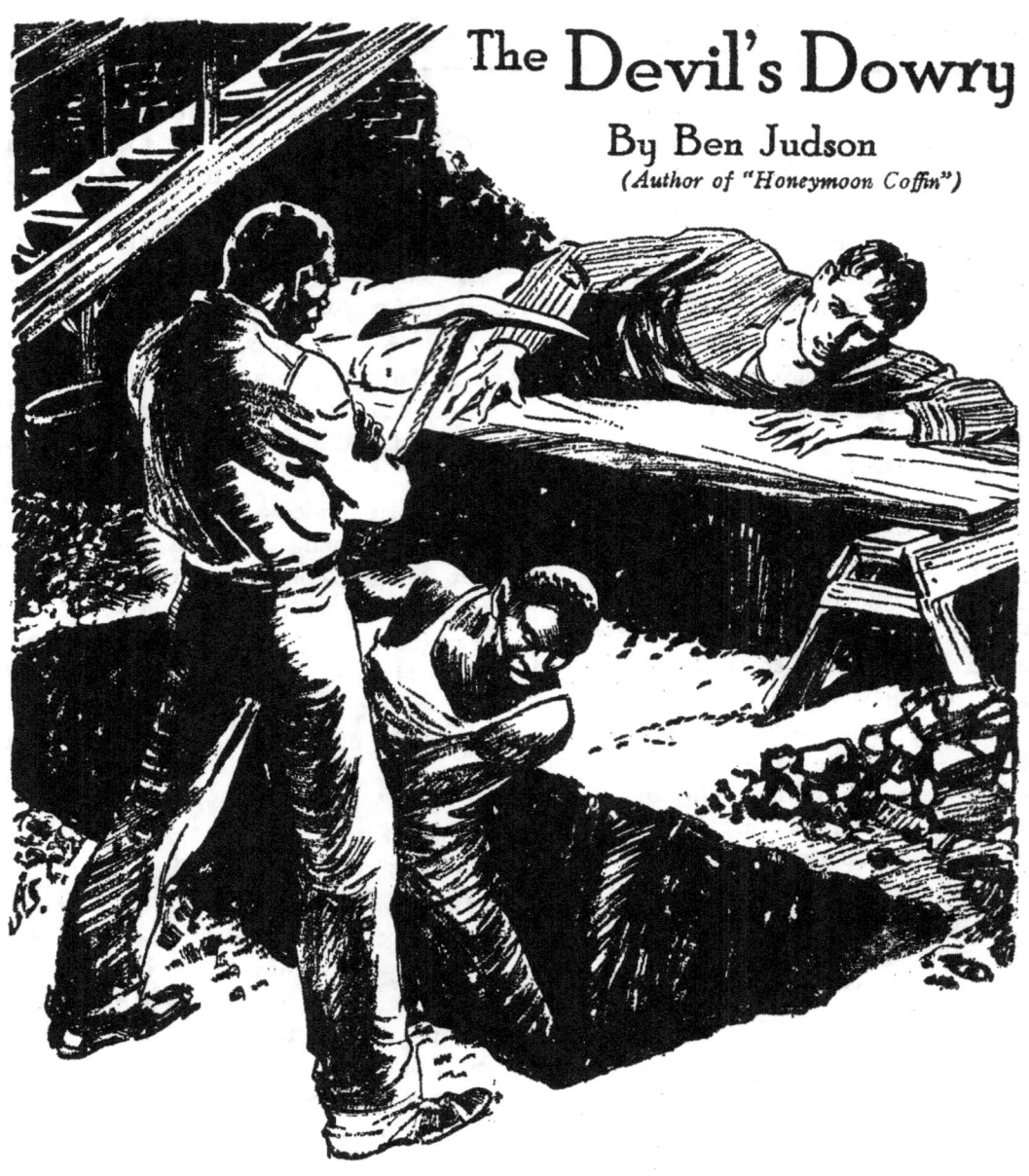

The Devil's Dowry

By Ben Judson
(Author of "Honeymoon Coffin")

Why did Julie Anthony die, on the eve of her wedding-day? Who was the fiendish voodoo doctor who offered to return her alive to her frenzied lover? And what unspeakable rite was performed each night in that dank, noisome tenement cellar?

SOMETHING knotted hard and tight in my throat. A feeling of eerie loneliness swept over me, though I was not alone in the room. The doctor fumbled with the sheet a moment, pulling it up over the sallow face on the bed. A low feminine sob convulsed from the bent, gray head of the woman slumped on the opposite bedside; a sigh rattled dustily in the old parson's throat.

Dr. Peleg's yellow, parchment-like visage gazed at the three of us. There seemed to be almost a leer of triumph in the cruel lines about his mouth, and I hated the man without knowing why. His impenetrable eyes glimmered with a strange, unholy light as they rested on the form beneath the sheet, and they seemed covetous and sinister.

They left me finally, Dr. Peleg with his shaking, knotted fingers; Julie's father, spare and grim as an old Puritan in his black cloth; and her mother, Lucy Anthony, stooped and stunned with grief.

I sat gently on the edge of the bed, and reverently uncovered the still, beautiful face. Julie Anthony slept peacefully in the misty twilight of the room. Why was it I refused to believe her dead? Was it because, even when death had scooped gray shallows in her youthful cheeks, those things we had shared in common kept her life alive *in me?* Because, only a few days ago, we had been joyously planning the details of our marriage?

I stooped to kiss the unfaded lips—crimson like a gash in her livid skin—half expecting to feel their warm response to my caress. But they were cold and motionless, and ever after their contact lingered on my mouth, cold, empty.

Standing up then, I replaced the sheet, and marched dumbly from the gray room.

The shadows gathered thickly on the stairway as I descended. In the circle of light at the foot a thin, dark-skinned man was standing, talking in a low tone with David Anthony. There was an angry frown on the preacher's dry, taut face. But it was the aspect of the Negro that caught my interest and suspended my descent on the steps.

There was something repulsively evil about the thick lips, the glaring, shadowed eyes. I had seen that sinister face before; I searched my memory quickly.

Presently the Negro bowed himself out deftly before the threatening advance Julie's father made. There was a sneer pregnant with evil on those grotesque lips. I rushed down as the door closed firmly.

"Who was that?" I demanded.

"Simone, the faith-healer," Mr. An-thony replied, and turned into the parlor where his wife sat huddled in an old, butterfly chair.

I stood by the rail-post, mouth half open. I remembered, then. A couple of weeks ago, my boss, the editor of the *Evening Mercury,* had sent me into the tenement district for a story about a Negro sorcerer who claimed he could raise the dead. But I came away with only a bruised shin when my foot crashed through a rotted stair tread. But I had seen the face, and recognized the man again as Simone.

What had the old Negro wanted? Did he think he could bring life into Julie's mute body with his witchcraft? My mouth settled grimly. There had been ugly, vague whisperings about black Simone's operations. I stuck my head into the parlor and motioned to David Anthony. He followed me back into the hall shortly.

"What did Simone say, exactly?" I asked.

The parson's long face gazed at me sternly. "You're not thinking, George —?" he queried.

"No—no," I replied hastily. "He's a fake, I know. But there are stories. Ugly stories."

"Of what sort?"

"That the people he has brought back have never been—natural—afterward. I have seen some of them. Negroes, mostly."

"He wanted money. Five hundred dollars. He said he would return it if he failed!"

We stood mute for several minutes. The feeling of emptiness descended heavily upon me. Finally I stirred. "I'm going—for a walk," I whispered, my voice husky.

I walked dumbly, for what seemed hours, not noticing the direction I took. I went as if in a dream—as if all that had happened before had been a horrible nightmare.

It was with a shock that I realized I was passing through Dwight Street. Dwight Street is in the downtown area, hemmed in by blackened tenements, littered with filth and the offspring of the dregs of the city. It was in one of these tenements that Simone lived and brewed his jungle magic.

I tried to analyze what I had been doing, and the revelation was startling. Searching, searching for some hope that Julie could not be dead, not dead forever! And the search had led me unconsciously to Simone's doorstep!

As I passed a blackened doorway, a finger beckoned to me. I hesitated, peering into the darkness of the opening. A voice hissed evilly. "Simone want to see you!"

I determined to go on again, then paused a second time. Finally I stepped into the hallway, searching vainly with my eyes for the origin of the voice. The air was dank and heavy with the odor of unclean bodies, and I shrank away from it, as if to compress myself into as little space as possible.

The darkness thinned out a little as my eyes became accustomed to the lightlessness. A small dark shape moved ahead of me, up the stairway.

"Come!" the voice demanded.

I followed, avoiding mechanically the hole in the staircase into which my foot had slipped previously. Three flights my guide and I ascended, passing rotted doors from which black, hostile faces peered out at me.

Simone waited for me in a dingy backroom. The Negro youngster hesitated on the doorsill, urging me inward. His eyes shown round and dead white; an unreasoning terror seemed to grip his features in an agony of indecision and shake his small frame with aspen-like convulsions. As I entered, he scuttled back down the narrow, tottering stairway.

Simone greeted me with a silent nod. He indicated a lone chair, and himself squatted on a disheveled cot. The place reeked with the mingled odors of decay, human sweat and strange herbs. A single, blackened oil-lamp flickered on the floor; its unsteady light, vaunting upwards, cast distorted shadows on the crumbling walls, and brought out the Negro's face in grotesque relief.

"I knew you would come," the thick lips muttered, "but have you faith in my powers?"

I stared through the gloom at black Simone. In the darkness his snug-fitting, American clothes seemed to fall away, and I saw there a half-naked savage, a voodoo high priest, mumbling his weird incantations.

A strange fit of trembling seized me, and I tried to shake off the halucination. The sickening realization came to me that I might almost believe in the powers he claimed!

Simone bolted up suddenly. There was a wild, barbaric bleam in his eyes. "You shall have proof of my ability," he promised. "Wait!"

I clung to my chair while the Negro vanished into another part of the tenement, for I was tempted to spring from my seat and rush madly from the room, down the treacherous stairs, and into the purer freedom of the street. But I waited.

Presently there were shuffling sounds outside the door. An old, wild-eyed Negro slouched in before Simone's prodding. He stared crazily about the room, fixed his bulging eyes on me momentarily, and then slunk like a whipped animal into a corner.

Simone gazed at me with a melancholy expression in his eyes. "A moon ago," his voice rumbled, "Old Lazar lay cold in death. But *he* had faith, his people had faith. Again he walks among the living!"

My eyes shifted to old Lazar, who gibbered incoherently in his corner. A shudder racked my frame. One could well believe Lazar had died! He seemed still dead! A black ghost, doomed to the shadowy vale between life and death, belonging to neither. Rather Julie dead than to exist in this state of unnatural obliteration!

I sat up with a start. My God, I was believing!

"But Lazar is mad!" The words vomited forth from my throat with jerky haste.

"Death is not a pleasant experience," Simone said gravely. "But Lazar will get over it. There is much to forget."

A maelstrom of fantastic thoughts swirled in my brain. What if Simone were a voodoo *hougan,* a votarist of black art? If he could call Julie back to my arms, was not that all that mattered? Could there not be something outside the ken of matter-of-fact understanding, whose cosmic, dark powers we could not realize, because we refused to believe in them?

I got up shakily. "I'll speak to Julie's father," I said, and my voice sounded unreal and hollow.

Simone bowed me out of the room, and I descended, clinging to the railing, the darkness swirling dizzily about me. In the dingy room it had seemed very natural that I should go to David Anthony and convince him that Simone's witchcraft was rational and moral. But now, relieved somewhat from that macaber atmosphere which seemed to emanate from Simone and Lazar, my courage to profess a belief in the Negro sorcerer's cult began to ebb.

At the foot of the rickety flights of stairs I paused abruptly. A figure which seemed oddly familiar to me blackened the doorway to the street.

The figure hesitated momentarily as I advanced into the light cast in from the street, started, and scuttled down the unlit hallway. I saw the face as it streaked through the blob of yellow light, and it was a face filled with the fear of discovery.

It was Doctor Peleg!

A hoarse cry of astonishment choked in my throat. I trembled by the doorway, not knowing whether to run from the insanity that I felt was pressing upon me, or to pursue the doctor and demand an explanation of his strange action.

I crept back into the hall, but nothing except blackness and closed doors reached my senses. Shortly I turned, walked into the street.

Maybe, I thought, Doctor Peleg had come, as I had, seeking the aid of the witch-doctor, his own powers having failed. The thought comforted me a little, but the evil, terrified glimmer I had seen on his face provoked sinister doubtings in my mind.

With quick, but uncertain, steps I strode back to the Anthony house.

DAVID ANTHONY gazed at me with grave concern. "Don't you think you had better get some sleep?" he inquired.

I tried as much as possible to erase the look of hysteria from my eyes. "I would like to talk to you—seriously—for a while," I asked, "if it won't disturb you and Mrs. Anthony."

"Mrs. Anthony has retired," the preacher informed me.

We sat in the dully lit parlor and I attempted to put an easy inflection in my voice, but the nervous gestures of my face and hands betrayed my lack of calm. David waited with a quiet resignation.

"How did you come to know Doctor Peleg?" I asked. "He wasn't your family physician."

"I saw him in church one Sunday about two weeks ago. He was new to the congregation, and asked me if he might talk to me some time. He came to the house

Monday evening, and we discussed our different religious beliefs. He called quite often after that.

"When Julie was taken ill, our regular physician confessed his inadequacy to handle her case. It was a disease he had never heard of, he said. A kind of sleeping sickness, but with unusual complications.

"Doctor Peleg seemed to show some knowledge of the disease, and suggested a possible cure. So Julie was put under his care."

The preacher slumped into his chair. His face stared vaguely at me, drawn, white and motionless. Then he demanded, "Why do you ask?"

"I saw Peleg at the tenement where Simone lives," I replied.

David started forward, his jaw unhinging. "What?"

I shrank into my chair. I had confessed more than I had intended.

"You were there?" David Anthony's voice was sharp.

* * *

Mr. Anthony was frowning meditatively by the time he had wormed from me the full details of my excursion to the witch-doctor's flat. "What possible connection could Peleg and Simone's acquaintance—if that is really so—have with Julie's death?"

"I don't know," I acknowledged. "But our first step is to find out *just what that acquaintance means!*"

I was silent a moment. A suggestion hovered on the tip of my tongue in cowardly embarrassment. Finally, hardening my jaw muscles, I blurted forth:

"Why not let Simone try his faith-healing? It might offer a clue!"

David gazed at me sternly. "That minister of the devil! A man of true faith would not demand payment for his healing."

"I will scrape together the five hun-

dred." There was a desperate tremor in my voice, and I clutched the arms of my chair in a vise-like grip.

"No!" Mr. Anthony was adamant. "If God willed Julie be returned to this life, he would grant me as much power as a —pagan!"

I wandered the streets listlessly, much as I had earlier in the evening. Late pedestrians glanced at me askance, some pityingly. In their faces I read: drunkard, madman. To a young girl who whispered concernedly to her escort I shouted suddenly: "I am not drunk!" They gaped at me in surprise, and I reeled off in confusion.

I could feel it urging me forward madly, that relentlessness and exasperation born of despair and inactivity. I must do *something*, if only to hunt out Dr. Peleg and twist a confession from his seamy, hateful throat. Otherwise, my reason would wither in a chaos of insanity.

Tomorrow they would bury Julie. Then she would be gone, forever. Was she not lost to me now? I could not seem to realize that. She still existed for me in flesh and blood, though she lay cold and motionless. Till tomorrow, then, I could have hope, though it were born of insanity.

I had a few hundred dollars in the bank. The rest I could borrow from the paper. The office would make me an advance. I had been there a long time. It would have to.

My pace quickened. Street corners slid by in a blur. The breath came short and excited in my windpipe. Simone would take my promise; I would write him a note. Tonight, while I engaged David Anthony in conversation, Simone would perform his miracle! How surprised the old preacher would be! I rushed on. . . .

Simone greeted me distrustfully. I

pushed the door in, and strode into the room. The place seemed to light up with the infectious delirium that raged in my eyes. I clung to the old Negro's hand, and my words tumbled forward in staccato confusion.

"I have the money!" I shouted. "Tomorrow—it's in the bank—I'll write a note. Come with me. I believe—I believe!"

Simone gazed at me, frowning. Then, shaking his head, he said to me in a low sepulchral voice, "It is too late!"

My hands dropped to my sides. My mouth slumped open. The world crashed suddenly about me, dinning in my ears with a horrible, threatening roar.

"But surely," I stuttered. "She has been dead only a few hours!"

"I cannot do it."

"I have faith in you."

The wicked eyes stared at me piercingly. "You are mad!"

I mumbled to myself. "Mad!" The black man seemed to hear me, and leered maliciously. Then something snapped in my head, as if a joint had sprung back into place. The air began to clear of the mist and headiness.

"Why," I demanded coolly, "did Doctor Peleg come to see you?"

Simone drew back into himself. He seemed to move away from me, though he made no step. "I do not know Doctor Peleg," he replied.

Shortly I descended from the tenement and made my way home.

JULIE was buried late the next afternoon.

The winches that lowered the casket into the grave ceased their humming. I turned, with Mr. and Mrs. Anthony, back to the car that had brought us to the cemetery. Another large chapter in my life had ended, I thought.

I returned to work the next day. To-wards evening, the editor called me to his desk. "There's been a throat-slitting on Dwight Street," he informed me. "I want you to cover it, George. It's in the tenement where the witch-doctor hangs out. An old black fellow got mixed up with a razor."

Not waiting to ask questions, I raced to the street and grabbed a cab. The hackie dropped me in front of the wooden building. It seemed to lean crazily over the sidewalk, threatening to crush us. There was a cop standing guard by the entrance.

"*Evening Mercury*," I flashed my card and leaped up the tottering stairs. On the fourth landing, outside Simone's doorway, two rookies were lifting the corpse into the wicker basket. A large pool of blood crept slowly over the uneven floor towards the stairwell. The dead Negro's head swung grotesquely from the shoulders by the cords in the back of the neck.

I peered intently in the basket at the distorted face. "Swing your light over here, Burke?" I asked a sergeant who was watching the work. Eyes, glazed and insane, stared at me from the police coffin.

It was Lazar, Simone's crazy patient!

"This was one of the witch-doctor's 'dead men,'" I whistled.

"That's one zombie won't walk again!" the sergeant remarked dryly.

"Get any suspects—any witnesses?" I demanded.

"Not a thing!" Burke snorted. "All these boogies can do is gape and roll their eyes!"

"What about the witch-doctor?"

"Not a smell of him."

"Looking for him?"

"Yeah, in a way. Got nothing on him, though."

"Listen," I confided in him. "I've got a hunch Simone knows plenty about this.

But if you hang around for him, I'll bet you anything he doesn't show up."

"So?" Burke gazed at me skeptically.

"So," I continued, "you and the rookies beat it. Keep the cop away from the street entrance, too. I'll wait in Simone's room, and grab him if he comes in."

Sergeant Burke pondered a moment. Finally he shrugged. "Suits me," he said.

I crept as unobtrusively as possible into the witch-doctor's room while the rookies bore the body outside. Presently I heard the police car drive off, and the darkness of night closed in about me completely. I waited, hunched forward on the cot, straining my ears for sounds.

Muted whisperings filtered in through the cracked walls. But no evidence of the black sorcerer. The minutes tramped heavily by, drawing themselves into hours. Presently I found myself nodding; a leaden apathy seized my eyelids, and my head slumped forward into my lap.

I DO not know how long I rested in that state of semi-consciousness. I was not entirely asleep, for I seemed to have some perception of the blackness and strange, hidden movements about me, betrayed by squeaking boards and ghostly rustlings. Slowly, a vague uneasiness pricked through my drowsiness, beating on the muffled alarm of some instinctive sixth sense.

Though the rousing seemed to take an age of effort, the final awakening came with a rapidity that jerked my remaining senses into a trembling awareness. My breathing came heavily, as if I had been running a great distance, my eyes strained through the thick blackness, and the beating of my heart thumped warningly against my ribs. Out of some subterranean depths, a low, muffled *boom— boom — boom* reverberated ominously against my eardrums!

Raising myself quickly from the cot,

I struck a match. The light flickered momentarily on the bare, crumbling walls of the cubicle, then dropped to oblivion onto the floor. Creeping to the door, I drew it open a few inches, and listened intently.

Except for the dull, muted thumping from below, the building slept in tomb-like stillness. The booming sounded weirdly savage and unholy, like the drumming of some heathen blood-rite. Under its awful threat, all my city-bred sophistication seemed to fall from me like rotted garments, and I stood naked and afraid, like a superstitious pagan in the black, specter-haunted forest.

Squaring my shoulders, I slunk to the stairwell, and descended, clinging to the railing, avoiding the shadowy doorways. Three banks of unlighted, creaking stairways can seem infinitely long when fear forces one to tread lightly and with unsteady feet. Thus sinners must descend into hell.

The thought never entered my head to escape into the street. The drums pulled me on and down with their relentless, hypnotic spell. I crept into the Stygian blackness of the rear hall, the booming growing louder and louder, more articulately savage.

Underneath the stair casing, a rectangular line of light discovered a flimsy door to me. I pulled it open cautiously, peered into the inferno of pagan rhythm and dancing lights below. The odor of sweating, straining bodies rushed up to sting my nostrils, and beneath the even booming, I heard the incessant thumping of naked feet.

I pushed unwilling feet down the stone steps. On my right was a solid brick wall which right-angled to the left beyond the landing at the foot. As I drew myself downwards, a sea of bobbing, black heads came into view. These formed a rough, thick circle about a small clearing, within which a smaller circle of naked savages danced, swaying and writhing in demoniac ecstasy. At the far edge of the clearing, three Negroes bent over long, slender drums, beating with the heels of their fists on the raw-hide surface. A wild, possessed gleaming shown in the eyes of the votaries, and they all swayed involuntarily to the heavy voodoo music.

But it was the object within the ring of dancers that started my mouth open, drew rigid every muscle in my body, and sucked in a gasp of fear and wonder in my throat.

Over a low, crude altar bent the thin, taunt face of the witch-doctor. A black robe covered his skeleton-like body, and in his extended hand he held a long slender needle like a hypodermic. His protruding lips drew back in a fit of ugly, devilish passion, and his nostrils swelled and deflated under the force of his convulsive breathing.

Slowly the hand descended. Under the advancing needle lay the exposed breast of a girl—a nude white girl, still as death!

It was Julie!

My crouched legs straightened under me, and a shriek of insane fury retched from my lungs. As I sprang forward, every head started around, the booming of the drums ceased, the dancers stiffened in their mad careers, and Simone's hand paused in its downward thrust.

I crashed to the hard, earthen floor; hundreds of milling bodies pressed about me; a titanic fist smashed against my cheek, and the chaos of light and noise faded from my senses.

A SOFT, grey light gradually flooded my senses. My eyes opened, and I gazed upwards. Over me tottered the unpainted front of the tenement building. The twilight of dawn slowly filled the sky. An intense aching gripped my body and head, and the sharp edge of a stone pressed against one shoulder. I was sprawled in the gutter of Dwight Street!

I got up shakily, attempting to brush the filth from my rumpled clothes with my hand. It was with pain that I hobbled onto the sidewalk.

How had I come here? What horrible nightmare evoked strange, fearful memories in my brain? I gazed into the ever-open doorway of the tenement. I had seen Julie in that weird jungle sprouted like a fungi in a modern city!

Or had I? I remembered clearly the order from my boss, the editor; the murdered body of Lazar; the long waiting in Simone's flat. But after that point, reality faded into the grotesqueness of an insane dream. Had it all been a dream, provoked by the murky, unlovely atmosphere of the tenement? Had Simone found me napping in his room, and tossed me unceremoniously into the gutter?

There was one way to find out—to re-enter the place and search for the subterranean mystery house where the witch-doctor performed his devilish rites. If I found nothing, I had but dreamed. If I found the altar—I prayed I would not—I had *not* dreamed!

I hesitated at the entrance. I hated to think of exploring the place alone. What could I do against a hundred frenzied blacks, the restraint of civilization forgotten in the orgy of savage mysticism?

The steady, irregular clack of a policeman's boot reached my ears. I waited, and shortly a blue-coated rookie approached.

The cop eyed me suspiciously. I showed him my press card, and explained I had been tossed out of the tenement for attempting to investigate old Lazar's murder. He agreed, a little reluctantly, to accompany me within, after a good deal of persuasion.

"How do I know you haven't been off on a drunk?" he grinned at me.

I assured him I hadn't and we merged into the blackness of the tenement hall. The rookie's searchlight revealed the door that opened into the cellar. He threw the yellow beam into the depths below, and we descended the stone stairway.

The cellar was there, just as I had seen it—brick walls, earthen floor, wide, low ceiling. But there were no blacks, no sacrificial altar, no dusky priest. Yet, clinging to the asmosphere, I could still detect a faint, acid stench of reeking contorted bodies.

"I guess I was wrong," I muttered.

The rookie snorted sardonically, and we proceeded up the steps and onto the street again. I left the cop at the doorway to resume his beat, and turned towards home. Half an hour later, I 'phoned into the office that the murder of Lazar was unsolved, and tumbled into bed, having left a note for the landlady to call me at eight-thirty.

IT WAS shortly after nine the next morning that I stumbled into the Anthony's parlor. He seated himself, and I swung into action immediately.

"I saw Julie last night—her body, at least."

"*What?*"

"In the basement of the tenement on Dwight Street where Simone, the witch-doctor, lives."

David Anthony eyed me narrowly. "You were there last night?"

"Of course!" There was an exasperated rasp in my throat. "I saw her, I tell you!"

"She was buried two days ago!" There was that look of cautious inquiry in his eyes, which seemed to question my sanity.

"But she is not in her grave now!" I shouted the last, and watched for the effect it would have on him. He cow-

ered back in his chair, wide-eyed and frightened.

Then I launched into the detail of what had happened last night. David stared at me unblinking, terrified lest I could make him believe. But I hammered home my one point. "I had never seen the basement before last night. Yet when I entered it with the cop, it was exactly the same as I had seen it during the ritual! The same—even the smell was there—except the Negros were gone; the altar, Simone, and Julie were gone!"

He sat thinking a moment. In a weak voice, then, as if uttering his last feeble defense against my argument, he quavered, "How do you know it was Julie? Might it not have been some other woman?"

I gazed at him sternly. "Is there anyone, except you and your wife, who would know her better?"

"No. . . ." his head shook infirmly. "But can you prove it?"

"Yes!"

David searched my face. "How?"

"Open Julie's grave!"

WE GROUPED anxiously about the slowly yawning hole, David Anthony; Carl Doran, the medical examiner; the caretakers; and myself. Finally the winches were let down, and the gray box rose slowly.

Doran raised the lid. David had turned his eyes away, not daring to look. It was with difficulty that I forced my own eyes into the—*empty box!*

The breaths of the caretakers and the medical examiner sucked in. David swung his head around, and his features were ghastly pale and taunt.

"God in Heaven!" I heard the old preacher murmur under his breath. He turned his pitiful countenance to me. "God, God, I prayed you were insane!" he whimpered.

"Come!" I yelped, swinging to the waiting car in the road.

"What's next?" barked the examiner.

"We drop Mr. Anthony, pick up a couple of dicks at headquarters, and lump it down to Dwight Street before dark."

But I noted with uneasiness the sun dip slowly into the horizon as I raced into the city. "We'll have to leave you at the station, Mr. Anthony," I shouted.

Sergeant Burke and Conway, plainclothesmen, slid into the rear seat of the car after I had helped David out. The preacher was pale and fluttering in a sort of dream, as if reality had suddenly vanished for him in the weird, chaotic subworld he had just glimpsed. I felt sorry for the old man.

But the visible minutes were slipping by. I jambed the shift into second, and we grated forward at a leap. Burke slid an automatic into my jacket-pocket.

Parking the car just off Dwight Street, we walked swiftly and unobtrusively to the entrance of the tenement. The shadows had already gathered thickly.

Light, invisible feet scurried up the stairways as we filed in the door from the street. We tramped up the shaking steps, lighting the ascent with torches. Caution was useless. Notice of our coming had spread as if we had entered with a brass band.

Simone's room was empty. We shoved our way into adjoining flats, but the occupants only stared at us with stolid, ill-concealed hatred, their heavy lips clamped shut. We gave up, finally, and trooped to the cellar. But the search of that fetid-aired cavern yielded no more than the motionless lips of the tenants.

Burke threw up his hands. "You're not finding anything *here!*" he exclaimed.

"Let's find Doc Peleg," I suggested.

"Who's he?"

"The guy that buried Julie Anthony.

I caught him snooping around here the night after her death."

"Let's go!" Burke started up the steps.

"Wait—!" I called. The sergeant paused. "I'm going to stick here, in case Simone comes in. The rest of you leave with plenty of racket, so the boogies upstairs will think we've all gone. Nab Peleg, if you can, and pump him for all you can get. Ought to be able to hold him for material witness. David Anthony might know his address."

They nodded assent, and clomped up the steps. Their feet resounded like thunder in the low cellar as they progressed over the hall. Squatting on the upper step, I waited in the dark near the hall door, my ear pressed to the flimsy panel.

I sat there, my hand on the revolver in my pocket, for perhaps half an hour. No unusual sound, no movements.

Suddenly the wind rushed away from my back. I started half around, jumping to my feet. The door had been thrust open without warning. A heavy pain shot into the top of my skull, I tottered down into an incredibly brilliant void of light, and felt myself bumping over the hard steps. The brilliance swiftly receded, and blackness swam over me.

A LONGITUDINAL seam of terrific pain shot across my pate, as if my head had been split open. My eyelids fluttered weakly, and dim light flickered in my brain. My body lay extended on a hard even surface, and my joints ached as if they had been wrenched suddenly out of their natural position. Somewheres to my right I could hear a regular thudding, repeated at short intervals, as of a pick-axe striking into hard earth.

I remembered waiting behind the hall door, the surprise attack from behind, and the vicious crack on the head that sent me toppling down the hard steps into oblivion. But where was I now?

A damp, earthy smell filled my nostrils. I opened my eyes cautiously. Above, heavy, cobwebbed rafters supported a rough wooden ceiling. Could I still be in the basement of the tenement?

I turned my head to the right, towards the sound. In a narrow, oblong pit, already several feet deep, a burly, sweating Negro, bared to the waist, was methodically chopping out the stony earth. At one end of the pit, which was assuming much the shape of a grave, stood Simone, his back toward me. A grave! For whom? Me? I shuddered. Simone then must have cracked me over the head, and thought he had killed me!

I inspected, with as little movement as possible, the object on which I lay. Three heavy planks, athwart a couple of sawhorses, formed a crude sort of table. My limbs were unbound, I noted thankfully.

Suddenly a voice—Peleg's voice—rasped on my left! My eyes snapped across the small, ill-lit room. The altar I had seen the night before—or had more time elapsed?—rested several feet away. It was a low, wooden affair, and on it stretched a body, wrapped in coarse sheeting, except for the head. But I could not discern the features distinctly, because of the dim light and because Peleg stood partly in the way.

"She's coming around!" the voice sounded exultantly.

She—could she be Julie? God, what monsters were these, giving and destroying life at will? Had Simone really succeeded in raising the dead?

Simone grunted, but did not stir from his post by the grave. Silence, marked off by the thud of the axe. . . .

"Ain' she deep enough fo' de body yit?" a puffing voice whined. No answer.

I knew I would have to act, and act quickly, if I intended to get out alive—and get *her* out. . . . *Alive,* I said mentally, and then wondered. Could Julie be *alive* now? Would, I asked myself, I want Julie alive now—would she want to be alive—alive like the gibbering Lazar?

A low moan came from the body on the altar. Now—now I must strike! I doubled my legs under me, whirled towards Simone, and leaped forward. The witch-doctor half-turned; the pick-axe suspended in the air. Surprise and fear shot across the Negroes' faces. My body shocked against Simone, and he tumbled into the pit, sprawling on the Negro workman. Both of them lay in a heap at the base of the hole.

The burly, half-naked Negro disentangled himself from the sorcerer and started up, cold, frenzied fear on his countenance. Simone lay inert. The falling pick-axe had cloven his skull. But the workman advanced upon me, despite his fear!

I whirled, seized one of the plankings of the rude bench upon which my supposed corpse had lain, and flung its further end at the Negro's head. He ducked, but his move was too late. His body thudded into the pit, and lay still.

"Reach for the ceiling!" Peleg's voice rasped behind me. I whirled and found myself staring into the muzzle of an automatic—my automatic, probably.

Peleg laughed, a short, horrid cackle. "That hole was made for you," he chortled, "and you're going to be put into it!"

THE doctor leaned back against the altar, watching with vicious pleasure for the effect this would have on me. The gun advanced in his hand, slowly, slowly. When his arm was fully extended, his already flexing finger would— An icy sweat broke over my body. Had I succeeded thus far to be mowed down by a bullet from my own gun?

The grin on Peleg's face became more cruel, more sardonic, more insane. In a few seconds that muzzle would bark once, twice, and I would fall backwards, writhing into the pit with the others.

The white form behind Peleg raised slowly. Wide eyes sprung to meet mine, snapped back to the doctor, and to the automatic. It *was* Julie! I lowered my gaze to the gun again, before its direction might discover her awakening to Peleg.

I heard the soft flurry of cloth whipping through the air; the gun spat: a leaden pellet spewed dirt at my feet. I sprang forward. Julie had flung herself upon the doctor's arm, breaking his aim.

The gun cracked again as Peleg jerked himself around, but I ducked it on the run, bursting through the remaining woodbench. We crashed together, and sprawled on the hard earth, the automatic flying through the air from the doctor's hand.

The struggle didn't last long. The doctor was old and not too strong, and despite my injuries, was soft game for my frenzied, hammering fists. He soon lay quiet, bloody-faced and mute.

I felt Julie's body press against me as I raised myself. I took her into my arms, and gazed into her eyes. They smiled back at me, though uncomprehending and frightened. There was no insanity there, as I had seen in Lazar's eyes.

* * *

We went over to the police hospital the next day, Burke, the D. A. and myself. The nurse had mopped most of the blood from Peleg's face, and he lay scowling at us from his cot.

Burke took the matter in hand in his characteristically rough manner. He drew a chair close to the bedside and glared at the doctor. "You gonna talk or no?"

Peleg flinched back. "What have you got on me?"

"Plenty! Simone told us practically everything. And every time you leave

something out, we're going to punch that nasty face of yours when we get you back to headquarters!"

Peleg didn't know Simone was dead.

"F'r instance," Burke said, "you might start with the white slave ring you been running!" That aspect of Peleg's activities had been turned up by the police just a few days previously.

Peleg's watery eyes roved over our faces, panic-stricken.

"Come on!" Burke growled.

PELEG talked. Simone's "dead people" had not really died. They had been induced to a coma approximating death by a drug Simone had brought to the United States from his native Haiti. In cases like Julie's, Peleg had administered the drug, first making himself acquainted with his victim and the victim's family. The victims were brought back to life by a powerful counteractant injected with a hypodermic, and restored to the family for a sizable fee, or, if the victim were a young and pretty girl, Peleg sold them into slavery on the Barbary coast. Lazar, who had been a maniac before his alleged "raising," had gotten to talking wildly, so Simone stopped his vague accusations with a razor.

* * *

Julie recovered quickly. I took her—with the ring on the correct finger—to a retreat in the pines of north Vermont the day after Peleg's trial. We kept the newspapers from her, in the little northern jungle now our paradise.

She is sane, perfectly. But every once in a while a vague, troubled expression comes into her eyes, as if to ask, "Where was I, those three days?" and I wonder just how much of a sorcerer Simone was. . . ?

The Cross of Blood

By
George Edson
(Author of "Food for the Devil")

FOR a fleeting instant Freeman saw in the old lady's eyes that same strange look of fear he had caught before in the eyes of each member of the Layton family. She stared at him while Christine—her granddaughter and his fiancée—proudly made the formal introduction.

"This is Robert Freeman, Granny. I couldn't wait until morning to bring him to you."

Novelette

of Endless Hate

*A curse was on the Layton blood, and a
dread fear in the Laytons' eyes. Was the curse
insanity—the fear of their own mad powers?
Was it a Layton who prowled the hallways, marking
his victims with the bloody cross? Bob Freeman, seeing
that look in the eyes of his own loved Christine, wondered
—and wondering, shuddered with fear. . . .*

"Robert Freeman." The old lady echoed his name in a hollow voice. "You want to marry my Christine . . . but it can't be . . . I see the cross—I see the terrible—"

"Mother!"

Freeman jerked his head around when Christine's father spoke. Henry Layton, a tall man with rounded shoulders and a prematurely aged face, had gone deathly pale. He shivered as if from a sudden chill.

"Yes—yes, Henry," his mother whispered. "I'm sorry." Then a little louder: "I—I'm glad to meet you at last, Mr. Freeman. Please—forget what I said."

Freeman returned his gaze to the massive four-poster, to the frail figure propped against a mound of pillows. She had veiled the look of fear in her eyes. Now she forced a feeble smile of welcome and lifted one shrunken hand a few inches from the coverlet. He bent, took it. It was as cold as the bloodless hand of a corpse.

"Of course, Mrs. Layton." He tried to make the works sound convincing. "And I'm awfully happy to meet you."

"Excuse me for not having been at dinner on the first night of your visit. But I—I haven't been able to leave my bed for nearly six months."

"You must say goodnight, Mother." Henry Layton moved across to the bed. "It's very late and you must sleep."

Gently Freeman lowered the icy hand to the coverelet, backed away a few steps to watch the solemn ceremony which Christine had described as a nightly occurrence. Each member of the family went in turn to the side of the bed and bid the old lady goodnight.

Julia Wilde, Christine's married sister, was the first. Then Christine. John Maillard, the son of Mrs. Layton's deceased daughter, followed her. And finally, after all the members of the family except Henry Layton, the little boy they called Conrad. Christine had told Freeman that the child was supposed to live with his grandfather in a shack up in the woods but preferred to spend most of his time with them.

At the end of the ceremony the younger people left the room. Christine walked with Freeman down the long hall to his door.

"Christine. . ." He gazed at her and saw deep in her eyes that same clutching dread. "What is it? Christine—darling, you're frightened. Two or three other times I've seen that. I've asked you why and you wouldn't tell me. Now—you must!" He caught both her hands in his. "Everyone in your family is afraid of

something. What? What did your grandmother mean when she said our marriage couldn't be?"

Christine lifted her white face and stared pitifully at him. "I don't know." Her tone held misery, anguish. "Bob —please . . . Goodnight, dear."

She rose to her toes, kissed him, pulled swiftly away from him. She spun and hurried back up the hall.

Lines of worry furrowed Freeman's lean face. He entered his room, switched on lights and closed the door. Some real or imagined horror hung over this Layton family—over the girl he loved. He had seen it in their eyes. He had felt it in the very atmosphere of this gloomy old mansion. What was it?

He climbed into bed. For a long while he tossed and twisted. Then at last troubled sleep claimed him. . .

He awoke with a start. He bounded out of bed and across to the door. From somewhere in the house came shrieks— shrieks of unutterable agony.

The hall was dimly lighted. Freeman peered up it, caught his breath, started to run. On the floor at the other end lay a body. Standing near it was the little boy, Conrad. And kneeling over it, sobbing now, was a figure in white.

The figure was that of Christine's grandmother—who had said that she hadn't been able to leave her bed for nearly six months!

Reaching the group, Freeman stopped and stared down at the prone body. It was Henry Layton. He was dead. He lay on his back, his face contorted into a terrible grimace of pain and his sightless eyes stamped with stark terror.

But it wasn't the face or the eyes which made Freeman's senses reel. It was the bared chest.

For on it was a crude cross, formed by blood welling from two long gashes in the flesh!

FRIGHTENED voices sounded; someone screamed. Freeman pulled his horror-stricken gaze away from the body; he wheeled, saw Christine and her sister coming up the hall.

"Oh!" Christine swayed. "Daddy!"

Julia breathed: "The cross . . ." and fainted.

Freeman caught her, lowered her gently to the floor. Straightening, he swung one arm around Christine and held her tight. He noticed that John Maillard had appeared. Then, with a little start of suspicion, he glimpsed the strange butler, Jaffray.

Jaffray was a squat hunchback with a massive head and weird yellow eyes that gleamed like the eyes of a cat. He had emerged from the darkness of a doorway giving onto stairs to the third floor of the house, was gliding on noiseless feet toward the group at the end of the hall. His face wore that same expression which Freeman had noticed at dinner and which had chilled him—an expression, bland and faintly mocking, that suggested knowledge of evil beyond the ken of normal man.

Abruptly Christine clutched Freeman's arm, choked between the terrible sobs of grief racking her body: "Bob — Granny. . ."

His mind jumped back to the startling mystery of the old lady's presence in the hall. In saying that she had not been able to leave her bed for nearly six months she had only corroborated what Christine had already told him. Old Mrs. Layton was dying. For three of those six months she had not even been able to raise herself to a sitting position in her bed without help. How had she managed to get out here?

Now she had lifted her son's head, cradled it in her arms and was rocking back and forth. She babbled incoherent words in a broken, frenzied voice.

"Bob," Christine whispered. "Help me carry her to her room."

"I'll do it, dear," he said. "You'd better look after your sister."

The old lady glared venomously at him when he tried to take her son's head from her arms. She struggled with surprising strength. Then, in the midst of her fury, she sighed and went limp.

He carried her to her room, laid her on the bed. The covers hung over one side as if flung off by a violent hand. He straightened them and pulled them over her.

When he turned from his task, he saw John Maillard bearing Julia's unconscious form toward a couch against the wall. And then Christine, her face drawn and pale, came through the doorway.

"I—I told Jaffray to telephone the doctor and Sheriff Carter," she said as Freeman reached her. Abruptly terror overwhelmed her obvious efforts to be calm. "Oh Bob! The thing—whatever it is—the horrible thing struck him! Just as it struck Grandfather and Great-Uncle John! The cross. . ."

"Steady, dear," Freeman said.

He held her hand tightly till she regained control of herself. Then she drew away from him and went to her grandmother. Freeman hurried down to his room then, and hastily dressed.

Returning, he saw that Conrad had crept nearer to the corpse of Henry Layton. He was staring down at it. But on his white face was no fear, no horror, not even grief—only morbid curiosity. . . .

THE unnaturalness of such a reaction to the death of a man who had shown the boy so much kindness made Freeman angry. He turned into the room he knew had been Layton's and pulled a sheet from the bed. For the sake of everyone it would be better to have the butchered figure covered. He twisted, strode out to the hall and spread the sheet over Layton's body.

"All right, Conrad." He put one hand on the child's shoulder. "Come down and sit by the table."

"Yes, Mr. Freeman," the child answered in his soft, girlish voice.

Freeman followed him down to the table and single chair opposite the top of the staircase. Something about this child gave him the creeps. Christine had said that the grandfather who lived in the shack up in the woods was a queer, brooding German. No one knew much about him; he rarely appeared in public and more rarely would talk to anyone. The Laytons had pitied the lonely child who had formed a habit of wandering down from the old man's shack to play on the banks of the stream near the Layton mansion. Through pity they had practically adopted him.

And he had adopted them—especially Christine. He was always anxious for her to play with him. When she couldn't, he curled up over a book in the big library and read. The precociousness of his reading had seemed to impress all the Laytons. At the age of ten he invariably chose works on the deepest subjects.

"Conrad." Freeman stood before the chair on which the boy had seated himself. "Did you see anything happen to Mr. Layton?"

"Yes," Conrad answered solemnly. He fixed his bulging eyes on Freeman. "I saw Mr. Layton killed."

Freeman started.

"I saw it," Conrad repeated. "I was reading in the room where I sleep when I stay here at the Laytons'. I heard a groan and peeked out into the hall. Mr. Layton lay there on the floor and someone dressed in a long white robe and white veil bent over him. Did something with a knife.

"I was afraid. I closed my door. But a few seconds afterward I heard shrieks and looked again. Mr. Layton was still there on the floor. And—and Grandmother Layton was bending over him

then. The veil. . . I—I could see her face."

"Bob." It was Christine's voice. "Bob, come quick. Granny wants you to hear, too."

As Freeman turned and started toward the girl standing in the doorway of her grandmother's room, horrible thoughts whirled in his brain. The person dressed in a white robe and veil . . . Mrs. Layton in her long white nightgown. Had Conrad recognized her that first time and tried to hide the fact? Had Mrs. Layton . . ? Good God, no! Not her own son! She would have had to be insane!

And then a chilling question blasted at him. The fear he had seen in the eyes of all the Laytons, the dread of a horror hanging over them. . . Was that horror—insanity?

Had old Mrs. Layton gone momentarily crazy and murdered her own son?

FEARFULLY Freeman looked into Christine's eyes as he drew close to her. If that had been what one dreaded, it was what they all dreaded. Even Christine—his sweet, beautiful Christine. But in her eyes now he could see only her misery.

Freeman followed Christine into the room. One glance showed him Julia, pale and trembling, in a chair near the bed; John Maillard stood behind her. Then Freeman looked at old Mrs. Layton.

She lay absolutely motionless. Death had crept upon her during these last few minutes and put his grey stamp on her wasted face. Life lingered only in her eyes that burned out of sunken sockets.

"Come close." Her voice was low, labored. "I must tell you before I go. You must know—now that it has struck again after all these years. You know how your grandfather died. And his brother—your Great-Uncle John. Just as your father died tonight—with Kurt Gilder's cross carved on each of their chests.

"You've all suspected something— feared it. But you didn't know what. I hoped you'd never have to know. I hoped the hellish curse had lost its potency. During this last month I realized it had not. In dreams I've seen the mark—the cross!"

She brought out the last two words in a louder tone. Then she paused a moment as if to muster her rapidly ebbing strength.

"Kurt Gilder was in business with your grandfather and great-uncle many years ago. And—and he wanted me. Over that the trouble started. One night Gilder tried to kill your grandfather. He didn't succeed. But as he was taken away by the police he cursed the Layton family. He swore that all those with Layton blood in their veins would die horribly until there was no more Layton blood in the world. And that on every victom would be his— Kurt Gilder's—mark.

"He had never learned to write. Your grandfather and great-uncle took care of that part of the business. He signed his name with a cross. A cross was his mark."

Again the old lady paused.

"Kurt Gilder was found to be insane," she went on finally. "He was sent to an asylum—escaped. The authorities learned that he died out West. But two years later your—your grandfather was killed by the curse. Your great-uncle on the very next day. And since then I've lived in terror.

"When your mother died a natural death, John, I began to hope. But recently I've had dreams and realized that there was no hope. Tonight I had another dream. I saw the cross hanging over my son. I awoke, pulled myself out of bed, ran to warn him. And I saw him. . ."

Her voice broke to a choked sob. Christine uttered a pitiful cry, dropped to her knees beside the bed. The old lady moved one bony hand, lifted it and touched her granddaughter's forehead.

"Now you understand, my little Christine. You understand why I didn't want Julia to marry—why you cannot marry. Not only are you doomed—but your children. All those with Layton blood in their veins are cursed. The Layton blood is— blood of death!"

CHAPTER TWO

The Cross Again

A STUNNED silence followed the old lady's last words. It was ended at last by Julia, who quavered out a stricken wail and covered her face with her hands. Freeman felt an added shock of horror as he remembered what Christine had told him shortly after he had arrived at the house. She had been so happy over Julia's happiness that she couldn't help telling him. The family were not to know until Jerome Wilde, Julia's husband, returned from a business trip.

That afternoon Julia had learned for a certainty that she was going to have a child.

Christine heard the wail, pushed to her feet, hurried around the bed. She knelt and clasped Julia in her arms. John Maillard, standing behind Julia's chair, stared stupidly down at the scene.

Freeman caught the sound of footsteps on the stairs. He twisted. The footsteps came rapidly down the hall and a thickset man carrying a small black bag strode through the doorway. He was obviously the doctor Christine had sent Jaffray to call. With only a brusque glance at the others in the room he crossed to the bed, bent over its occupant.

"Please." The doctor straightened, turned his head. "Will you all leave the room?"

Christine looked anxiously over Julia's

shoulder at him. "Is—is she—?"

"She's very weak. Please hurry. There must be absolute silence."

Freeman went over to help Christine with Julia. They took her down to her room. John Maillard followed. Freeman noticed, too, that Conrad slid off the chair in the hall and tagged after them. He clutched at Christine's hand as soon as Julia sank on her bed.

"Oh, Conrad! You—you poor child!" For an instant Christine gazed pityingly down at the boy's white face. Then she looked toward her cousin. "John, he must be taken home to his grandfather. He can't stay here—now."

John Maillard scowled, muttered sullenly: "Let him go alone. Or have Jaffray go with him. Why should I—"

"John. Please. You know he's afraid of Jaffray."

"Oh, all right." Maillard shrugged. "Come on there, kid."

"Do I have to go, Christine?" Conrad asked. "I—I don't want to go."

Freeman restrained a sudden impulse to grab the child and propel him out of the room. There was something he didn't like about the way Conrad's bulging eyes crawled over Christine's body. They seemed to be worming through the wrapper that covered it.

"Yes." Christine flinched, edged back a step. "Yes, you must."

Reluctantly Conrad turned away from her and walked across to the door where John Maillard waited.

"I—sometimes he makes me uneasy," Christine said after the door had closed behind them. She twisted toward the bed as Julia mumbled her name. "Yes, Julia. I'm right here."

"I'll be out in the hall if you want me, Christine," Freeman told her. "I'll leave the door—" He stopped at the sound of a motor outside the house.

"It must be Sheriff Carter," Christine said. Then in frantic despair: "What can he do? What can anyone do? The curse. . ." She caught herself. "Bob, will you see him and—and keep him away from Granny's room?"

"Yes, Christine." Freeman's face was lined with worry. "Dear, don't lose hope like that. You can't! There isn't any such thing as a curse. Someone hated your father, knew the belief about the curse and used it to divert suspicion. Someone. . . I don't know what this Sheriff Carter can do but I'm going to get that killer!"

For just a moment the terrible dread deep in her eyes seemed to go. But then, slowly, it returned. It had been there too long to be so easily conquered.

DREAD was in Robert Freeman's heart, too, as he went out of the room and down the hall toward the stairs. He had said that he was going to get the killer. But what if the killer had been Henry Layton's own mother? Then it would really have been insanity—homicidal insanity. God! The thoughts screaming through his head were horrible!

Homicidal insanity—a strange mania to kill, to kill even loved ones. This Kurt Gilder had been a homicidal maniac. Old Mrs. Layton had said that Gilder was dead. Was it possible, as some people claimed, for the spirits of the dead to control the living? Or was there a Devil who had transferred Gilder's disease to the blood of the Laytons? Was the curse going to work itself out that way?

Gruesome pictures flashed into his mind. Julia—a new life within her and a murdering knife in her hand. Christine—a bloody cross. . .

No! No! He drove his reason at the madness he was thinking. Old Mrs. Layton hadn't killed her son. She had waked from a nightmare and found him dead.

There wasn't any such thing as the power of a curse.

He had reached the top of the stairs when he saw the doctor come out of Mrs. Layton's room. With a slow nod the doctor pronounced the verdict. The old lady was dead.

"What's that?" The doctor pointed toward the white mound at the end of the hall. "It looks like—"

"It is," Freeman told him grimly. "Henry Layton."

The doorbell below jangled. Freeman turned away from the doctor, caught sight of Christine emerging from Julia's room and stopped.

"I heard you talking," she explained. She looked first at the doctor and then at Freeman. "Granny. . . ?"

"Yes, dear," Freeman said softly.

With a little sob Christine ran past him. The doorbell rang again. He twisted and started down the stairs. Where the devil was Jaffray?

Freeman frowned as he strode across to the door, opened it. A burly man with a red face and grey hair showing beneath the brim of an ancient felt hat surged into the hall. He didn't have to announce that he was the sheriff from the Village of Chatham; he looked every inch the bluff country official.

"I had a telephone call that Henry Layton'd been murdered," he said. "That right?"

Freeman nodded.

"Where's the body? Who did the killing?"

"The body's upstairs." Freeman drew in a slow breath. "God knows who did the killing."

"Umph." The sheriff slipped a flashlight he had been holding in one hand into a pocket. "Well, let's—"

He stopped short, jerked up his head. From upstairs came the sound of a frenzied voice.

"Julia! Julia!"

Freeman had wheeled at the first cry, rushed to the stairs and charged up them. The voice was Christine's. She was running down the corridor toward him when he reached it. He grabbed her arm.

"What is it?"

"Julia! I—I remembered I couldn't leave her alone and went back to her room. She—she's gone!"

"Gone!" Freeman pulled her after him as he hurried up the corridor. "How could she?"

But she had. Her room was empty. Freeman looked into the closet, then opened another door and peered into utter darkness.

"Yes!" Christine exclaimed. "She could have gone through that vacant room to the rear hall!"

Christine found lights and they followed the route Julia might have taken to a rear flight of stairs. They went down to the lower floor, kept calling her name. They went outside and shouted. But always there was no answer. . . .

MINUTES later the four remaining at the Layton mansion—Christine, the doctor, Sheriff Carter and Freeman—stood worriedly in the lower hall. They had searched the entire house and the lawns; yet they had been able to find no trace of Julia Wilde. During that minute she had been left alone she had vanished as if from the very earth.

"Where's that hunchbacked butler?" the sheriff asked. "He's the one who telephoned me."

Freeman, on the point of speaking, abruptly stiffened. From outside the house had come a quivering, high-pitched yell! He twisted, sprang to the door, yanked it open. A figure ran from the darkness into the light spraying out from the hall.

But it was not Julia. It was Conrad.

"Mr. Freeman!" The child's bulging

eyes rolled over the gathering as he glided through the doorway. "That—that person in white again! I hurried to tell you!"

"Where? Who was it—did you see?"

"I—I couldn't see. John and I were going—"

"Maillard!" A chill of foreboding crept over Freeman. "Where is he? What happened to him?"

"I don't know. I—I ran."

Christine had uttered a cry and rushed up beside Freeman. In a sideward glance he caught the look of dread in her eyes.

"Julia!" And there was terrible dread in her voice. "We—we must find her! Before something happens!"

The sheriff lumbered up behind them. "What's this?" he grunted.

"Give me your flashlight," Freeman said.

The sheriff handed over the flash. "Sure, but—"

"Doctor, will you come along with the boy and me? Christine, you stay here with the sheriff and—"

"No—no, Bob. I'm coming with you."

"Please, dear. . . Julia may wander back and someone should be here. Sheriff, please step outside a second before the rest of us go."

Bewildered, the sheriff complied.

"Sheriff," Freeman said, "anything might happen outside and I don't want to take Christine into any more danger. A killer is loose somewhere around here. Stay in the house with her. Guard her. Don't let her out of your sight for a second. Will you do that?"

"Why—why, sure."

"Ready, Doctor?"

The doctor had gone to his car parked just beyond the porte-cochere and returned with his flashlight. He nodded.

"All right, Conrad," Freeman told the child. "Lead the doctor and me to the place where you last saw this person in white."

It wasn't far. Out through the ancient trees which surrounded the dismal Layton mansion, down over the hill and along one bank of the brook.

"There," Conrad said. He pointed to a clump of brush ahead of them.

Freeman ran forward, probing the section with the beam from his flash. Suddenly he stopped. Once more horror clutched him, rocked him, made his very brain whirl.

Sprawled on his back at the edge of the brush was John Maillard. Death had frozen his face into a mask of mingled terror and agony. His clothes had been ripped from the upper part of his body. And on his chest had been carved a bloody cross!

THE doctor came up behind Freeman, stopped short. For a moment he stood there in silence. Then he choked: "Another cross! God! The—the killer must be a maniac!"

Maniac? Thoughts which brought with them ravening dread flashed through Freeman's mind. Again Conrad had said he had seen a person in white. . . Julia was out here somewhere and she had been wearing a white negligée. . . No! She couldn't have done this!

Once more he told himself that someone knew about the curse this Gilder had laid on the Layton family and had used it to divert suspicion. Someone who hated the Laytons as much as Gilder could have hated them, who had nursed that hate over all these years since he had murdered Christine's grandfather and great-uncle. But who?

Jaffray? Why had the butler disappeared? Yet why, if he were the killer, would he have waited so long after murdering his first victims before murdering these others?

Freeman twisted his head to glance at little Conrad. The child stood staring down at the butchered corpse of the young man who had so recently been his living companion—just as he had stared at the corpse of Henry Layton. Expressing no fear, horror, grief—but with a sort of ghoulish fascination.

There was something eerie about him, something unnatural and—yes, unclean. Freeman remembered the way those eyes had crawled over Christine's body. And suddenly he had a desire to see the grandfather of Conrad, who was so mysterious.

"Conrad," he said, "I'll go on with you in place of John. You know Christine wants you to go home."

Reluctantly the child pulled his gaze away from the corpse. He answered in a meek tone: "Yes, Mr. Freeman."

"Stabbed in the back first." The doctor had been examining John Maillard's wounds. "Twice. The skin on the chest is only cut deeply enough to let a limited amount of blood ooze out to form the cross."

"Doctor, let's leave the body here for the present," Freeman said. "I'm going to take this lad home to his grandfather. You can find the way up to the house?"

"Oh, yes. Easily."

"You go ahead, Conrad," Freeman said. "I'll follow and throw the light over you."

Conrad turned and started trudging along the bank of the brook. Presently he veered off to the left, led Freeman up a sharp rise and into the woods. For about half a mile they kept to what must once have been a logging road, then cut off that onto a vague trail through dense young evergreen growth. At last they came to a clearing and could see a flickering light.

The grandfather wasn't in bed yet, then. That surprised Freeman for he knew it must be after three o'clock. But it helped his plan; now he could have a look at the man without being seen.

"This is where my grandfather lives," the boy announced.

"Run inside, Conrad," Freeman said brusquely. "I've got to hurry back."

"Yes, Mr. Freeman. Goodnight."

Freeman said, "Goodnight," and walked back along the trail. Over his shoulder he could see the little figure go toward the cabin. For a second the figure was etched against light as the cabin door opened; then the door closed behind it.

FREEMAN snapped off his flash, swiveled, returned to the clearing. Following the edge of the woods, he circled to the rear of the cabin and crept around to the front. Stealthily he peered through the one window.

A first cursory glance showed the interior to be crudely furnished and filthy. He saw Conrad on the floor. Then he saw the grandfather, sitting by a littered table on which stood a kerosene lamp.

Freeman stiffened. The man looked more like some kind of a monstrous beast than a human being. His body was a massive, shapeless hulk. Matted grey hair hung down to his shoulders and a dirty grey beard hid the lower part of his face. His eyes were fixed on his grandson; they were dark, ugly, possessing in their depths a brooding madness.

Freeman could see that Conrad was talking. Presently the child lifted one small white hand and traced a cross in the air. His grandfather jumped out of his chair, cuffed Conrad with one huge paw. He pointed and Conrad scrambled toward the corner.

The grandfather turned back to the table, reached for the lamp. And then Freeman noticed the blotches on his tattered coat. Blotches which might be filth —but which looked like dried blood!

Darkness flooded the interior of the hut.

Freeman twisted, returned to the rear of the cabin and followed the edge of the woods to the trail.

He tried to sort all the confusing evidence as he hurried toward the Layton mansion. Still not to be stifled was the insidious fear that he might in the end discover something too horrible to bear.

Conrad had started the fear by his story of seeing the veiled person in white bent over Henry Layton with a knife.

Everything fitted so hellishly well. Old Mrs. Layton might also have murdered her husband and his brother; there appeared to be no evidence to the contrary. And Julia, another figure in white, had been missing when John Maillard was killed.

On the other hand, there was only Conrad's word for his stories. The child was precocious, capable of shrewd guile; maybe he had fabricated those damning tales to hide some other person. Whom would he be more likely to hide than his own grandfather? And there were the blotches on the grandfather's coat—though those blotches didn't constitute proof of guilt.

Then Jaffray. . .

Freeman sighed. He had reached the house. He stepped through the doorway into the hall. It was empty. He heard voices on the second floor, mounted the stairs. He spotted the voices as coming from Julia's room. He walked down the corridor to the door—and halted abruptly on the threshold.

Julia lay on her bed.

"Oh, Bob!" Christine saw him, hurried over to him. "She came back by herself just a few minutes ago. She'd been outside somewhere. She—she must have had sort of a—a fit. She can't remember anything."

CHAPTER THREE

Gleaming Eyes

THE remaining hours before dawn were for Freeman an eternity of mental torture. Nor did daylight bring relief. Nothing happened; no progress toward bringing a sure end to the horrors of the night before was made.

The doctor had finally left, saying that only rest could help Julia. At Freeman's insistence he had sent out a nurse. Freeman had commanded her not to leave her patient for a single moment.

He himself had clung to Christine and guarded her every minute until late afternoon. Then he had left her in the care of Sheriff Carter while he went to see Conrad's grandfather. At a closer view he could tell whether or not those blotches were blood. If they were. . .

But he found the cabin deserted. He searched it, discovered nothing. He waited until an approaching storm brought early darkness; by then he had begun to grow uneasy. Something might happen down there at the house while he was up here. He started back.

Rain began to fall before he had gone far along the trail. Thunder rumbled in the distance. Luckily he had brought his flash, for the woods were as black as in the middle of the night.

His thoughts jumped to Jaffray. The sheriff had sent a description of him throughout the entire northern part of the state but had received no report. An exhaustive search of the grounds had resulted in nothing. Jaffray had vanished without leaving a single trace.

All Christine knew about the butler was that he had worked for the Laytons as long as she could remember and that he couldn't have killed any of them. She insisted on the last. He was too loyal.

But why had he disappeared? What. . . ?

Then Freeman heard the padding sound behind him. He stiffened, whirled. He caught one glimpse of gleaming yellow eyes coming toward him through the darkness. He got the beam of his flash around just far enough to catch a glittering knife clutched in an outflung hand.

He dropped the flash, ducked, lashed out with both fists. One found nothing; the other grazed his assailant's body. The blade of the knife nicked his cheek as it drove past him. He jerked up his shoulder to take the shock of his assailant's forearm, then grabbed at the forearm with his left hand.

He grasped it as it was pulling up for another thrust. He twisted it, heard a grunt of pain, a little clatter as the knife dropped and struck a rock.

He landed one blow—another glancing one. Then, suddenly, he slipped. For just an instant—yet long enough for those animal eyes to see the opportunity and long enough for the creature to spring.

Freeman, not quite on balance again, went down when the hurtling body struck him. He felt powerful hands clutch his throat. He heaved, tried to roll. He grabbed at the throttling hands, tore at them. But he could not dislodge the creature or break his hold.

Agony burst in Freeman's head. He felt his eyes bulge, felt a thousand hammers start to pound behind them. His lungs ached. Hot fire flamed in his throat and mouth.

MADNESS seized him. He worked his heels up under him, dug them into the ground. With all his remaining strength he lifted his body. He threw himself over and at the same instant smashed both fists against those iron forearms.

The creature's hold broke. He toppled sidewise to the ground.

Freeman dragged air into his lungs, pushed himself toward the spot where the yellow-eyed creature had fallen. He found nothing but damp earth. Then he heard a dead branch crack, pulled to his feet, stumbled in the direction from which the sound had come.

Sobbing for breath, he stopped and listened. There was only the lashing of rain on leaves and the soughing of wind. His head whirled. He knew that his knees were buckling, yet could not stiffen them. He was falling. He tried to break the fall; his arms were rubber. His temple struck something hard.

One thought throbbed in his brain. Those gleaming eyes could have belonged to but one person—Jaffray.

He sighed, sank into oblivion. . . .

He came to slowly, painfully. His head hurt like hell. He lifted one hand and touched his temple, felt sticky blood. Only then did full memory of what had happened a little earlier return to him. Forgetting pain, he scrambled to his feet.

Jaffray! It was Jaffray! It wasn't what he had dreaded!

His first sensation was one of wild relief. But abruptly terror surged up to replace it—frenzied terror which sent him staggering toward the trail. He didn't know how long he had been unconscious. By now Jaffray might be down at the Layton mansion.

Pure luck let him find the trail in that thick darkness, find the flashlight he had dropped. It wasn't broken. The switch had merely clicked off when it had hit the ground. He saw the knife he had forced out of Jaffray's hand and stuck it in his belt.

It had stopped raining but the ground was slippery. Yet he ran most of the way down the trail and old logging road to the brook.

He reached the hill on which the Layton mansion stood; he climbed rapidly to the ancient trees, started through them.

Then he jolted to a stop. His eyes had caught something revealed by the beam from the flash. A grey thing— lying in mud stained red.

Horror gnawed at his stomach. The grey thing was the Layton's cat. The animal's neck had been slashed so viciously that the head had almost been severed from the body.

Freeman rolled the cat over on its back. On the animal's chest had been carved a cross!

Freeman shuddered. Good God! Even this poor pet that belonged to the Laytons! Jaffray's hatred must have driven him truly mad with lust for blood!

Abruptly frenzied terror returned to supplant horror. The cat's body was still warm. That meant this fiendish atrocity had happened not long ago. Even now Jaffray might be. . .

An icy claw clutched Freeman's heart. Through the night had quavered a faint cry!

FREEMAN twisted, fairly hurled himself in the direction from which that cry seemed to come. He slipped in slimy mud, fell, clawed himself up with a frantic groan. He heard the cry again and thought he recognized the voice as Christine's.

Merciful Father! What had happened? He had to find her—find her!

"Christine!" he shouted. "Christine!"

A muffled answer came from behind the house. He ran across the lawn and into more woods. Ceaselessly he kept the beam from his flash raking through the darkness.

Then he saw a form run into the light. It was Christine. He uttered a tearing sob that changed to glad relief.

She was unharmed! Fear filled her eyes, distorted her face. But she was unharmed!

"Oh, my dear!" He rushed to her and caught her in his arms. "I thought—thought—" A lump clogged his throat.

"Bob—you're hurt! Your head!"

"It's nothing," he said quickly. "What—"

Freeman stopped, stiffened as he heard

footsteps pound toward them. He started to swing her behind him. Then the burly form of Sheriff Carter lumbered into view. His red face showed quick relief at sight of Christine.

"Lord, I was worried," he panted. "I lost you when you ran out of the house. I've been hunting all over the place for you."

Christine clutched Freeman's wrist, stammered: "She—Julia's gone—again!"

"Gone! But the nurse—"

"She fell asleep," Christine said. Despair was in her voice. "She says that Julia was sleeping and she just dozed off for a minute. But when she woke up, Julia had disappeared. Oh, Bob! She—she must be having another fit! We've got to find her! Anything could happen to her out here!"

Gradually the insidious dread that Jaffray's attack on him had stifled crept back into Freeman's brain. Jaffray had tried to kill him. But that wasn't proof he had killed the others. Julia had slipped out of the house just a little while ago. The mutilated body of the cat had been still warm. . . .

"We will find her," he said grimly. "Come on."

He turned, went rigid. Into the shaft of light had glided little Conrad.

"Christine." The child's bulging eyes rolled over her. "Julia—she's spoiling my village in the sand. She's making the water wash it all away."

"Julia!" Christine tore from Freeman and went to the child. "You've seen her! Where? Take me there!"

Freeman moved swiftly after the distraught girl, swung his arm around her. He said: "Steady, dear." Then to Conrad: "Yes, lead us to her."

A chill of foreboding settled over him as they followed the boy through the woods and down toward the brook.

Reaching the brook, Conrad turned and led them along the bank for a short distance. Finally he stopped, pointed.

Freeman shot the beam from his flash over a narrow sand beach on which stood the remains of a tiny play village. His hand tightened on the flash when the beam showed what had diverted the water.

Lying on her back in the sluggish stream was Julia Wilde. One glance told Freeman that she was dead. Her throat had been cut. Her head was twisted. But her body, stripped to stark nakedness, was wedged between two rocks and only partially submerged.

Her chest. . . Freeman's senses reeled. . . . The white skin had been slashed from each shoulder down through her breasts, so that oozing blood had formed a crude cross! . . .

HE CAME out of his horrified stupor at last, jerked the beam of light away from that gruesome spectacle. But he was too late. Christine had already seen.

"Oh God!" Mounting hysteria was in her cry. "Julia! Julia!"

Freeman held her tight, tried to comfort her. But his own heart was a cold weight in his breast. There remained only one of the Layton family, only one possessing doomed blood—his Christine. She would be the next to die. . . .

"Holy Mother!" Sheriff Carter whispered over and over again.

"Bob!" Suddenly Christine clutched Freeman's arm, dug quivering fingers into it. "Take her out of the water. Maybe she—she's still alive!"

"No, Christine, she isn't alive," Freeman said gently. "But we'll carry her up to the house. Can you hold the light for us?"

Christine choked back a sob, extended one shaking hand for the flash. "Yes —yes, Bob," she answered. "I'll hold the light."

Admiration for her pluck swept over Freeman and a lump formed in his throat. He spoke to the sheriff, stepped down to the beach and waded out into the stream. He slid his hands under Julia's shoulders; the sheriff took her legs. They lifted the clammy body over to the sand.

It was then that Freeman noticed little Conrad. He stood where rays from the flash touched his white face, stood absolutely motionless and stared down at the naked corpse. Freeman could not help remembering the way the child had looked at Christine—as if he were seeing the feminine body beneath the wrapper she had been wearing. Now his bulging eyes roved over Julia's nakedness with greedy curiosity. He was like a foul little ghoul defiling the sanctity of a grave.

Revulsion welled up inside Freeman. He yanked off his coat and spread it over Julia's torso.

"Oh!" Christine's voice was shrill with horror. "Bob! That knife!"

Automatically Freeman glanced down at his belt, saw the knife with which Jaffray had tried to kill him. He had forgotten it until now. There was a dark stain on the blade from the blood it had drawn from his cheek at the beginning of the fight.

His throat went dry. Christine—she couldn't think that he. . . And then he saw the sheriff move toward him, saw the ugly accusation in his eyes.

"No!" He shouted the denial. "Jaffray tried to get me a little while ago. This is his knife." Ignoring the sheriff, he went up the bank toward Christine. "You believe me! You must!"

"Oh, I do," Christine told him quickly, shakily. "I do believe you. Bob— my dear! I—I was just startled when I saw it."

"Christine!" The name was hardly

more than a sob of relief. "Thank God! I thought—"

He stopped short at the sound of rustling brush. He grabbed the flash from Christine's hand, whirled, probed the darkness with the shaft of light.

Into that light lumbered a massive figure. Conrad's grandfather.

Silently he came toward them. He raked his brooding eyes over each of them, held his gaze on Christine for a moment and then lowered it to Conrad. He muttered something which Freeman recognized as German but could not understand.

Conrad shook his head. His grandfather muttered again and raised one huge fist. Conrad twisted, ran off into the darkness.

"I send him home." His grandfather looked at Christine once more. "He should not bother you now. *Ach, Fraülein* Christine, I am so sorry these terrible things happen."

And then, before she could have answered, he followed Conrad.

CHAPTER FOUR

Cavern of Death

FREEMAN and the sheriff carried Julia's body into the Layton mansion. They took it to the gloomy library, laid it on a couch. Christine knelt beside it.

Clicking footsteps sounded on the stairs. It was the nurse. She saw the corpse on the couch, uttered a terrified shriek. She sank into a chair and covered her face with her hands.

The sheriff nudged Freeman, motioned with his head. Freeman followed him out into the hall.

"What's this about Jaffray trying to get you?" There was still a faint glimmer of suspicion in the sheriff's eyes. "Where'd it happen?"

"Up in the woods," Freeman told him bitterly. "He got away from me. He jumped me with this knife." And then a frenzied tone leaped into Freeman's voice. "He's the damned murdering maniac! By God, he isn't going to murder Christine!"

For a moment the sheriff looked intently at Freeman; he seemed finally to become convinced that his story was the truth. He said: "Well, there's no sense in both of us sitting here and waiting for him to come to us. Now we know the killer. It's my job to get him; so I'm going out after him. You'll stay with the girl?"

Freeman's face tightened into a grim mask. He answered: "I'm not going to let her out of my sight until I can get my hands on that fiend."

"Okay. First I'm going to call the village and get some men started out here. If I don't catch him before they come, we'll search very inch of these woods."

The sheriff went up the hall to the telephone and put through his call to the village. That finished, he stalked purposefully out the front door.

Freeman crossed the library to the couch on which was Julia's body. Christine had sagged into a quivering heap, was choking out terrible dry sobs. Freeman lifted her to her feet and helped her to a chair.

"Oh, Bob . . . Bob. . ."

"Don't dear, don't," she begged.

She jerked up her head, said wildly: "Bob, you've got to go away from here! Oh, you must! The Layton curse . . . it may strike you!"

"Christine." He bent and put his arm around her shoulders. "There isn't any curse. Don't believe that there is. That's a myth—a foolish myth. Jaffray did these fiendish things. I know because he tried to kill me up there in the woods. For some reason he hated the Layton family and wanted to wipe it out of existence. His hatred has driven him mad. But we're going to get him. He's committed his last insane killing."

Christine shook her head, whispered: "No—no, it isn't Jaffray. It's the curse." Awe made her whisper hoarse. "It's Kurt Gilder's curse. I know it—I can feel it. I've always known there was something fearful hanging over this family. I—I almost forgot it in loving you. I was so happy. But now . . . all that is done. We can never—"

A shrill scream from the nurse cut off her last words. Freeman straightened, whirled. And for just a split second he saw the gleaming yellow eyes at the window.

Jaffray!

FREEMAN reached the window in one bound, unlocked it, opened it. He saw a shadowy form running through the darkness toward the woods. Twisting, he wormed his body over the sill and dropped to the ground. He started in desperate pursuit.

The man had almost made the cover of the woods by the time Freeman was halfway across the lawn. Calling up all his strength, Freeman increased his speed and began to gain.

Then, abruptly, he jerked to a stop. Terror stabbed to the very depths of his soul as he spun and rushed back toward the house. For from the house had come a chilling shriek—a shriek of mingled horror and fear!

It seemed to take him interminable hours to reach the open window. He shot a wild glance around the room as he pulled himself inside. Except for the corpse of Julia Wilde, it was empty!

Empty? Oh God! No, it wasn't!

Freeman's eyes saw the thing on the floor beyond the couch as he straightened. Another corpse—the corpse of the nurse. Her throat had been slashed. And —Freeman groaned—on her breast was another mark. Showing sharply against the white of her uniform was the cross of blood! . . .

In that moment madness swirled in Freeman's brain. Christine . . . could she have. . . ? Damning thoughts blasted at him: He had found Christine out there in the woods, separated from the sheriff, after the killing of Julia. And now she had been alone with the nurse while Jaffray, whom he had thought the killer, was outside. . . .

Sobbing, he lurched across the room and out into the hall. Where had Christine gone? What would she do?

To fulfill the hellish curse there was only one thing she could do. . . .

"Christine! Christine!"

His hoarse shouts reverberated through the dismal mansion, faded. And only silence answered.

He stumbled wildly down the hall, started up the stairs. Maybe she had gone to her room. He reached the corridor, rushed to her door and flung it open. The room was empty.

Oh God! Where was she? She couldn't have done the thing more than two or three minutes ago. Where would she have gone? Out into the night as Julia had when the fits of insanity had seized her?

He twisted, reeled back into the corridor. Then, abruptly, he halted and listened. Had he heard footsteps? Yes— somewhere on the first floor.

Hope stabbed through the despair in his heart. She hadn't killed herself yet. He could prevent her.

Swiftly and silently he crept to the stairs, down them. It might be wiser not to let her hear him until he could get the knife away from her. He paused at the bottom of the stairs and listened again.

The footsteps were approaching from

the rear of the house. She would reach the hall in a moment. He stole across to the dark doorway of a front room, waited. . . .

HIS breath came in jerky little gasps. Blood pounded in his head. His eyes throbbed as they strained to see her moving through the shadows at the other end of the hall.

And then he did see. . . . It wasn't Christine! It was Conrad's grandfather!

Freeman uttered a hollow moan, threw himself out into the hall and toward the massive figure. "Christine—" he demanded frenzily. "Have you seen her?"

"*Die Fraülein* Christine?" The man's brooding eyes fixed on Freeman. "She —she is gone, then?"

"Then?" Freeman said wildly. He grabbed one huge arm and twisted it. "What do you mean? You expected her to be gone? Why? Where is she?"

"I—I take you."

The giant tried to pull away from Freeman. For an instant Freeman failed to comprehend the meaning of the words; he gripped the huge arm tighter with one hand and clenched the other into a fist.

"Wait. I tell you I take you. *Ach*, the little Christine, she has cared for me when I was sick. She has saved my life when no other has come near. She is a good angel. She must not die."

Then Freeman loosened his hold on the arm, lowered his fist. He said harshly: "Take me! God! Hurry!"

Conrad's grandfather turned and lumbered back up the hall. He led Freeman through a succession of dark rooms to a rear door, out and across a narrow lawn to the woods.

Mingled emotions swept over Freeman. Suspicion of this madman's intent, his word—for how did he know where to find Christine? And doubt—*did* he know? But overwhelming these lesser emotions was his terrible fear for the girl he loved. He had to grasp at any faint hope of reaching her. Would he reach her in time?

The massive figure ahead of him heaved to a stop, peered searchingly around them.

"What's the matter?" Freeman demanded. "Hurry! We haven't got a second to lose!"

"*Ach, ja,* now I know the way," the old man muttered. "It is not far."

They went on again, ploughed through a patch of brush and pounded down over a steep hill. The giant slowed and signaled for silence. He dropped into a crouch, crept toward what looked like a wall of solid rock.

But it wasn't solid rock. Suddenly Freeman saw the cracks of flickering light. In his eagerness to reach Christine he forgot the giant who had led him here. He sprang past him.

He saw now that the light filtered through a crude little door of logs. He peered through one of the cracks.

A wave of sickening horror swept over him. The blood in his veins turned to ice. A soundless cry tore to his lips.

Beyond the door a low tunnel opened into a small cavern lighted by a candle. And on the ground in this cavern, half her clothes ripped from her body, lay Christine.

Bending over her with a blood-stained knife gripped in one white hand was little Conrad!

FREEMAN'S hand went to the door— then stopped. He couldn't do that! Conrad would plunge the knife into her breast. And the little fiend did not intend to kill her yet; he was absorbed in pawing at her.

She was still alive. Unconscious—but alive. Freeman could see her bared breasts move with her slow breathing.

God! What could he do to stop that inevitable thrust of the knife? The tunnel was so low he would have to crawl along it to get into the cavern. That would give time for a dozen thrusts.

Now Conrad was ripping off more of her clothes. Gibbering crazily, he ran curious fingers over her soft flesh. . . He straightened and lifted the knife.

And then Freeman did seize the handle of the door. He yanked it open, clawed his way into the tunnel.

Conrad uttered a snarling cry. He twisted and saw Freeman. He hesitated for but a second, then yelled shrilly, a yell of rage, and leaped toward him.

Freeman squirmed over on one side and flung out a hand. If he could catch Conrad's arm or take the slash in the shoulder. . . .

But fate jumped ahead of him and struck. Conrad stumbled, fell — and gurgled out a horrible groan of pain.

Freeman stared as the boy struggled to his knees. His arm had twisted under him when he had hit the ground. The blade of the knife had dug across his chest.

Conrad fixed his bulging eyes on the bloody gash. He mumbled something, mechanically raised the knife and drew it over his chest to make a cross. His arm dropped. The knife slipped from his hand. For an instant he swayed back and forth on his knees. Then he crumpled into a motionless heap.

Freeman saw that he was dead. He did not hesitate longer, then, but hurried to the spot where Christine lay. She was conscious now. He held out his arms to her.

"Oh, Bob. . ." Sobbing, she clutched at him.

He held her tight. Wild relief surged over him. She was safe—and sane! The ghastly things he had imagined were not true! He uttered a silent prayer of thanks.

It was not until he turned to lead Christine out of the cavern that he remembered Conrad's grandfather. The giant had wormed his way in to where the little figure lay. Now he gathered it in his arms and backed out again. He was standing near the entrance when Freeman reached it.

Freeman watched him warily, expecting an attack. None came.

"*Ach,* little Conrad," the guttural voice was saying. "Did I not tell you enough was enough? Did I not tell you to spare the good Christine?"

The giant, still holding the little figure cradled in his arms, lifted his head and gazed at them. There was only grief in his eyes.

"The curse is finished," he said. "I tell you now—I am Paul Gilder. Yes, the son of Kurt Gilder. And Conrad is my son. Not my grandson, as you have thought. He is twenty-six years old. When he was ten, a thing grew on his brain. A thing you call a tumor. The doctors, they operated and by mistake destroyed the gland which develops the body. He has not grown or changed in body since that time. Except—yes, he is very strong. And his brain has become very great."

Freeman felt Christine shiver. He pulled her closer to him.

"I—*Fraülein* Christine, I am sorry for these things." The giant shook his shaggy head. "I did not want them like—like my son. My father, Kurt Gilder, did not die as you have thought. No, he had the revenge on your grandfather and his brother. Then he fled to Germany. He brought me up to finish the curse he had made, though I did not want to. In the end it was my son who did it. He was strange to me—this son. He lived only to do his grandfather's bidding. Lived —and now he is dead."

The giant looked down at Conrad, mumbled something in German. At last he straightened.

"*Fraülein* Christine, you saved my life and I wanted to save yours," he said. "The curse is done. My little Conrad is dead —and I. . . ."

He did not finish. A strange gleam crept into his eyes. He wheeled and rushed off into the night.

FOR a long moment after he had gone, the two stood there, silent. Another storm was coming; lightning flashed and heavy thunder rumbled. Abruptly it began to rain.

"Christine. . ." Freeman dropped his head, buried his face in her hair. "My darling! My darling!"

"It's all over," she whispered as if she could not yet believe it. "The curse—it's broken. Oh, Bob!"

Presently he sighed, said: "We must go back to the house."

They did not talk on the way. They did not need to talk; each knew what was in the other's heart.

Thoughts skipped through Freeman's mind. Conrad had, indeed, lived for the fulfillment of his grandfather's curse. Craftily he had posed as the child he appeared to be, in order to gain entrance into the family he planned to destroy.

He must have acquired a mad fixation on carving those crosses in flesh. He had carved one on the pet cat, one on the nurse who wasn't a Layton—and finally one on himself.

They reached the house as the full fury of this second storm broke. They went inside, found Sheriff Carter and Jaffray in the hall.

"I picked him up easy enough," the sheriff told them with a touch of pride. He laughed. "He's still trying to make me believe he didn't do it. Says he took to the woods because he thought he'd be suspected and tossed into jail. He wanted to be free to get you, Freeman. Says he thought you were the killer."

Freeman gazed at Jaffray. Suddenly the butler's face didn't seem so evil as it had. And deep in the weird yellow eyes glowed a light of savage loyalty.

"So that's why you jumped on me, Jaffray? You thought I was the killer and I thought you were the killer. I'm sorry." Freeman shifted his gaze to the surprised countenance of the sheriff. "He didn't do it, Sheriff."

"What the—"

Freeman told him what had happened. Then, while astonishment still held the sheriff speechless, he followed Christine into the front room. She was weeping, but she smiled wanly through her tears.

"Darling." Gently he took her in his arms. "You've had too much horror and grief to bear. But now it's finished. There'll never be any more."

"Never any more," she said.

He kissed her.

* * *

The storm that night was the worst in many years. The next day the dead bodies of a huge man and a little child were found. Two trees had fallen, crushed them. The two trees had fallen in such a way that over the bodies they had formed a great cross.

THE END

Moon Mania

By
Robert C. Blackmon

Two bodies lay there on the path-
way, lighted by the blood-red moon,
and none of those left living knew
when Death would strike again. . . .
Had a deed of the long ago tainted
the noble Castletons, making them
half man, half beast . . . ?

U NDER the motorcycle headlights,
the concrete highway stretched
like a smooth pathway of white,
crushed bone between the black hull of
the trees on either side. And above the
jagged tops of the trees on the right
showed the red rim of a slowly rising
moon—a huge bloody eye peering over
the trees.

"Blood moon!"

Nat Hough's wind-dried lips formed the words; then his broad shoulders lifted in a shrug. He was nervous, he muttered low to himself, nervous from an uneventful patrol. He hadn't seen a car for the past three hours, not a soul since eight-thirty P.M., and the quietness was getting him jumpy. Well, he'd be off duty at midnight.

He throttled the motor to a purring mutter, coasting along the highway between the black trees, his lithe body hunched comfortably in the saddle, his big, freckled fists loosely gripping the handlebars. The cool, night wind burbled noises that were almost words in his ears, tugged insistently at the goggles screening his keen, grey eyes, and pulled the State Police uniform snugly about his deep-chested figure.

Another mile slipped past, and he heard a long-drawn mournful howl coming from the trees to his right—a dog howling.

Nat's strong fingers tightened on the handlebars, a cold prickle racing along his spine, and he pushed erect, listening. The howl came again, throaty, chilling. He shuddered. It sounded like a dog baying at the blood-red moon—yet, somehow, it carried a wilder note, almost like—

For a moment, he thought of wolves, then grinned tightly, twisted the handlebar throttle until the motor speeded to a throbbing roar.

Fat chance of wolves, especially along that side of the road. The Castleton Estate ran for over a mile on that side. The howl was probably one of the Castleton hunting dogs yelping at the blood moon.

Abruptly, Nat spun the throttle closed, jammed his feet on brake and clutch, his dry lips hard, grim. Impaled in the livid beam of his headlights was the ghostly figure of a woman, clad in white. She had darted out of the trees on the right side of the road and was running toward him.

Nat rolled closer, dropped one foot to the ground to balance the machine as it lost headway; then every muscle in his body went taut. His mouth felt dry and salty.

THE woman was Ethel Castleton, only daughter of the paralytic widower who owned the big estate. Her white dress was smeared with a ghastly spotch of blood directly below her slim, white throat. The crimson stain pulled Nat's eyes like a magnet, made cold chills race through his body.

She ran toward him, little whimpering noises bursting from her lips, and Nat almost cried aloud in horror as she came closer.

Red smears of blood marred the girl's white skin about her mouth, stained her slim fingers as though she'd been dabbling in the scarlet fluid. Her lips were parted, baring little, white teeth, and her dark eyes stared wildly from a small, oval face from which horror had drained every vestige of color. She reached Nat, caught at his arm with blood-tipped fingers.

"He's dead! His throat—Oh God! I —" Her voice broke. Hysteria threatened to overcome her.

Nat gently disengaged her hands, deliberately got off his motorcycle, kicked down the stand. For a moment he'd thought she was injured, but in the headlight's revealing beam, he'd seen that she wasn't. The blood had come from someone else. He stepped to the girl's side, caught her quivering shoulder in hard fingers.

"Steady, Miss Castleton," he rapped. "What's wrong?"

"My—my brother Ronald! He's dead. His throat—oh!" Her hands fluttered to her face, further smearing her cheeks with thickening blood.

Nat looked toward the place from which she had come, saw a narrow gravel walk entering the woods. The moon had lifted higher, was bathing the landscape with a faint, blood-colored light. He gulped, grasped the girl's arm and led her toward the walk.

"Ronald and I went on the porch," the girl choked as they walked toward the house located some distance back in the trees. "He'd heard one of the dogs whining. He told me to go back in the house, but I watched him go down the walk. Suddenly, he stopped. I heard a strange whirring noise. Ronald jerked backward, grasped his throat and fell. I ran to him, saw that he was bleeding from the throat. Then I heard your motorcycle on the road and ran out. He—he's there!" She pointed a slim, bloody finger.

NAT stopped, every nerve quivering. The mournful howl came again, and in the red light of the rising moon, he couldn't place it, couldn't tell from which direction it was coming. It seemed to fill the air for a moment; then it was gone. The Castleton house, a three-storied, balconied affair, loomed as a shadowy bulk about a hundred feet ahead; fifty feet from the porch, sprawled in the center of the gravel walk, was a body.

Nat released the girl, stalked forward, legs stiff, body taut. He fumbled for his flashlight as he walked, pressed the switch, directing the beam downward. The light spread in a livid circle about the thing on the walk, bringing every macaber detail into sharp relief.

It was the body of a young man huddled upon the gravel, lying partly on its side, head thrown back, face upward to the reddened sky. The hands were raised as though they'd clawed at the throat. A surging wave of nausea swept over Nat

as he stared at the ghastly slash beneath the clean-shaven chin. The throat had been torn open as with sharp fangs, and gushing blood had stained the man's fingers, soaked his white shirt-front. The gravel beneath the body was washed with the crimson fluid which formed a dark blot about the corpse. The face, which must have been rather handsome in life, was drawn, contorted, and the dark eyes were glassy with a ghastly horror and terrible surprise.

Nat sank to his knees to feel for signs of life, a purely mechanical gesture. He knew that Ronald Castleton was dead, but he had to think. He swept the light over the gravel walk, but could tell nothing about footprints in the crushed stone of the pathway. He got to his feet, a deep frown biting into his forehead, queer thoughts seething in his mind.

That wolf-like cry in the darkness. . . . The girl with her mouth and hands stained with blood. . . . What—?

"You—you saw it happen?" His throat felt queerly dry, tight, and his voice sounded strained to his ears. "There was no one near him but you?"

The girl's head moved. "No one. One of the dogs had run to him. But when he staggered and fell, the dog ran back to the kennels, howling. I—" She started sobbing. Nat caught her arm and led her toward the house.

As they reached the steps, the heavy front-door opened and a young man clad in a blue dressing-gown came out, his stocky body silhouetted against the light from the living room.

"What's the matter, Ethel? Who's that with you?" His deep voice was sharp with alarm. He stalked toward them.

"My cousin, Everett Davis," the girl choked. "He—he lives here with us. It's terrible, Everett!" She stumbled across the porch toward Davis, would have fallen had he not put an arm about her shoulder, held her close.

"Miss Castleton found her brother Ronald on the walk, dead," Nat explained crisply. "If you'll show me the telephone—"

"Dead? Ronald? Good Heavens, man! Why—"

"What's happened out there? Ethel, who's that with you?" A deep, harsh voice came from the open front-door. A strange rumbling sounded, and a frail, old man in a wheel-chair was framed in the open doorway. It was Castleton, the paralytic. He reached to the wall, clicked on the porch light and rolled the chair through the doorway. His bright, deep-sunk eyes widened at the sight of Nat's uniform, spotted the blood on his daughter's dress and hands. The girl ran to him, knelt beside the wheelchair. Castleton swung a wrinkled half-bald head toward the officer. "What is the matter?" he demanded hoarsely, and Nat had the queer feeling that Castleton already knew!

Rapidly, he explained what Ethel had told him, and what rôle he had played. "Your daughter," he finished quietly, "must have stained her hands and clothing trying to help her brother. Now, if you'll show me the telephone, I'll report this to—"

"Haven't a 'phone," Castleton broke in harshly, a fierce intensity causing his voice to quiver. His thin hands gripped the chair arms until the bony knuckles showed white, and his skin seemed almost transparent in its paleness. "Ethel," he rasped, "go upstairs and wash that blood off yourself. Everett, get Martin and Oscar out of bed and tell them their brother Ronald's been—been killed. You," he stabbed a bony finger at Nat, "come in here." Then before Nat could protest, Castleton wheeled the chair about and rolled back into the living-room. The girl entered the house next and Everett and Nat followed. Everett and the girl went upstairs.

"Now, if you'll show—" Nat started as soon as he and Castleton were alone.

"Sit down!" Castleton indicated a chair. Nat eased into it. Without a word, Castleton wheeled his chair to the wall, pushed aside a picture, opened a wall-safe and took out a tattered, canvas-bound book. He rolled back to the officer, the book lying upon his bony legs. "Ronald's throat was—was torn, wasn't it?" he queried hoarsely.

THE blood drained from Nat's heart, leaving it cold; it pounded in his temples. Icy fingers plucked at his vitals. The howling dog, the girl's face, dress and hands bloody, the mutilated corpse. He managed to nod.

"I knew it. Been expecting it. I'm the cause of it." Castleton's frail body slumped, pale lips quivering. The deep-set eyes burned with a strange light. He opened the canvas-bound book. "This," he said, drawing bony fingers across the yellowed pages, "tells why—why I've been expecting it for years." He swallowed noisily, went on slowly, brokenly. "It's the log-book of a ship, a ship that foundered in the mid-Pacific years ago. I was on that ship. Before she went under, four of us cast off in one of the small boats. She took the rest of the crew down with her. We four drifted—weeks — months — God! — years! I've lived it over and over again ever since. The other three died. I lived." Castleton's eyes were sunken pools of torture, horror. "Thirst — hunger — exposure." The pale skin seemed to cleave to his skull, outlining every bone. His eyes seemed to sink deeper into shadowed sockets. "The others—died—and I ate them—drank their blood to stay alive!"

Nat's breath stuck in his nostrils. Outside, a dog howled. The officer felt cold sweat crawl down over his stiff cheeks, streak his set jaws. His eyes were balls of ice in his head. Blood pounded in his ears. The living-room seemed filled with the scent of death, a chill reek that struck to the marrow, left him weak, trembling. Rigid muscles ached from their sudden tautness.

"I—I had to. You would have done it too. Anybody would have done it. I had to live." Castleton was still talking, his voice harsh, expressionless. "But—God! I've—fought it. I've—" He stopped, plunged on, mad despair in his words. "I—I've wanted to taste blood ever since! Whenever the blood moon came, I felt that I had to have hot, rich blood! But I fought it. I married, without telling any-one. I've never told anyone. My children, Ethel, Martin, Oscar and Ronald have the taint in their blood. They—they're were-wolves! Ethel was all bloody! God, she—"

Nat pushed to his feet, fighting a grow-ing horror that threatened to blast his reason—a horror that flowed like liquid ice in his veins. The wolf-like howl. It could have been— The girl *was* bloody . . . blood-stained fingers . . . scarlet-flecked mouth. Ronald's throat had been torn by fangs, sharp teeth. . . . And the girl's—the Blood Moon . . .

His teeth ground together; hard bunches of muscle bulged at the angle of his jaws. His hands clenched until the nails bit into the sweat-beaded palms.

"Nonsense!" The shrill, strange voice made him jump, and then he realized it was his own. "That's impossible!"

He forced his taut muscles to relax, resolutely pushed the mad thoughts from his brain. There was some other expla-nation. Ethel Castleton couldn't have—

Footsteps clattered on the stairs. Everett Davis, Ethel Castleton and her two brothers came down into the living room. Everett Davis seemed to be the calmer of the four, though his broad face was pale, his wide-set eyes bright, and the movements of his stocky body reflected his nervousness.

The girl was dazed with terror; yet the unnatural whiteness of her soft face, the strange brightness of her large, dark eyes, couldn't detract from her wistful beauty. Her slim figure moved almost me-chanically, and Nat knew that she hadn't yet recovered from the shock of seeing her brother's mutilated body.

Oscar and Martin Castleton were twins, apparently, being built almost alike. Their thin faces bore a striking likeness to their father. Both of the boys were about twenty years old, Nat figured, younger than the dead Ronald. Their staring eyes were filled with wonder as they stood side by side near the foot of the stairway. Both of them clasped thin, nervous fingers in front of slimly built bodies. Nat catalogued them as slightly eccentric, studious and reserved.

Rapidly, crisply, he explained the cir-cumstances which had brought him there. "And now," he finished, "I want Mr. Da-vis to get a car and report this to the local authorities. I want one of the brothers to go out to Ronald's body and stay there until the police get here. The other'll go with me, show me around. Miss Castle-ton, I want you to stay here with your father. I'm going out to the kennels. You mentioned something about one of the dogs being near Ronald when he fell. I hope," he added, his lips drawn into a straight, grim line, "that we'll be able to settle this thing in a very few minutes."

NAT HOUGH walked toward the kennels some distance from the side of the house, Oscar Castleton walking quietly at his side. A moment, and Nat heard a car start, heard it roar along the drive at the back of the Castleton house. Everett Davis was on his way to get the local police.

The moon had risen higher, and its blood-red light was faded to a yellow glow that bathed the Castleton grounds with a sickly, but strengthening light. Nat could see Martin Castleton standing beside his brother's body on the gravel walk in front of the house, see the lighted windows of the living room; and strangely those lighted panes made him think of the horror crawling in Castleton's deep-set eyes.

A horrible picture of the old man gnawing at the shriveled corpses of his ship-mates flashed through his mind, and he shuddered with revulsion, forced himself to think of the weird facts connected with Ronald Castleton's death.

If, as the old man feared, his daughter had suddenly been overcome with the mad lust for blood and had killed her brother, she would hardly have run out to the road, knowing that the motorcycle meant a state-police officer.

If it had been any of the others, either the boy walking beside him or his twin brother, the girl would have seen them. She'd said that Ronald was alone, that there had been not one living thing near him except the dog.

Nat's lips tightened. That was his purpose of visiting the kennels—to see if any of the animals had blood about their muzzles.

Everett Davis. The cousin couldn't have had anything to do with it, according to the girl's story. She was the only person near Ronald, unless she was lying to screen someone. Abruptly, the thought of her going to Davis, the cousin holding her closely in his arms, flashed through Nat's mind. Almost as quickly, he rejected the idea. That was a natural action under the circumstances, yet—

Old Castleton? A chill swept over Nat's body. The old man had confessed to eating human flesh, had admitted that he'd had to fight a ghastly craving for human blood, even feared that the ghoulish taint had been transmitted to each one of his children. Could old Castleton have—?

"How—how was Ronald ki-killed, officer?" Dully, Nat was aware that Oscar Castleton had asked the question twice. The boy was staring up at him with horror-bright eyes. Nat shook his head slowly.

"I don't know—yet," he admitted. "He wasn't killed by—well, any immediately obvious methods. Your sister said she saw absolutely nothing." Nat paused. "There've been no violent quarrels in the family? That is, between Ronald and any of the others?"

"No." Oscar's voice was grave, scholarly. "We Castletons are notably congenial." He smiled thinly. "There has been no discord here for years."

"How about Everett Davis?" rapped Nat. "He gets along all right with everybody here?"

"Splendidly. All of us like Everett. He's our fourth cousin. A really expert fisherman and equally as good hunter. He was Ronald's favorite, for my brother was extremely fond of hunting and fishing. Martin and I—" His thin shoulders lifted expressively, "are so constituted that we are not particularly adapted to sports." He hesitated. "You're inclined to believe the whirring noise Ethel heard was purely imagination?"

"I don't know." Nat walked on toward the kennels, his mind seething with thoughts. Oscar quickened his pace, went ahead as they neared the place.

"Why—why—" The boy's startled exclamation made Nat stride forward, hard-heeled. Oscar Castleton was standing beside the open gate of a wired enclosure at the back of which were low houses. "The kennel gate was open!" He looked up at the husky motor-cop, and his eyes were strangely white in the strengthening moonlight.

NAT pushed in past the boy. "All of the dogs inside?" he rasped, whipping his flashlight about. Gleaming eyes burned in the semi-darkness as his light touched them. A dog barked sleepily, snarled, then five husky animals sniffed and whined about the two men, long tails wagging.

"I'll look around the other kennels. Just a moment." And Oscar Castleton disappeared in the deep shadow between two of the kennel houses.

Nat stepped outside the wired enclosure, latched the gate, and strangely, he felt as if someone was watching his every move—watching and waiting. He shrugged broad shoulders, turned to face the house. From where he stood, he couldn't see Martin Castleton, for the corner of the house cut off his view. Behind him, he heard a dog whine softly for a moment, then stop.

There was a chance, he thought, that one of the dogs had—

His thoughts chopped short, cold horror squeezing them from his mind. His scalp twitched, every hair rising as a shrill, nerve-jangling scream cut through the night. It was the terrible cry of a woman confronted by a ghastly horror. It mounted to a chill, piercing note, then trailed into a sobbing gasp.

Nat stood frozen motionless for a moment, then broke into a run toward the house. That scream had come from Ethel Castleton!

He rounded the corner of the house, feet digging into the turf of the lawn as he skidded to a halt. Running footsteps pounded behind him. He half-turned to face the sound, and someone crashed into him, driving him to his knees. Nat jerked to his feet, right hand streaking to the heavy gun holstered at his hip, then stopped. Oscar Castleton sprawled upon the lawn beside him. The boy scrambled up, then his shrill cry blasted in Nat's ears.

"God! Look!" The boy pointed with a thin finger.

Nat stared with aching eyes.

There were three bodies now upon the gravel walk in front of the house where but one sprawled before, and one of them was Ethel Castleton!

Nat pounded forward, his flashlight stabbing toward the walk, splashing the gravel with livid light. He picked out Ronald Castleton's body, saw another body beside it, recognized Martin Castleton's slight frame. The girl sprawled beside Martin, her body limp. Nat reached them, knelt beside the girl.

She lay on her back, white face upward, arms outflung. Nat whipped the light over her, upward over slim, silk-clad limbs, a narrow circle of white thigh bared by her disarranged clothing, firm breasts thrusting against the soft fabric of her dress. Then the light reached her face. Nat choked back an exclamation of horror.

Flecks of blood stood out as damning red splotches against the white skin about her small mouth. Her slim white fingers were daubed with the crimson fluid, and splashes of it showed on her dress. She was alive and uninjured. Nat decided that she had fainted. He went to Martin's body.

The boy sprawled upon the gravel, thin fingers clutching at the crushed stones. His dark eyes were wide, staring, and a gushing stream of blood had burst from his throat, drenching his clothing and the gravel walk. The sweetish smell of it rose in Nat's flared nostrils and made him sick. The boy's throat had been torn just as Ronald's had been.

Nat heard Oscar Castleton's whimpering breath behind him, heard the boy whispering a prayer. He swung about.

"Where," he rapped, "were you when your sister screamed?"

"In—in the farthest kennel." Oscar wrung pale hands. His slight body was jerking nervously. "I—I found only four dogs in it. The gate was open. Three of the dogs are loose in the grounds."

"I—" started Nat, then stiffened, every faculty concentrated into listening. He'd heard the short, muffled bark of a dog somewhere in the night. It came again, ended in a pained yelp, then everything was silent.

HE jerked to his feet and pounded toward the sound, loosening his heavy, service pistol in its holster as he ran. Abruptly, the spot of his flashlight, racing before him, picked out the limp body of a dog. Nat stopped, dropped to his knees.

The dog was dead, its head crushed by a blunt instrument. Mechanically, Nat rose to his feet, whipped the light about, seeking the weapon. It was nowhere in sight. He listened for a moment, heard nothing, then turned and went back to the front of the Castleton house.

Old Castleton had switched on the porch-lights and was sitting in his wheel-chair which he had rolled to the very edge of the top step of the porch. He started shouting questions as soon as he saw Nat.

"For God's sake tell me what's happened! Has Ethel—?"

Oscar Castleton had picked his sister's limp figure up in his arms and was carrying her toward the porch. He pushed past his father and went on into the house.

Nat mounted the steps, dropped a hard hand on the old man's shoulder.

"Steady, Mr. Castleton," he rasped, his voice grim. "There's been another murder."

"Murder!" Castleton's bony fingers clutched his wrist; the old man half-rose from the wheel-chair, and Nat thought

of those talon-like fingers rending the dead flash of his ship-mates. He stiffened to keep from shuddering. "Did—did—Ethel—?" Castleton's strained voice stuck in his skinny throat.

"I don't think so." Nat flashed a searching glance toward the front door. Oscar had placed his sister upon a leather lounge and was bathing her face with water. Nat swung back to Castleton. "Tell me what happened," he directed crisply.

"We—we were sitting there, neither of us talking. Ethel was staring out of the open door, her eyes sort of glittering strangely. I—I was thinking of the—blood lust. I—I had to get out of the room because—" Castleton stopped, bony fingers twining nervously. "I—I—well, I've thought of killing my children to keep them from becoming were-wolves! And seeing her staring—God! I—"

"How long," rapped Nat, his lips drawn in a grim, white line across his grey face, "have you been confined to the wheel-chair?"

"Why—why—!" Castleton's pale eyes snapped wide, showing blood-shot eye-balls. "Why—I've been paralyzed for years, fifteen years. I can't move from this chair. I can't—"

"You raised up a moment ago." Nat's eyes slitted.

"God! You don't think that I—?" Castleton's voice rose to a shrill scream.

"Perhaps not." Nat's grim eyes whipped back to the doorway. Ethel Castleton was sitting up on the lounge. He swung back to Castleton, turned the wheel chair about and pushed it toward the open doorway.

Oscar was kneeling on the floor, rubbing his sister's wrists. She looked up, staring wildly as Nat pushed the wheel-chair into the living-room and strode toward the lounge.

"Listen, Miss Castleton," he said

quietly, "I dislike to be insistent, but I want you to tell me just what you saw before you screamed."

"I—I sat in the room with father for a few moments after you and Oscar left for the kennels. Father excused himself and rolled his chair toward the back of the house. I was sitting where I could look out of the door. I could see Martin. He was standing near—near Ronald." Her breath caught in her throat. "He was looking toward the kennels. Suddenly, he reached for his throat, just as Ronald had, then he staggered and fell. I heard the same whirring noise. I knew something terrible had happened. I ran out—and—I guess I screamed. I—I must have fainted." She buried her face in her hands, sobbing. "His throat—was bleeding! Oh—h—"

Nat's forehead ridged. "You didn't see anyone near Martin?" he asked. The girl shook her head. "You didn't see the dog this time?" She shook her head again, her face still buried in her slim fingers. Oscar had washed the blood from her hands. "Now, where was your father," Nat went on quietly, "just before Ronald was killed?"

He heard Oscar Castleton's sharp intake of breath, noted the boy's startled glance toward his father. Castleton sat slumped in his wheel-chair, his bony face deathly white, pale lips drawn tight across stained teeth.

"I—I don't know." Ethel Castleton dropped back to the lounge, her slim body shaking with sobs.

Nat strode hard-heeled from the room, went out to the two bodies on the walk and examined them again. Both had their throats torn in almost the same manner. He searched, but could find no sign of a weapon, not a trace of footprints. He rose to his feet, sweeping the wide, moonlit lawn with narrowed eyes.

A grey shape slunk out of the trees on his right, moving with a silent, padded step. Moonlight glinted on green animal eyes, and Nat grunted. The shape was one of the missing dogs, unless—

Sucking in breath through set teeth, he stabbed his light toward it, pressing the switch with suddenly cold, stiff fingers. He relaxed as the light showed the thing to be one of the dogs. For a moment he'd thought of what Castleton had told him—the taint of blood-lust transforming his children into were-wolves.

Unconsciously, Nat swung his eyes toward the living room door. Oscar, Castleton and Ethel were still in the room.

He turned to stare at the bodies on the walk, strode stiffly around them, stopped a few feet away, frowning, eyes squinted as he tried to make all the queer facts fit into a logical whole.

There was Castleton's mad story—his admission that he'd thought of killing his children to keep them from becoming were-wolves. The thoughts of that ghastly experience in the small boat fifty years ago had unsettled the old man's mind. Castleton had left the room a few moments before Martin's death. Well, for that matter, Oscar had gone to one of the other kennels before his brother's death.

Nat rubbed his hard jaw with a muscular fist.

Ethel Castleton was alone at the time of her brother's death. Oscar was alone. Old Castleton was alone. No one to check on any of them. Everett Davis was not on the premises, having gone after the local Police.

He turned his attention back to the bodies on the walk. The thing, whatever it was, had struck from the darkness without warning. Both men were well over fifty feet from the house, the nearest cover. A razor-edged knife on a cord, flung, then drawn back to— He shook his head. Not likely. It was something else.

Absently, Nat's hard fingers fumbled a cigarette from his uniform coat pocket. He reached for a match, flicked it alight with his thumbnail, thrust the cigarette into his mouth, lighted it and puffed for a moment, the still flaming match held in his fingers. Then abruptly, a choked curse burst from his lips.

He was standing upon the exact spot where the two men were killed. The thing might flick rending fingers at his throat!

He spun on his heel, half-crouched, right fist glued to the slick butt of his service gun, slitted eyes probing the shadows about the house.

SINISTER, threatening things seemed to lurk in the dark shrubbery against the brick walls. No light showed except in the living room. The rest loomed dark, forbidding. He saw the bulk of a balcony thrusting out from the second floor over the porch, its brick rail barely touched by the rising moon. A queer thought flashed through his mind. He started toward the front steps, then stopped as the throb of an automobile motor sounded toward the back of the house. Headlights swung through the trees, brakes squealed as a car stopped behind the house.

A few moments and Everett Davis, followed by four local police officers came around the corner of the house, headed toward him.

Introductions over, Nat stuck around a few minutes, explaining things to the local cops. Then he touched Davis on the arm.

"If you don't mind, Mr. Davis," he said quietly, "I'd like to ask you a few questions about the Castleton family. I've an idea, a queer one, and I'd like to know what you think about it. Suppose we go to your room?"

"Sure! Good Heavens! I can't get over Martin being killed while I was away. Why, Lord, I've only been gone a few minutes. I hardly know what to think."

Nat followed him through the living-room, upstairs and into his room on the second floor well toward the back of the house. Davis stood aside as the motor-cop entered the room.

The light showed the place to be adorned with various hunting and fishing trophies. A deerhead thrust from the wall over the bed. A life-like tarpon hung over the door. Various other smaller trophies and weapons were placed about the room.

Nat took the proffered chair, lighted another cigarette. Davis sat on the edge of the bed and mopped his forehead with a handkerchief.

"Have the Castletons," Nat asked abruptly, "any skeletons in the closet? Something rather bad that's not generally known?"

Davis stiffened, came half to his feet, then dropped back, white about his heavy lips. His eyes held a strange gleam.

"Why—why! I don't know what you mean," he whispered hoarsely. "There's no scandal, if that's what you mean. They—"

"I mean quarrels, bickerings, any cause for any of the family to hate each other enough to try—well, murder."

"Well, no—o." Davis seemed reluctant. "I shouldn't say that any one had cause to do—what was done tonight—but—"

"Big tarpon you have there." Nat jerked a hard thumb toward the mounted fish. "Catch it recently?"

"Two years ago, off the Florida coast." Davis leaned forward earnestly. "About the hidden family affair—" he started.

"You're considered an expert with any kind of a gun, aren't you, Mr. Davis?" broke in Nat, muscles bunched, right fist rigid near his holstered gun. "And you're an expert fisherman, aren't you?"

"Yes." Davis cleared his throat, got to his feet, and started toward the massive bureau. "I've taken several prizes for—"

"Stay away from that bureau!" rasped Nat. "Get back to the bed! Move!" His hard fingers wrapped about the butt of his gun, started lifting it from the holster.

Davis leaped with the swiftness of active muscles, fingers clawing open the bureau drawer, whipping out a long-barreled target pistol.

Nat jerked his service gun up, squeezed the trigger, unconsciously squinted his eyes as the blasting roar filled the room with crashing waves of sound. The acrid reek of burned powder filled his nostrils.

Davis was on the floor, knocked flat by the heavy slug in his right shoulder. His target pistol lay within reach of his left hand. He clawed for it. Nat coolly put a slug through his left forearm, grinning tightly as mad curses drooled from Davis' writhing lips.

GETTING deliberately to his feet, the motor-cop picked up the target gun, shoved it into his pocket, then strode toward the door of a clothes closet in the corner of the room. He was back in a moment with a heavy surf-casting rod and reel in his hand. The reel was wound with extra-heavy deep sea tackle, strong enough to lift a man, and attached to the end of the heavy line was a queerly constructed device. The thing was clotted with scarcely dried blood.

Nat's lips tightened into a grim line and he strode to stand over Davis.

"So you figured to murder Ronald, Martin and Oscar *before* old Castleton kicked off or was sent to the asylum," he rasped. "Taking a chance on your ability to fool Ethel Castleton into marrying you and bringing you the Castleton money and property as dowry. If she hadn't, you'd have murdered her. You knew of the log-book in the safe—probably opened the safe and read it. You were ready to tell me all about the blood taint of the Castletons when I asked about the tarpon, weren't you?"

Davis nodded, his face drawn, eyes flaming with agony and hate.

"You were going to tell the Castletons enough to make them think the taint was working, that they were killing each other. Your black brain figured out the way to rip out their throats. You stood on the balcony. Ronald was easy. Martin was harder, but you went a short distance in the car, came back through the back of the house, killed Martin, then slipped back to the car. Gone for the police would be your alibi, and you might have worked it, but you killed a dog that was about to give you away. You left the body where I found it." Nat held the heavy rod and reel out in his hand.

"You stood on the balcony and ripped out Ronald's and Martin's throats with this." He pointed to the queer treble hook at the end of the thick line. The curving section of each steel hook was in reality a curved, razor-edged knife. The shank of the hook itself was encased in a heavy lead weight. In the hands of an expert angler, the thing was a terrible weapon, its killing distance limited only by the length of the cast.

"You cast this hook, snagged it in their throats, then jerked. The sharpened barbs did the rest. You reeled in the line. The whirring noise that Ethel heard was the line on the reel."

"You were lucky, too, in that Ethel, in each case, got the blood on her hands, and smeared it from them onto her face. That fooled me for a long time."

Racing footsteps were clattering down the hallway toward the bedroom door. Some one outside shouted hoarsely.

"So it was, after all," Nat said softly, as there came a pounding on the door, "—a blood moon!"

THIRST OF

By
Nat Schachner
(Author of "They Dare Not Die!" etc.)

A strange girl it was whom John Carson married—one moment pure and wholesome, the next a demon of greedy passion. Yet not till he had followed her to the home of her ancestors, till he had seen the withered, horrible ancient making ready for his feast, did John Carson guess the fearful truth. . . .

IT WAS almost three months since I had married Elise Delsart. Over and over again, I told myself that I was very happy—though when I was with her I needed no such assurances. Her strange, haunting presence enmeshed me in a fiery web that hazed my senses and beclouded my mind. I knew then only that I loved her, loved her with a strange dual love which was, I realized later, but a counterpart of the dual nature of her own being.

There were times when she was everything that a lovely, normal young bride should be. Her caresses were pure and

THE ANCIENTS

Novelette

of

Evil Passions

wholesome, her face alight with tenderness. The haunting dread that seemed so often to shadow her eyes would vanish like smoke.

But there were other times—and they followed like snapping, snarling wolves on the very heels of sweet normality—when a stealthy shiver would tremble over her body from crown to toe, and that strange, greedy look I had come to know only too well would creep into her eyes.

Then, like a will-less automaton, like a man in a dream, I would sink into those warm-tinted, rounded arms that tightened fiercely about me, stare into the fathomless depths of those jet-black eyes, see the dark wine of her slightly parted lips, behind which gleamed whitely the even, sharp teeth—too sharp, almost.

In such moments there was always the queer prickling sensation that perhaps this time was the last. Horrible similes made lightning tracks through my brain. I thought of the strange nuptial flight of the queen bee and her mate; I thought of the praying mantis. In such moments it seemed to me that my very soul was being sucked out of my body, that one more instant of madness and the slender strands that still held its whispering tenuity would part irrevocably.

Yet I could do naught else. For it was always Elise, my wife, who would finally release her strangling embrace, and, with panting breath and swift horror in her eyes, push me from her as if—as if—God help me for the thoughts that crept unbidden into my mind—she had recoiled from the very edge of some dark and dreadful deed too hellish for human comprehension.

Once, in the hothouse passion of such a transformation, Elise had bitten me with those sharp little teeth of hers. It was just a mere bruising of the skin, the tiniest of lacerations; but a small globule of blood had welled forth. It had been salt on her full carmine lips. A convulsive shiver permeated her being. Her arms were whipping snakes about my form, her passion-flower mouth nuzzled against the unprotected line of my throat. I felt her teeth edging, edging . . . oh God, I could not move nor breathe!

Then she pushed me away violently, so violently that I all but lost my balance.

"John, darling!" There was shrinking dread, desperate fear in her voice, not justified by the trifling hurt. "You are bleeding! I have hurt you!"

She hurried away, came back a moment later. The iodine applicator in her hand trembling like a leaf in a shrieking hurricane. Her face, pale now as new snow, was stiffly averted.

What, after all, did I know of Elise? Nothing! I had met here at a Bohemian affair, where one's only passport was the ability to hold one's liquor. She qualified. So did I. No one knew her, but all eyes followed her pantherish grace, the Mona-Lisa mystery of her smile. She was lushly exotic; she was ageless, she was woman incarnate!

From that moment the spell was on me.

I courted her with whirling ardor. She seemed to return my love, and yet, strangely, she seemed at the same time to flee my advances. That haunted look which later was to be a perpetual part of her, crept into her eyes the first time she refused me. I persisted, such being my madness; at last I won and married her. I had not known her antecedents; I still did not know them. She evaded my fumbling questions, and I felt a strange, unaccountable reluctance to press the point.

There was no question, however, about the fact that my friends no longer visited me, no matter how urgent the invitation, no matter how sweetly Elise insisted when we chanced casually to meet in the street. They would mutter hasty, indistinguishable excuses, look queerly at me, then in slanting sidewise fashion at the exotic loveliness on my arm, and would quicken their pace almost to a run as they left us.

It was also true that something had happened to me. I was no longer the sane, eminently practical lawyer I had always been. I seemed to walk in a perpetual haze. My mind, once keen and alert, fumbled and groped in a dark world peopled with hideous shapes and sounds. My clients gradually fell away from me; my office became an empty desolation.

In a vague fashion I connected my malaise with Elise. I sat alone, head in hand, for hours, trying to analyze the situation. It was no use. My thoughts would not function. I knew afterwards that subconsciously I was afraid—afraid of the woman I had married, of what she was, of what she might have been.

THEN, I noted after weeks had passed, with a great wave of thankfulness a gradual change in Elise. The dark cloud that overlaid her with brooding strangeness was gradually disappearing. Her spells of shuddersome passion grew more and more infrequent, and she even sometimes laughed—wholeheartedly, girlishly. She had never laughed before. A black shroud seemed lifted from both of us.

It was not quite three months since our wedding now. I came home that night cheerfully from the office. Whatever it was that had threatened our existence was gone. I was sure of that.

Elise met me at the door. Her manner was distraught. Her midnight hair made a disordered cloud and there was a frantic glitter in her deep-shaded eyes.

"John!" she cried huskily. "I just received a telegram. My—my uncle is dying!"

I kissed her and released myself gently. I stared at her a bit puzzled. Why such abandoned sorrow over an uncle? Then it struck me. It was the first time my wife had said anything about a family.

"That's too bad, honey," I murmured sympathetically. "But don't take on so. After all, uncles *do* die."

She clenched her hands convulsively. The knuckles were drained white. Something showed in her eyes, something more than sorrow, something more than dread, than terror even. It was frantic, supreme determination. I fell away a bit, afraid.

Elise must have seen that. She veiled her eyes. "You don't understand," she said very low. "My uncle is all I have—besides you. He brought me up from earliest childhood. My father died before I was born; my mother six months after. I must see him before it is too late."

I patted her shoulder, ashamed of certain dark, unbidden suspicions. She loved her uncle who had been father and mother to her. That was natural. It made her human; it—I started, shuddered. That very phrase flitting through my mind showed the frightful abyss, the vile foulness of my thoughts.

Aloud I said: "Of course, honey, we must go. We'll leave at once."

She shrank back from me as if she had been stung by a poisonous snake.

"No, no!" she panted. "You must not! Never! I must go alone!"

All my old suspicions flared again. What was she hiding from me? What was wrong with her family? Once and for all I determined to find out.

"I repeat," I said angrily, "I am going with you."

For a long moment there was silence. The veil dropped again over her eyes. Then, very low, she said: "If you insist. . ."

Would to God I hadn't! But in my madness, in my new-found determination to pierce the truth, I answered: "I do."

I DID not like the looks of Satanstoe. The gloom of approaching dusk hung thick on the wavering backdrop of mountains, and the red clay clung clammily to our shoes as we trudged up the snaky road. The bags were heavy in my hands. Dark, dilapidated cabins lined the path.

I was irritable, and more than a bit uneasy. Two days and two nights on the train had not helped. Nor the fierce restrained eagerness of my wife, the hectic flush that dyed her cheeks, the eerie, unfathomable look she turned on me. Nor the tense, electric atmosphere of this backwoods village. It dawned on me that I had not seen a soul—except one.

"What was the matter with that hackdriver?" I asked Elise. He had come forward eagerly enough as we left the train—the only arrivals. He had jerked a thumb toward a battered Model T.

"Any place I kin take ye, stranger?"

I motioned to Elise. "All right, honey. Here's our taxi."

My wife had emerged then from the shadows of the train shed, in which she had unaccountably lingered. The man jerked his eyes around. They widened. I thought at first it was because of her loveliness, because he was glad to see her.

Glad? Oh, my God! If ever I have seen terror limned indelibly on human countenance, it was on that lean, heretofore placid face. His eyes bulged, his lips writhed. His hands went up as if to fend off a thing of unutterable evil.

With a strangled incoherent moan he had whirled, darted for his ancient machine, and bounced off as if all the devils in hell were after him.

At my question the spots of color darkened on my wife's face. Her cheekbones were hard and glittering. She kept her eyes directly ahead.

"I am not responsible for all the fools in Satanstoe," she said with hard huskiness.

I did not mention the incident again, and we went on. But the strange unease grew on me. A little, half-naked child ran out of a cabin door with that natural curiosity which all children have in infrequently visited places. She dug her small toes in the clay and stared at me. Then she saw my wife.

A shrill baby cry split the silent air.

"Mammy! Mammy!" The tot wailed out its frightened little heart and tumbled back into the cabin. I thought I saw arms reaching out in the shadow doorway to clutch it tight, but no one came out.

Elise kept her face set straight on the road. She did not seem to have seen or heard. I said nothing, but strange thoughts wound like corpse-cloths around my flogging brain.

Boots made thumping sound behind a windbreak of trees. A man slouched into view. He was dressed in faded overalls and his face was long and sallow.

"Howdy, stranger," he waved friendly greeting. Then he stiffened, bit off something he was about to say. He whirled —face averted, he clumped down the road. The beat quickened; it was almost a run. Then it stopped.

I turned my head. He had hidden behind a tree. Only his face showed, peering whitely at me. There was fear, there was desperate warning in that glance.

Anger surged within me; anger—and something else. What the devil did it mean?

Before I could assemble my fumbling thoughts a wagon lumbered slowly down the road. Three men were in it, lean, hard-bitten, typical mountaineers. The horse plodded wearily along, ears drooping, too spiritless even to swish his tail at the buzzing flies that settled on his flanks.

The driver was telling a story. It must have been funny, for hoarse guffaws rose startlingly above the creak of ungreased axles. They had not seen us. I turned aside to let them pass. Elise stood quietly at my side.

The horse's heaving flanks almost brushed me. The large sad eye that fixed blankly on me was red and streaked with white. It was blind. Its head drooped more than ever.

Then it was abreast of my wife. The red-pitted nostrils sniffed, twitched violently. A long whinny of terror burst from the broken animal. It skittered away so violently that it all but overturned the wagon.

The driver grasped the lax reins, pulled.

"Whoa, consarn ye! What the devil. . . !"

Long trembling shudders ran over the horse's body. It fought with bared teeth against the bit. White lather flecked its mane.

The man next the driver swallowed the plug he was chewing. The stubble showed black against the sudden pallor of his skin.

"By God!" he blurted. "Seth! She's back!"

Then the horse bolted. The wagon careened from side to side down the red clay road. I gaped after it. Had I heard

—or was it just imagination—chopped words from Seth: "Another . . . poor devil . . ."

SOMETHING clutched my throat. I turned. Elise was smiling a slow, strange smile.

"Something scared that horse," she said.

"Yes," I answered. And I said nothing more. God knows I should have stopped then and there, and demanded an explanation. Perhaps I should have gone back, caught up to that runaway team, found out things. My hair might yet be jet-black instead of grey; my face might still be youthfully unlined. And nights might be repositories of sleep, instead of gloating little animals with evil red eyes.

But I was at that moment afraid of Elise. I dared not ask. I was afraid of the answers. Besides, she was the woman I had married, had lived with, had embraced. How *could* one acknowledge to her the fearful, impossible thoughts that swirled in my brain—round and round, until I seemed twisted into hard, tight knots.

Night had fallen. Faint stars were out, but no moon. We went on. Elise said cheerfully: "We're almost there, darling." She walked with sure, quick tread. She seemed an uncanny shadow flitting at my side; she seemed to see in the dark.

At the next dim bend of the road she turned off into an overgrown path. I followed, stumbling. A house loomed across a weedy tangle. It was huge, somehow ominous. No lights showed.

We crunched over cinders, climbed the three steps that were blurs in the starlight. My clumsy footsteps thudded hollowly like a skeleton's. Elise made no noise.

The portico was supported by faded, sagging columns. Once they had been stately; now they were grey with death, ready at a touch to crumble into dust.

Elise was making doleful reverberations with a brass knocker on an arched door that hung crazily askew. There was still time for me to turn back, the maggots crawling in my brain seemed to whisper.

The door swung open with a squeak like that of a gibbering bat. A black hole yawned behind. There was a moment of dull silence in which the darkness peered out at us. Then a match scraped, burst into thin flame, and gave yellow luminance to a swinging lantern. The glow crept upward to disclose the holder.

The marrow seemed to freeze in my bones. What was it—monster or man? For a great hairy face leered out at us. Black greasy hair fell in a mop over a sloping forehead; a broken nose bulged darkly from squat, unformed features, and yellowish, malignant eyes drilled holes in my shuddering soul.

He held the lantern high. The light swept over my wife. He licked his lips and a slow grin spread over his evil countenance.

"Miss Elise!" he said, forcing the syllables out of his throat as if he were unused to speech. "So you come back!"

"Yes, Lem," she answered. Her brittle tone was a hardness that had been growing on her since we started South. "And this is my husband, Mr. Carson."

Lem's brutish eyes turned slowly on me. I did not like it; I felt a quick shudder at what I saw, or thought I saw, in those yellow flares.

"Take me to Uncle Philip," my wife said quickly. "I want to see him before he—dies."

A low growling chuckle, that raised the hackles on my spine, rasped its way from Len's throat.

"Afore he dies, hey?" he cackled. "Yeah, Miss Elise, you sure would."

Without another word he turned and led the way through the cavernous reaches of the entrance hall. I looked stealthily at my wife, but her face was hard and rigid and pale with some strangely fixed determination. I found myself afraid to talk.

THE light made the shadows retreat, only to gather with more intense blackness in the corners. Dust was on everything, dust and the decay of death. I shivered and followed Elise.

We plodded up a winding stairs. The treads groaned hollowly under my feet. Blackness greeted us at the top, against which the little flare of the lantern beat with unavailing rays. Lem paused and cocked his brutish head to one side.

"Hey, there!" he shouted.

The echoes rolled shrieking through interminable darkness. Then there was silence, in which I could listen to the slow *drip, drip* of my heart's blood.

Abruptly I jumped back, almost fell down the stairs. A shape had materialized out of impenetrable gloom. It had come with uncanny silence, and now it rolled into the dull yellow light.

It was a wheel-chair on rubber tires, dexterously propelled by means of a lever. But the man who sat in it! Good God! If Lem had sent shivers down my spine, the man in the chair made my body one frozen mass of horror.

He slumped in its hollow like the sloughed skin of a snake from which the meat and flesh and bones had already wriggled. The fingers that rested loosely on the chair arms, the legs that dangled uselessly in the chair well, were mere dried husks of blown thinness. But the head, that supported itself from the high stiff collar of an older day, was incredibly alive and incredibly malignant. Yellow parchment skin clung hairlessly to a small round skull and whispered like dry leaves in a wind. Deep sockets burned twin holes from which, as from the bottom of a well, something eyed us stealthily. His fleshless lips writhed in fixed laughter, baring red gums from which protruded long, startlingly white fangs. There was no other way to describe those four tusks, two on each side, that locked hideously on each other.

"It's Elise come back to her poor old uncle Philip," the old man whispered. His voice was like the creaking of a rusty gate.

Hard spots of color burned in my wife's cheeks. Her eyes flared with strange lights as they clashed with the almost invisible orbs that lay in the deep socket pools.

"Yes," she said in a flat, controlled voice. "I have come back."

"Ha! ha!" he cackled. "She must have heard I was dying, Lem. That's filial affection for you. First she goes away and leaves me. I call and call and she doesn't come. Tonight she comes. Why, Lem?"

The brutish servitor grinned thickly. "I think, Mister Delsart, 'cause she's the dark o' the moon t'night."

Philip Delsart cackled and wheezed, "Exactly, Lem. Dear Elise was twenty a week ago, and the moon is dark for the first time tonight."

He bobbed his horrible head so that it seemed about to drop from the confines of his collar. "And she brought a man with her, too, like a sensible child." His hollow sockets fixed on me. "Married her, didn't you?"

I TRIED to open my mouth to answer him, but my jaws refused to function. Cold, freezing horror swept over me in great waves. I wanted more than anything else in all my life to get out of this frightful house, away from these frightful denizens, yet I could not move.

Elise answered for me. For the first time I detected a tremble in her voice. "John Carson is my husband."

That little tremble—of concern for me, was it?—was the spring that released my body from the stiff mold into which it had been poured. I turned halfway, to grab her by the arm, to flee with her into the night. Then down the black, unfathomed hall I heard the swift patter of feet.

A girl burst panting into the lantern glow that enveloped us all in a tiny island of light. Even in the first shock of her appearance I noted her slender prettiness, the deep blue of her eyes, the glint of gold in her wind-bobbed hair.

"Oh, Mr. Delsart," she cried. "You had no right to leave your room. It will be the death of you. I told you—"

She stopped abruptly as she saw us. Her eyes widened with alarm. She shrank back with quick, fluttering movements from my wife.

"Oh! Oh!" she gasped. "Miss Elise! You've come back! I thought—you were gone—forever!"

A long shudder had rippled over my wife at sight of the girl.

"Nancy Tennant!" she said sharply. "What are you doing here?"

The girl threw back her head defiantly and moved closer to the horrible old man in the chair.

"I'm taking care of poor Mr. Delsart," she said. "He is dying, and needs a woman's care." Strange, the intonation she placed on that word!

My wife laughed. The sound of that laugh sent shivers of apprehension down my back.

"He has died before this, you poor fool!" she cried wildly. "He will die again, when you won't be here to witness it. Get out of here, Nancy Tennant! Get out before it is too late!"

The old man huddled in his chair like an empty sack, but I felt his hidden eyes staring—staring. Lem rocked his apelike head with foul, fierce merriment. He was in back of us, blocking the stairs, cutting off the flight I had meditated.

The girl, Nancy, gripped at the arm of the wheel-chair for support. Her bosom heaved and her breath was coming very fast. But crawling fear gave way to anger born of desperation.

"Elise Delsart!" she shrilled. "You—you have no power over me. I know you—everyone in Satanstoe knows you. You want me out of the way so you can work your hideous deeds without hindrance." The words were tumbling from her lips in a blazing fury of haste.

"You, Elise Delsart, dare accuse your uncle!" She was laughing wildly, and it was more terrible than Lem's sinister cackle had been. "Poor old man, he has but hours of life left. You, you have done that to him. You have drained him of life, you who have lived, a loathsome, despicable creature since the world began. We know your history, we people of Satanstoe. We know you for what you are —a hideous, blood-lusting vampire!"

CHAPTER TWO

"You Die Tonight"

VAMPIRE!

The dreadful word exploded in my skull and shattered my reeling brain into a thousand shards of flesh. All the strangeness of my married life came back to me in flooding horror—all the fearful suspicions, the swift alterations of mood on the part of my wife, the pierced blood from my neck that had lain salt on her tongue, her strong even teeth. . . .

Vampire! I had married a vampire! God in Heaven! The shattered fragments of my being cried out frantically in denial, absolving, defending—but the dim spark of reason rose up in me with horrid, damning, conclusive evidence.

And the voice of the girl, the accuser, went on inexorably, with hysterical speed, crushing me with her young, shrill tones farther down into the depths of hell.

"Yes, a vampire!" she cried. "You

were Sheba's Queen, the Lamia, the Medusa who turned men to stone; you were Lilith herself, who drained Adam of immortality and flaunted her love for the Devil. Every twenty years you must renew yourself, otherwise you die a mortal. Every twenty years you seek a victim, and, in the dark of the moon, you suck his blood to fatten your own filthy body, so fair of surface."

The dark of the moon! It was that tonight! I was going mad, stark, ravening mad. I had loved this woman—there had been times when she had been so warm and loving and sweet. God! Were they but webs of deceit to enmesh me further until the appointed time, when the moon was dark, unable to see the foul deeds perpetrated on a shadowed earth?

Nancy Tennant whirled on me. She was exalted with her accusing passion, she was beyond fear now.

"Go, poor fool!" she cried, "before it is too late! Run from her while there is time. Hide from her as you would from the face of destruction itself. Don't you see—don't you understand—why she has brought you, her victim, to Satanstoe? This is the seat of her power, the place of her filthy re-creation!"

I reeled like a drunken man. I felt the evil eyes of Lem boring into my back; Philip Delsart nodded and cackled approval like a horrible bird of prey. And Elise—my wife— A great groan burst from me. If I believed this I would surely go mad. I turned desperately to her who had lain at my side—to her who, in spite of everything, had shown flashes of what, to my deluded mind, had seemed true love.

"Elise!" I cried. "In the name of all that is sacred, deny these frightful things! Tell me they are not true. Tell them all to their gloating faces they are foul, damnable liars. I shall believe you, Elise. Do you hear? *I shall believe you! . . ."*

I waited a moment. "Only your word," I begged abjectly, "only two little words. Say only: 'They lie!' and we shall go out of this house of evil, together."

I gazed into the face of my wife imploringly, while my heart's-blood pounded madly and the cold sweat rolled on my clammy forehead. All about us the blackness of hell beat down with engulfing wings.

Lifetimes passed and no one moved. Then, very slowly, Elise turned her shapely head, the head I had loved to fondle. Her olive face was drawn and white, her lips a livid gash of red against the pallor. Her eyes, jet black, deep-shadowed pools, met mine.

I staggered back. I must have cried out, though I do not remember. The world, the universe itself, crashed in flaming destruction about my tortured brain.

I had read the truth in her eyes! Elise—my wife—was a vampire!

I MUST have gone mad then, completely, ravening mad. Bursts of idiot laughter shrilled from my lips; I cursed, I yelled, I screamed. I called on the heavens to fall and blast us all to destruction.

Then the fit left me, and cold, weakening horror wrapped me in a shroud. Nancy pitied me with fear-struck eyes. Delsart cackled like an obscene chorus. Elise had not moved or said a word under the floodgates of my loathing.

"I am going!" I said. "I leave this accursed place to the demons of hell. And I'll kill the one, vampire or mortal, who tries to stop me!"

It seemed to my bewildered mind that Elise's head dropped at that, but no word issued from her tight-locked lips. Then a thought pierced the haze. "Nancy Tennant," I whispered fiercely, "come with me. You, too, are mortal and in danger. Come . . ."

Dread flamed in Nancy's blue eyes. She

shivered, yet she made no move. I could hardly hear her voice, so low it was. "I cannot. I must take care of Mr. Delsart. Go, please, quickly, and do not think of me. I am safe."

I groaned and turned on my heel. I took swift strides toward Lem, who blocked the stairs. My fists made desperate balls, ready to lash out if he tried to stop me. God! How I yearned for the clean, fresh air of night, for the feel of icy water on my fevered skin!

I heard Delsart's rusty, grating voice behind me. It was harsh with urgency.

"Elise Delsart, your husband escapes you and it is the dark of the moon. You die tonight—a mortal. Do you hear, dear niece?" He chuckled hideously. "For thousands of years you have lived, yet tonight you die for want of a husband's blood."

I felt the impact of something almost like a physical blow on my back. Lem, hairy face aflame with cruel quiverings, crouched at the head of the stairs, awaiting my onset. Yet it was not that which stopped me dead in my tracks.

Elsie would die tonight! Even in my maddened state it came as a shock. She *had* been my wife.

Then realization of what she was, of what she had intended, flooded my being. I exulted, I bathed in fierce joy. The face of the world was well rid of this idiot, of this foul cancerous thing that had roamed its surface too long, taking hideous toll. I turned to tell her so, to scream the last dregs of my loathing.

Something seemed to snap, some invisible web of influence of which I had not been aware. A strange smile fluttered over the skull-like features of Delsart.

Elise swung slowly from her locked gaze. I shouted something—what it was I do not know. Then her eyes met mine. No longer masked, no longer veiled, but filled with longing, with a yearning that

enveloped me and tingled down to the very depths of my being. Her arms went out in imploring gesture, even as they had done so many times when I had thought she loved me.

"John!" she murmured, and there was a sweetness in her tones that I had never heard before. "John! Do not leave me! I need you, John; I shall die if you go."

Her face glowed with a strange light, her voice tugged at me with queer harmonies. I felt myself filled with a surge of strange sensation. Her voice was sweet —too sweet. It was cloying, with a poisonous syrup that seemed to cling round my heart. I knew that it was evil, I knew that I was doomed to destruction if I stayed; yet all the madness, all the revulsion, flowed like water out of my being.

Elise, who was my wife, had called on me. Tonight she would die, die for lack of blood to revivify her and make her beautiful and glowing and immortal. Only *I* could furnish that blood.

But I suddenly did not care. I read more than lust for my blood in her tender eyes. She loved me! Elise, vampire or not, loved me! Loved me, I was sure, more than she had ever loved anyone else through the centuries.

ALL my loathing turned to love. God! She *was* beautiful! She had a right to live, to exist for all eternity. What did it matter what means she employed to achieve immortality? What did it matter that I should die, that hundreds of other men had died before me, would die after me? We were mortals and our terms were limited. A few years more or less meant nothing.

But she, the glorious, the beautiful, would go on forever, a shining being through the ages. And she loved me, would pity me even as she drank deeply at the wellsprings of my being.

I would stay, I cried inwardly, and offer

up the wine of life to her luscious, poisonously sweet lips. A surge of self-sacrifice tingled ecstatically in my veins.

Philip Delsart darted his shriveled head around to me. He seemed to read what was in my mind.

"Go, fool!" he shrilled. "She has you in thrall again. Lem, let him pass."

"John, darling!" the woman I had married called to me. Her head was thrust back and the pale yellow light of the lantern made a sinuous curve of the line of her throat. "Don't leave me. I love you, I want you!. . ."

Unutterably vibrant, compelling that voice—filled with the tenderness of our unclouded moments. I knew that evil crawled underneath; I knew that I had but a little while to live; yet I did not care.

"Elise!" I cried. "I am staying; I am yours. Do with me what you will!"

She swayed a little at that. For one instant her eyes were full on me with strained fear, with dreadful warning. Then she was rigid again and subtly alluring, with red parted lips that panted and showed the white line of her teeth.

I took a step toward her.

Like a small beating whirlwind Nancy Tennant was upon me. She pounded upon my chest with frantic fists, she pushed me with all the quivering strength of her slender body.

"Blind! Blind!" she cried passionately. "You are lost if you listen to her. Run, run for your life!"

Then I saw Elise, arms still outstretched. I thrust the frantic girl violently away. She stumbled and crashed against the wheel-chair. I even laughed.

"Life!" I cried. "What is my life compared to the immortal loveliness of my bride?"

Nancy righted herself with difficulty. Her eyes were wide on me, her face death-pale.

"Oh!" she gasped. "I see it all now.

The whole damnable thing! It is too late—we are doomed, both of us!'

She whirled suddenly and ran down the hall. The darkness swallowed her. But I heard the desperate drumming of her feet on the pine-board floor, the sobbing of her fading voice: "Too late! Too late!..."

A door slammed, and there was silence.

Delsart took his cavernous eyes off his niece. His hairless skull was ghastly with sweat, as if the flickering life within him were exuding its ichor under groaning pressure.

"Nancy is tired and overwrought, poor child," he whispered. "And no wonder. Lem!"

The apelike man shambled forward. "Yes, Mister," he snarled.

"Leave the lantern here. Go watch over Miss Nancy. See that she is safe."

Lem grinned thickly. Then he hesitated, looked at me with sidelong glance.

"Don't worry about him," Delsart said. "I've advised him to go, but Elise is too strong for him. It is a pity."

The slow sweet smile of my wife penetrated my heart.

"It is no pity," I said, and fell into her enfolding arms. . . .

I OPENED thick-lidded eyes and peered vainly about me. There was nothing I could see. The darkness pressed on my burning eyeballs in dense folds. All light had been withdrawn from the universe.

I stirred my addled brains and tried to think. It was hard. Little hammers pounded sharp nails into my skull. Blood roared in my ears. My tongue was a great furry ball in my mouth.

I shifted a head that was sizes too large for me. It scraped over corpse-cold cloth. I twisted slowly on a lead-weighted leg. I was in a bed, somewhere.

The sickening sensation in my head slowly lifted. I flogged my brain into remembrance. Scenes pierced my consciousness like mocking ghosts. Horror beat soundlessly about me. As in a dream I saw a fantastic, endless procession of men —always men—death-pale, their starved lips working in the gloom.

A cold sweat bathed my limbs. I remembered now. My wife—Elise—I had cast myself into her arms; I felt a cloying sweetness enfold me. Then I had known no more.

Without knowing, I opened my mouth. I shrieked.

The tremendous sound beat gibbering at the darkness, sprang full-throated around encircling walls.

I jerked under the impact. God! I was not dead, I was still alive! Only the living could scream like that.

Then the truth flashed on me. I had been drugged, and brought to this unknown place. But why? Very quietly I told myself the answer. It was not yet time—it was not yet midnight.

Only at midnight could the awful ceremony take place. Only at midnight could Elise dip her eager mouth into my life blood, and arise, refreshed, for twenty years more.

I lay as in a shroud, savoring that with my tongue. I was not dead yet, but soon —horribly soon—the vampire would glide into the room. My skin was a tight mask, too tight for my body. I burned with bursting fever, yet I was cold as ice.

My lungs labored as if I were running; my flesh shrieked for life, for the warmth of a new sun, never to be felt again. I did not want to die! I half rose, to spring from my bed of death, to run blindly through halls and corridors, yelling, shrieking out my thirst for life.

I half rose, I say; I thrust a whipping leg over the side. Then, out of the clamoring silence, came a sound. A succession of sounds. I paused and listened.

Deep, guttural, clangorous. Somewhere in the hollow depths of forgotten time, a clock was striking. I hearkened to those sullen grim reverberations. My heart's blood ebbed with each succeeding stroke.

I counted. Twelve doomful hammerings. . . .

Midnight! The dark of the moon! Death to me—or to Elise.

Even now I could have escaped. My body jerked forward under the irresistible urge for life. But in my mind's eye I saw Elise. Elise, who was my wife, whom I had sworn to cherish until death did us part. I laughed wildly—that vain oath held hideous meaning now.

I saw her lovely form. I remembered the pure gold of certain days. I beheld as in a glass darkly the pleading of her eyes, the pallid sadness of her face.

Click—click—tap—tap. Down some unknown corridor came a steady noise, closer and closer. Elise was coming to claim her sacrifice.

My heart was a thudding pile-driver, my blood a mill-race. Terror seized me. But I clenched my chattering teeth and forced my shrieking body back on the bed.

Elise—vampire though she was, must live!

I lay very still, waiting . . . waiting. . . .

The tapping sounds were very close now. A tiny light ebbed into the room, making the darkness more terrible. Behind it loomed a form. The candle glowed brighter, and held in a round circle of illumination the gliding figure of Elise.

She moved silently toward me, her beautiful form half-revealed through filmy silk. Her exotic face was set in a queer stiff mask. She walked as one asleep. But her eyes were blazing coals. They reached out for me, held me shuddering in a fierce, unyielding grip. For the first time I noticed the long curve of her fingers as they closed around the candle.

DREAD of the final consummation swept like an avalanche over me,

This was Elise, yet it was not Elise. It was a stranger whom I had never seen; it was some demon in her lovely form.

I shivered as with ague, yet I did not move. Soon, soon it would be over. And Elise, the real Elise, would be reborn.

Her stiff, too-red lips opened. "John, darling!" Her beautiful arms went out suddenly, bare to the shoulders. Warm breath fanned my cheek. The candle sputtered on a night table. My wife's arms pressed back, exposing the line of my throat.

My body squirmed in shuddering revulsion. Almost I burst that embrace of death, almost I smashed furious fists into the soft, strangely cold cheek that rested on mine. I lifted, and dropped back trembling and sick.

I could not break away! *I could not!* To gain life for myself, Elise must die! I knew then that I loved her, fully, completely. Even at this moment when the world was at an end. I loved this vampire, I loved her with my life! Had I twenty lives, she could have them one by one, to feed on and make herself whole.

I fell back, passive. Silence grew enormous wings and overlaid me. The candle guttered and hissed out. I heard only the slow beating of my death-sick heart, the faint rustle of the woman as she thrust her head closer to mine.

A muscle twitched in my bare neck. My head was rigid, my eyes were closed. A burning iron entered my throat, just above the jugular. A tooth! Warm stickiness flowed out of me, was draining . . .

In spite of steeled will, I jerked uncontrollably. The cold bare arms tightened on my body. Sharp teeth nuzzled hungrily deeper, closer to the jugular.

Her hand loosed its hold, then pressed my throat back. I felt the greedy crunch of bone through cartilage. My blood spurted. I felt faint, sick with irrepressible horror.

Yet still I did not move. Something deep within me sang and exulted. I was dying so that *she* might live. What happier fate for any man who loved!

Already unconsciousness was claiming me. The dimness of approaching death filmed my eyes, hazed my thoughts. Soon the rending pain would be gone, and I would know no more.

A shrill scream made a slashing sword across my consciousness! It slapped ice water over my face, hurtled my numbing brain back to normal. It was a woman's scream, filled with unutterable terror! Again and again it rose, in a wild crescendo of tearing agony. Then it was gone, wiped out as if no sound had ever existed.

The eager sucking mouth at my throat lifted, and warm blood flowed down my neck. Elise was taut above me, listening. It was deathly quiet.

But I—I had heard. I had recognized. It was Nancy Tennant who had screamed in the last extremity of terror. Life flowed back into my veins. The truth made blinding concussion inside my skull. I knew now what Nancy Tennant had discovered out there in the hall, when she had fled sobbing and shrilling: "Too late! We're both of us doomed!"

I leapt out of bed, from under the still-clinging arms of Elise. I heard her startled cry, natural, but filled with alarm: "John! What's happened? Don't go!"

I did not pause; I raced through the darkness, every nerve-end quivering, every drop of blood left in my body clabbered with fear. Somehow I found a door and flung it open. Far away, down a long black tunnel, a tiny flickering light made dim illumination. I smashed headlong for it.

Behind me my wife was crying: "John! John! Come back!"

But I did not stop. Nancy had called for help and there was no one else to save her.

For one thudding second I stared into that murky hell, frozen by the horror of what I saw. My skin crawled and my scalp prickled. The very blood dripping from my wounded throat congealed into thick clots.

"Oh my God!" I gasped.

The monster I saw there looked up quickly from his dreadful pleasure, stared past me. I slammed around on the balls of my feet, in time to see a huge black arm descending.

I tried to duck, but it was too late. The weight crashed against the side of my skull, and I went down in a shower of blinding stars.

CHAPTER THREE

Ancient Thirst

I WAS like a swimmer coming up through green depths with lungs bursting and ears pounding with pressure. Light shot through the murkiness in my brain; light and the grumble of voices. Something acrid stung my nostrils. They twitched violently. I came to my senses.

I found myself flat on my back on a wooden pallet. A ghastly yellow-green light wavered over the dank, dripping walls of a stone chamber. Whitish fumes, sharply acid, billowed up endlessly from a vat in the corner. I turned my head and groaned from the splitting pain in my skull, from the raw, tearing ache in my throat. Then I forgot the pain in the horror of what I saw in that vat.

An oily yellow liquid bubbled furiously in its depths. The boiling vapors rose along the eroded stone of the wall to disappear into a black hole in the ceiling. My eyes smarted and twitched insupportably; my nostrils were raw from the wisps that floated over me.

I knew what that deadly liquid was. Sulphuric acid! Acid that could eat human flesh and bones into horrible dissolution without a sign that they had ever existed. I knew now what was in store for me in this subterranean chamber.

I screamed and tried to rise. Something was holding me down. I jerked vainly at the copper strands that cut cruelly into my flesh. My head seemed held in a vise that was squeezing with gigantic pressure. I fell back exhausted.

Then a shadow fell across my body. A huge bulk obscured the seething cauldron. I opened my pain-swept eyes to see Lem bending over me. His black greasy face leered at me, his black malignant eyes were darts of hate.

"So ye're awake, hey?" he grimaced through slobbering lips. "Good thing I didn' hit you harder; else I'd 'a' spoiled the fun."

I steeled my sick flesh. Blinding memory of the monstrous thing I had glimpsed before I had been struck down came to me.

"Where—where is Nancy?" I gasped.

Lem grinned with evil malice.

"Look the other side of you," he mocked.

I twisted my head painfully. At the farther end of the chamber, his wheelchair flush against corroded stone, sat Philip Delsart. Like an obscene vulture he sat, crouched over his prey. I groaned with sick revulsion.

For his snarling, writhing lips were dabbled with gore, and the curved tusks were no longer white. Thick red liquid dripped with horrible slowness from the corners of his mouth. Was it delirium or approaching madness that made me imagine a horrible similitude of plumped-out fullness in that skull-like head, in those empty, shriveled sacks that had been hands and feet? Was the hectic glow that dyed the parchment of his cheeks the dawn of a new and more hideous youth?

I shrank against the strands that held me, and groaned dully.

Vampire blood! The ageless monster had already feasted on, his living prey, and was renewed. I was too late! Nancy was dead!

As if he had read my thoughts, Lem thrust his foul face closer to my shuddering vision.

"She ain't dead—yet," he croaked. "The Master's jes' started when you came along. He wants you to see it all."

Just then I heard a faint, piteous moan, a whispering.

"Oh, my God! What are you doing to me? Why do you torture me so? I want to die. Kill me quickly. Oh!"

On the other side of Delsart, spread-eagled on a table, arms and legs lashed tightly to bolted iron rings, was Nancy Tennant.

Her dress had been stripped from her shoulders and her nude torso shook with terrible gulping sobs. Her blond head lolled over the edge of the table so that her bare throat was level with Delsart's avid, bloody mouth. There were four hideous punctures in the tender flesh, and the welling blood dabbled her shoulders with ghastly red.

I WENT mad again. I shouted, I screamed, I cursed that ageless vampire with every curse there was. I threatened horrible things if he did not release the girl; I called on all the devils in hell to drag their brother kicking and screeching back to the pit. I threw myself again and again against the cruel wire, until my body was a bleeding crisscross of gouged flesh.

Delsart sat like a green harpy in the ghastly light. Green flares burned in the hollow sockets of his eyes.

"I have been cursed before." He grinned, and the grin pierced my senses like the Gorgon's deadly smile. "I have been cursed for five hundred years. Ever since the scared villagers of Olain, in the south of France, forgot to drive a stake through the dead heart of Philippe Delsart, who had fed on their wives and daughters. Yet I still remain to mock at the world of stupid men who live their petty lives and die.

"I too would die, if I did not drink the warm rich blood of a young girl whenever I feel dissolution steal upon me." He laughed horribly, and bent his fiend's body over the half-conscious girl.

I was bathed in icy sweat. Wild loathing submerged my being. I strained futilely. Nancy was doomed. Already the snarling avid lips were close to the open wounds. I was doomed too. There was no escape for me. Searing, frightful dissolution in the oily bath of the acid was to be my lot.

Unless . . . and I froze at the terrible thought. Unless I was to be saved for Elise, the monster's niece, to complete the unfinished draining of my blood . . .

Taut cords snapped within my brain. God! I had forgotten that! Elise was a vampire too, fit mate for Delsart. Together they had roamed the world, together they had sought their victims.

In a twinkling all my love turned to unutterable loathing. I revolted at what I had done, at the dreadful sacrifice I had gladly made. Already my untainted blood was coursing through her veins. The gash in my throat throbbed with horror; I shuddered with agony at the thought of that contact. Not until now had I seen the whole hideous truth.

"You filthy beasts of hell!" I shouted insanely. "You and your mate—your pretended niece—who tricked me into blind sacrifice. With all my dying breath I curse you—curse you both to eternal damnation!"

I was raving, altogether mad. There was no doubt of it. But that last discovery, as I thought, of the pair of them linked through the ages in unholy couplement, had burst the last thin thread of my senses.

The vampire lifted his head from his dreadful feast. Nancy moaned slightly and lay very still. Her face and neck were marble white, and the dark red of her blood made ghastly contrast.

There was a gloating grin on Delsart's evil countenance. Lem, stirring the sizzling acid with a paddle, laughed harshly, as at some horrible jest.

"You poor fool!" cackled Delsart. "Still you do not know the truth. It is the cream of the jest, the last irony that makes an otherwise tedious eternity of existence worthwhile. I would not have you die without knowing the full impact of that truth. It would give the final delicate touch of my chucklings over the years."

Dimly I heard through the red haze that clouded my brain. I did not understand, did not comprehend at first. But as the cackling voice went on . . .

"Elise Delsart is no kin of mine," the vampire gloated. "The last of my race is dead five hundred years. Almost twenty years ago I fed on a woman, young, beautiful." He smacked his dripping lips with dreadful glee. "She had a little baby daughter. I took her and reared her. I would feed on her when the time came, I thought. But then a brilliant idea burst on my dazzled vision. It would be sport, gigantic sport to make me laugh and hold my sides for ages to come.

"I would make this little baby girl into a vampire, even as myself."

I LAY as one beyond madness. The words were like leaden weights, dropping into the shuddering pool of my consciousness.

"I set to work," Delsart went on gleefully. "I exerted the power of my ageless mind on her tender brain. She grew up, believing, thinking herself the female counterpart of me. She grew up, beautiful but damned. She thought herself doomed to drink blood in the dark of the moon on her twentieth birthday," he went on. "She became restless, moody as the time drew near. Then one day, somehow, she burst from my influence. She disappeared.

"I tried to bring her back by the force of my will. I failed. Then I felt myself dying. I too needed blood. I sent her a telegram, knowing she would come. I had told her what it meant." He laughed with hideous concatenation of sound. "She brought you, her husband, whom she had married to escape the nightmare taint in her blood. She has drunken, she will continue to drink, but the greatest jest of all is this: *She is mortal still. She can never be a vampire!"*

Waves beat upon my brain, crashing waves that somehow were flooded with delirious joy.

Elise was no vampire! My failing blood sang it over and over in a paean of happiness. I forgot my bonds, the cruel fate that awaited me, the crueler torture of Nancy; everything but that one overwhelming fact. That was why I had loved her, in spite of all the hideous evidence. She was mortal, and dear and sweet, and . . .

She had drunk my blood! But that didn't matter. Now that the vampire was engrossed in his frightful pleasure, she would emerge from his influence, even as the dawn came up with the kindly, blessed sun. She would escape into the normal world of men once more and live out her normal life, one among many.

Then Nancy shrieked. I jerked back to reality. Delsart had plunged his tusks into her neck. They were closing, crunching with hideous sound. The girl's head whipped from side to side like a broken-winged bird. Scream after scream of agony whipped from her tortured throat.

God! The sound went through me like red-hot knives. If only I could get my hands on that monster; if only . . . I threw myself against the wires in final desperation. My body shrieked its pain; it blazed with coruscating agony. Lem stopped his paddling to smirk brutishly over my vain twitchings. Nancy screamed horribly. It was almost over.

I turned my head away, deathly sick. My glaring eyes fell on the arch of the door. I choked incredulously.

Elise was framed in the doorway.

I shouted with frantic terror. "Elise! Go away! Run for your life, out of this place of hell. You are not a vampire, Elise! Do you hear me?" I screamed. *"You are not a vampire!"*

She stood there, immobile, her blank eyes on me. Her face was cast in a tight, rigid mold. Her lips were paper white, and unspotted with blood.

"Go away!" I cried again. But she did not seem to hear. She glided into the room with slow sinuous movements, straight for me.

"Oh God!" I gasped, as the full horror of it exploded in my brain.

Elise was coming to complete her frightful meal. *She was coming to drink the last remnants of my blood.*

Lem slapped his uncouth thighs and howled with hideous laughter. Delsart raised his gory head, licked with red pointed tongue at his blood-besmeared lips, and cackled.

"The cream of the jest," he gloated. "My will has prevailed. She believes she is a vampire; she will not hear you shout as loud as you wish. She will plunge her fangs into your throat; she will suck and suck. When she is through, and your drained body has vanished in the bath, then——" and he rubbed his dry hands to-gether with a grating sound— "I shall have more blood for myself—from her pretty neck."

I watched with shrieking horror her slow, doomful approach. I cried out, I prayed, I pleaded with her, trying to pierce the dread spell that fogged her senses; I recalled our love, our happiness.

It did no good, even as Delsart had said. Her expression did not change; her head swept down to my neck, seeking . . .

In that last extremity of madness, I fainted. . . .

I AWOKE to a sharp, needled pricking of my side. I opened my eyes dully. Elise was still bending over me. I shud-dered and was about to cry out when she put a quick finger on my cracked, weary lips. Urgency was in her gaze, swift warning and human tenderness.

I started incredulously, thinking I was dreaming, or dead.

"Quick!" she whispered very low. "I've cut your bonds with a knife. You're free. Hurry, before they turn around. Get Lem. I'll take care of Delsart."

Still not believing, I tried my leg. It moved! Strength flowed through my shrunken veins. I leaped madly from my bed of death.

For a moment I staggered. In that in-stant, Lem, who was facing the vat, swung around. A great animal roar filled the room.

I roared in feral answer and charged. We locked in death embrace, his long ape-like arms whipping around my weakened body. I felt a rib crack; I was being lifted off my feet. In another second I would be thrown bodily into that boiling vat.

I struggled, I clawed, I gouged. The hairy brute laughed and tightened his crushing hold. My senses swam.

Then I saw Elise, knife in hand, lung-ing for the vampire who had pretended to be her uncle. Delsart's startled face was lifted from his feast; he shrieked in terror.

For one infinitesimal moment Lem relaxed his grip, swinging around toward his master. One tiny moment—but that was enough. Mad strength surged through me. I crooked my leg behind his knee; I placed both palms against his massive chest, and shoved.

Lem staggered, tried to recover himself. I shoved again. There was a long-drawn howl of agony. He teetered and fell headlong into the deadly liquid!

There was a great splash, a gurgling shriek, followed by silence. I stared down, sick and trembling, at the gruesome sight.

Then Elise's cry came to me. I whirled and pounded crazily for the other end of the room. Somehow the vampire had wrested the knife from her hands. He had my wife on her knees, one bony hand clutching her throat, the other with gleaming steel uplifted.

I crashed into him with a wild curse; my balled fist smashed with every ounce of my hatred and loathing into that evil countenance.

It crumpled almost like thin plaster under the impact. The knife dropped with a clatter. The vampire, with the horrible screech of a lost soul, collapsed like a pricked balloon.

Philip Delsart was dead!

AFTERWARDS, our wounds bound, we rested awhile before leaving that abode of Satan. Elise nestled warm and human and tender against my heart, stroking the bandages that swathed my neck with remorseful murmurings. Nancy Tennant, pale and drawn, her throat hidden under layers of wadding, lay on a bed.

"All the while I was married to you I struggled against the spell," Elise said with a shudder. "I wanted to die on my twentieth birthday, as Delsart had threatened, a normal human being. I thought your love would help me. But when I got that telegram, I knew that once he drank afresh of blood, his power over me would extend even to where I was. Then and there I determined to kill him before he could fill his shriveled veins with the blood of Nancy.

"When you insisted on coming, too, I was afraid, but dared not refuse. I realized you had uneasy suspicions. Once here, Delsart proved stronger than I anticipated. He willed me to hold you, and like a puppet in his hands, I did." She shivered. "I even drank your life blood as—as he willed."

"That makes you more than ever a part of me," I said softly.

She smiled tenderly into my eyes. "It was when Nancy shrieked, and you leaped up to rescue her," she added, "that I awoke to the full realization of what I was doing. I followed you here, and pretended I was still a—a—" Her tongue stumbled on the frightful word.

"I know the rest," I said. "Don't talk about it."

Nancy raised her bandaged head. "Delsart had spread tales about his supposed niece," she said weakly. "No doubt it was to divert suspicion from himself." She closed her eyes, as if reliving the horrors she had been through. "Do—do you think," she asked, "he was really and truly a vampire, or just a madman whose disordered brain had conjured up horrible imaginings?"

"I don't know," I said. Then I added grimly, thinking of the sharpened stake I had driven through the dead man's heart: "But I took no chances."

THE END

THE BLACK CHAPEL

WHENCE came the Devil? What mind first recognized him as a living entity? Whose eyes first saw him as he is now portrayed? Over the answers to these questions, men have disputed much. There are those who maintain that he was indeed but a fallen angel. Men of science insist that his origin must have been much farther back, in the dark pages before history, before even Christianity was born. They point to the horned god of the caveman, to the blood-hungry spirit the Druids worshiped in the dank woods of Gaul, and say that here was Satan, under another name.

Whatever the means by which he came into being, whenever he was born, there is no doubt that once men worshiped him. They bowed down to him, gave him fiendish homage, on a thousand desolate hilltops, in myriad dark forests. This much, the records of innumerable witnesses seem to prove.

Now, some people say that the Devil is dead. Some say that he was never more than a fantasy in disordered, fear-racked minds. This latter may be true—but it is hardly true to say that he is dead. For in the sense that he once lived—in the minds of those who feared him and in the twisted brains of those who sought to do his bidding for their own gain—he still lives.

He lives in the power of such a fiend as he who, in that blood-chilling tale by Hugh B. Cave, *Enslaved to Satan*, all but brought young Paul Norton to madness. He lives in the clawing hands of that monstrous child who left his fearful mark on the Laytons in *The Cross of Blood*. And in that hideous voodoo worship whose rites you saw enacted in *The Devil's Dowry*.

No, as long as men live who seek in devilish ways to gain their own evil ends, one cannot truly say that the devil is dead. And until he is dead, not only physically but in the minds of men, there will be fear and clutching terror to walk with us in the dead of night.

And as long as this is true, men will wish to know of these things. They will wish to know the truth behind them and the fear that is in them. And they will find the answers in such stories as we have printed, and will continue to print, in TERROR TALES!

125

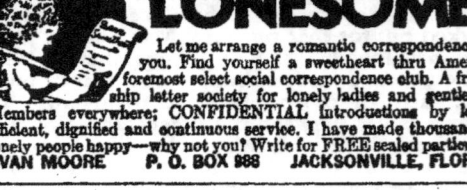

127

128